ROSEDALE

BY

JT HENDRICKS

This is a work of fiction.
Names, characters, places
and incidents either are the product
of the author's imagination or are used
fictitiously. Any resemblance
to actual persons, living or dead, events
or locales is entirely coincidental.

Special thanks to:

my friend,

Heather McFall

For your unwavering support and periodic

threats,

as you encouraged me to keep writing

… or else

R. Anita Owens

For cover photography and editing.

Dr. Phillip St. Louis

Dr. Kenrick Spence

Daryl Guillemet

and

Kay Bruhn

1

Purple. She always liked that color as far back as she could remember.

'They'll be pretty in front of the house.' she thought to herself as she dug a small hole in the dirt and placed yet another plant with tiny purple flowers gently into the ground, brushing the soil back in around it and then pressing the dirt firmly into place with her hand. Another perfect spring day in Rosedale. As perfect as the day before and probably as perfect as the day to come.

Maggie loved living there - in fact, she couldn't imagine living anywhere else.   The house was exactly what Maggie had always wanted ... a buttery yellow cottage with white trim. She even had the white picket fence she had always dreamed about. Large oak trees not only framed the house, but also lined the quiet, picturesque street.

Maggie took a deep breath. The scent of flowers and freshly cut grass. She looked back at the house. The window boxes she had just filled were bursting with color. They would be beautiful as the flowers took hold and started to spill over. A warm, cozy place to call home. The perfect home in the perfect town - Rosedale. Maggie couldn't imagine herself living anywhere else. She smiled and reached for another tiny purple flower.

"Those are pretty!"

Maggie turned and saw her daughter, Jordan, standing behind her, admiring the garden. "They are aren't they? Just a few more to plant. Do you want to help?"

"Ah no, that's ok. I don't do well with plants remember?" laughed Jordan.

"So how was school?"

Jordan was 15 and seemed to excel at everything she did. She was lucky that way. Pretty, athletic and smart. Maggie couldn't have been more proud of her. Her long, blond hair moved gently in the breeze, her backpack dangled from her arm. She shrugged. "Same old stuff. I'm starved, when's dinner?"

Maggie smiled, "You're always starved! I thought you and Susan were going to grab something before practice."

"We did!" replied Jordan with a sly smile. "We grabbed a burger at Pop's Diner, but that doesn't mean I'm still not hungry!"

"Okay ... well if you can hang on a little bit longer before you pass out from starvation, it's in the oven. Your father should be home soon. I wanted to wait for him before we ate. Why don't you set the table?"

"Okay!"

With that, Jordan turned on her heels, walked up the front steps and vanished into the house.

Maggie couldn't help but smile as she watched her daughter. She was growing up so fast. She and Sam had waited to have children, although at this moment, Maggie couldn't remember why they had waited so long. But now, in her late 40s, her life was complete. A husband she adored, a daughter she couldn't love more and the home she had always dreamed of. A bead of sweat started to slowly trickle down Maggie's forehead and as she used the back of her hand to wipe it away, she glanced up and noticed a teenage boy walking down the street. He seemed out of place somehow, a little confused maybe, although Maggie couldn't understand why she felt that way. She had never seen him before. He was maybe 17 or 18, dressed in blue jeans. Perhaps he was visiting someone.

Maggie reached for another plant from the plastic tray and glanced back up, curious to see where the boy would turn, but he was gone. Maggie looked up and then down the street, but there was no sign of him. It was as though he had vanished.

'That's odd.' Maggie thought to herself. She stood up hoping to get a better view of the street. It didn't make sense. She had only looked down for a second. It couldn't have been enough time for someone to completely disappear. He had to be somewhere.

"What's so interesting?"

Maggie jumped at the unexpected sound, dropping a tiny plant to the ground. "God! Don't sneak up on me like that!"

There, standing behind her, was her husband, Sam. Sam was Rosedale's Sheriff. He, along with his two deputies, Jason Moyer and Rebecca Sanchez, kept the residents of Rosedale safe. It wasn't a particularly daunting task however. Rarely did anything actually happen in Rosedale. A periodic traffic violation, a cat up a tree, maybe an argument between neighbors, but that seemed to be the extent of it.

Maggie couldn't help admiring her husband as he stood there - that one lock of hair that was forever falling onto his forehead. Tall, handsome with a warm smile and sparkling blue eyes. Over time his hair had become the most beautiful shade of silver Maggie had ever seen. He would joke that it was the stress of elementary school that made his hair change so early. That always made Maggie laugh.

Whatever it was, it was one of the things she loved about him from the first moment she saw him. But it was his eyes. She could lose herself in those ice blue eyes.

"I'm sorry, Babe." said Sam grinning. "I didn't mean to sneak up on you. I'm surprised you didn't hear me when I pulled into the driveway. What's so interesting?" He nodded in the direction she was looking.

Maggie glanced one last time at the street and shook her head. "Absolutely nothing." she laughed. "Just losing my mind I guess."

Sam pulled Maggie into him and smiled down at her, wrapping her in his arms. "Well I'm thinking maybe later, I could sneak up on you for real ... maybe frisk you a bit. I've been thinking about frisking you all day. How does that sound?"

"Oh have you now?" said Maggie, grinning. "Well I do like when you frisk me, but will that help me if I'm losing my mind?"

Sam's smile broadened. "Funny you should ask! I just read that they think a good frisking might cure a number of medical issues."

"Really? Well then - in the interest of modern medicine, I think we need to give it a try!"

Maggie smiled as Sam leaned down and pressed his lips into hers. At that moment, she felt the familiar flutter run through her body. No matter how many times he kissed her, it always felt like the first time. He could still leave her breathless.

"Ewwww. Gross!" Jordan was standing on the front porch. A look of disgust etched on her face. "Would you PLEASE try to control yourselves? It's embarrassing! At least not in the front yard where everyone can see you!"

Maggie and Sam tried to hold back their laughter. Sam draped his arm over Maggie and looked up at Jordan. "Well if you would like us to do something REALLY embarrassing ...," Sam's eyes were twinkling as he spoke.

"Just get in the house!" Jordan said with exasperation. "You act like teenagers! It's awful. Anyway, I came out to tell you the table is set and I'm really starving. Can we eat now?"

"We'll be right in." answered Maggie as she started collecting her gardening tools.

Jordan headed back into the house as Maggie turned to Sam.

"If we can just put this stuff on the porch, I can finish up tomorrow." she said, as she picked up the tray of remaining plants and handed them to him.

"Be my pleasure to help you Ma'am." he responded, doing his best small town southern accent. Maggie gave the garden one last look.

Darkness was beginning to envelop the tiny town of Rosedale. The old fashioned street lights had just started coming on. Gradually the warm, welcoming lights from inside the houses began to spill out onto the street. Off in the distance, a dog barked. Slowly they started walking towards the house, taking a moment to breathe in the night air.

"So how was your day?"

"Pretty quiet." responded Sam. "Just the way I like it."

With that, they reached the front porch, carefully stacking everything in the corner.

"Babe, I want to change out of my uniform before we have dinner. I'll just be a minute."

"Yeah that's okay. It'll take a minute to get everything on the table anyway." smiled Maggie. "What do you want to —"

Suddenly out of nowhere, Maggie was overcome with a feeling of panic. She heard herself gasp. Her heart was pounding.

She spun around looking behind them, then at the street, but there was nothing. No one. No reason to be afraid. Nothing was any different. And then as quickly as the fear struck, it vanished.

"Maggie what's wrong?" said Sam wrapping his arms around her. "What is it?" A look of concern was etched on his face.

Slowly her breathing returned to normal. She was left shaken and confused. What had just happened? "I'm fine ... It was like some sort of panic attack but that doesn't make sense."

"You're probably just exhausted and over-heated. You've been out here gardening all day and I'll bet you didn't stop for lunch, did you?."

Maggie shook her head.

"Come on, let's get you inside. Have a nice dinner and a long shower. You'll feel better."

"You're probably right." agreed Maggie. But deep down she wasn't convinced. Something had just happened to her. Something she could't explain and she didn't think dinner and a shower was going to be the answer.

Sam held the door open for her. As she past by, he looked out onto the street. There was nothing. He turned and entered the house, shutting the door behind him. The dog was no longer barking. It stopped the moment Sam shut the door. There was only silence.

2

Downtown Rosedale was still. Darkness had pressed down upon it creating a suffocating quiet. The only sign of life was a traffic light in the center of town, that relentlessly went from red to green to yellow over and over again, keeping the invisible cars under strict control. The storefronts were, for the most part, dark. There was one exception however - the storefront that housed the Sheriff's Office.

Bernice had been with the Sheriff's Office for as far back as anyone could remember. An older woman with short, curly, grey hair, a stocky build and a warm smile. She threatened retirement every time she felt under-appreciated, even though everyone knew it was an idle threat. She loved working at the Sheriff's Office. They had become her family.

She always felt she should have had children ... but she hadn't ... although, try as she might, she couldn't remember why she hadn't. Obviously it just wasn't meant to be. She worked dispatch, answered the phone, made the coffee and took care of everyone who walked through the door - especially Sheriff Cooper. "If only I was 30 years younger and 30 pounds lighter," she would jokingly say from time to time. "I'd give Maggie a run for her money!"

The office was old and tired looking. A lot of dark wood and dull lighting. Not the most high-tech operation around. But at least they had a photocopier, a fax machine and a couple of computers that worked most of the time, some old and dented filing cabinets and a couple of plants that Bernice would talk to when no one was around to see her.

Rebecca Sanchez sat at her desk finishing paperwork. She faced the now empty desk of her fellow Deputy - Jason Moyer. He had just left a few minutes earlier to take his nightly drive through the empty streets of Rosedale. He wouldn't be gone long. When he got back, Deputy Sanchez could finally go home. A hot bath and soft bed were calling her.

She was the newest member of the Sheriff's Office and at only 24, the youngest. Being in law enforcement was a dream she had had as far back as she could remember. Always a tomboy, her decision came as no surprise to anyone. While her friends were deciding what dresses they would wear to the prom, Rebecca was at her kick boxing classes. Her father was always proud of her. So was her mother, even though secretly she had wished her daughter could have been at least a little interested in prom dresses.

"Bernice, why don't you go home? I have to wait for Jason to get back before I can go anyway. No reason for both of us to stay here."

Bernice glanced over at Rebecca and smiled. "Well that might not be a bad idea now would it? I'll just clean out the coffee pot and get to goin'. Sure you'll be okay?"

But before Rebecca could answer, the phone rang.

"Do you want me to get that?" Rebecca asked Bernice.

"Naw, I can do it." she replied, as she put down the coffee pot and reached for the phone. "Probably a wrong number anyways ... Sheriff's Office, Bernice speaking."

Rebecca watched as she saw the expression change on Bernice's face. This obviously wasn't a wrong number.

"Now Ann, just calm down. What did you say the address was again?" asked Bernice as she quickly wrote down the information she was being given. "5548 Lincoln Way. The name again? ... I think I know her. Ain't she that nice lady who baked them blueberry pies for the Church bizarre last week? ... I thought so. I'm sure everything's just fine. She probably doesn't hear the phone. Now don't you worry. I'll get Deputy Moyer to take a drive by there and check things out. Okay then ... Yes I'll let you know."

Bernice hung up the phone. A confused look had spread across her face.

"Who was that?" asked Rebecca.

"Ann Barnes. She said Mary Haskins was supposed to come by her place today but never showed up. She and her husband have been calling her but there's no answer. They want us to send someone over to the house to make sure everything's okay. I'm sure it is, but I'll radio Jason and get him to swing by."

As Bernice reached for the radio, Rebecca hurriedly grabbed her keys and headed towards the door. "Let Jason know that I'll meet him there."

Bernice nodded and pressed the button on the radio.

Outside, Rebecca got into her patrol car and pushed the key into the ignition. She felt a chill run down her spine. There was no logical reason to meet Jason at the Haskins house. 'Probably nothing, just like Bernice said.' she thought to herself. Yet still - she had an unsettled feeling.

Rebecca pulled out into the street and headed towards Lincoln Way. It would only take a few minutes. Rosedale wasn't that big to begin with and after dark, there was rarely anyone out on the streets. She wished though she could understand why she felt so anxious. Nothing ever happened in Rosedale.

After just a few minutes, she found herself turning onto Lincoln Way. Up ahead she saw Jason Moyer's vehicle parked on the side of the road in front of the Haskins house. She reached for the radio.

"Bernice?"

"Go for Bernice." the familiar voice said on the other end.

"I just arrived. Jason is already here. I'll let you know what we find."

"Sounds good. You be careful."

"Will do." replied Rebecca as the radio made the usual static noise. Rebecca replaced the radio and pulled in behind him. She shut her car off as Deputy Moyer opened his car door and stepped out onto the street.

"This 5548?" Rebecca asked as she stepped out of her vehicle and motioned towards the darkened house.

"Yup." answered Deputy Moyer, glancing down the street. Jason Moyer was in his 40s - a thoughtful, quiet man. The touch of grey at his temples made him look even more distinguished. He wasn't the type you'd think of if you imagined a Deputy Sheriff. There was just something about him that screamed history professor - although Rebecca knew that under that quiet exterior, was a seasoned deputy who excelled at every aspect of his job.

She could learn a lot from him and she was planning on doing just that.

"The house sure is dark." said Rebecca quietly.

"Yup, sure is." replied Deputy Moyer. "Seems it's the only dark house on the street too. Real dark. There's a car in the driveway, so unless she went somewhere on foot ..." His voice trailed off.

Taking out their flashlights and resting their hands on their guns, they slowly made their way around the outside of the house. Even though there was a full moon, the clouds blocked whatever light it would have offered. The dampness in the night air caused Rebecca to shiver. She took a deep breath trying to settle herself. The house was a beautiful, old, three story Victorian. Surrounded by trees and a well tended flower garden, to Rebecca it always looked like one of those elaborate doll houses that some little girls played with. Perfect and enchanting. But tonight, shrouded in darkness, it had a very different feel. It felt as though the house was watching them. Or perhaps it wasn't the house, maybe it was someone or something in the house. That's when she heard it. It was faint, but it was definitely coming from inside - music.

"Do you hear that?" whispered Rebecca.

"Yup, sure do." replied Deputy Moyer. "This doesn't feel right."

Slowly they made their way around the house and back to the front door. Deputy Moyer knocked.

"Ms. Haskins?" he called out. "Deputies Moyer and Sanchez from the Sheriff's Office. Just checking to make sure you're okay."

But as he knocked on the door for the second time, it opened. Deputy Moyer nodded to Rebecca as she took out her revolver. He did the same. It felt awkward in Rebecca's hand. Unbelievably heavy. She practiced her shooting regularly, but this was the first time she could remember ever pulling it out for real. She released the safety and looked back at Deputy Moyer. Her heart quickened. With a nod from him, they slowly entered the house, the beams of light from their flashlights, slicing through the darkness.

"Ms. Haskins?" called out Deputy Moyer for the second time. "Sheriff's Office."

The house was completely dark. Had it not been for their flashlights, they wouldn't have been able to maneuver. Off in another room, the sound of Frank Sinatra singing Fly Me To The Moon, added a little touch of insanity to the situation. Rebecca fought the urge to switch on the lights. It would give away their position and possibly make them easy targets if there was someone other than Mary Haskins in the house. She could hear the sound of her heart beating and just prayed it wasn't as loud as it seemed.

Deputy Moyer motioned to her and they slowly followed the music, clearing rooms as they went, calling for Mary Haskins, until they found themselves in the kitchen. There, in the center of the table, sat a small CD player. Frank was starting to sing an encore. The large kitchen with its pristine maple cabinets and lace curtains covering the window over the sink, looked tidy ... nothing on the stove, no dirty dishes in the sink. There was, however, one thing that seemed somehow odd - other than Frank, of course. A shiny red apple sat at the edge of the counter. Nothing more, just an apple. An apple looking out of place. Rebecca stared at it wondering why it struck her as it did. There was really nothing to indicate anything was amiss.

Suddenly they heard the sound of running on the second floor. Guns ready, they hurried back into the foyer and looked up the grand staircase. The beams of their flashlights revealed nothing. They stood motionless waiting for another sound, but there was nothing, nothing other than Frank, who was still busy entertaining in the kitchen - oblivious to any of the drama unfolding around him.

"Ms. Haskins?" Jason Moyer called out into the darkness. "I'm Deputy Moyer with the Rosedale Sheriff's Office. Checking to make sure you're okay. Folks are worried about you Ms. Haskins. Ms. Haskins can you hear me?"

Nothing.

Deputy Moyer motioned to Rebecca and they slowly began to climb the stairs to the second floor. Rebecca kept her eyes and gun trained behind them as Deputy Moyer focused his attention ahead. And then abruptly, Frank stopped singing mid sentence.

3

Maggie was looking out of their bedroom window as she dried her long brown hair with the over-sized towel. With her old, comfortable robe wrapped around her, she felt relaxed. She actually did feel better after eating and having a hot shower. Maybe Sam was right. Maybe it was nothing. Maybe it was just the result of not having eaten and working too long in the garden.

Suddenly she felt silly. Of course it was nothing and luckily they had even managed to finish dinner without Jordan passing out from hunger. Everything was as it should be.

The view from the second floor bedroom was beautiful. The full moon was starting to peak out from behind some clouds and from the corner of her eye, she saw a shooting star trace through the night sky.

She cracked the window open so that she could hear the chorus of crickets which at times, could be almost deafening. Maggie sighed. It was so peaceful, so perfect. A cool breeze caressed her skin.

"Jordan is in her room studying, the kitchen is clean, the house is buttoned up and you — you look beautiful." smiled Sam as he walked into the bedroom, shutting the door behind him. "How do you feel?"

"Much better. You were right." said Maggie smiling.

"Think I could hear that again?"

"No!" laughed Maggie. "You should have paid more attention the first time! But I do feel better. Thank you. So, Sheriff, am I still on the books to be frisked?"

Sam walked up to Maggie.

"Absolutely." he whispered into her ear as he untied her robe and let it drop to the floor. "Have to make sure you're not hiding anything."

A soft groan escaped Maggie's lips as she felt his hands move across her body. He pulled her into him and gently kissed the corner of her mouth.

"I want you." whispered Maggie.

He kissed her again, but this time as he kissed her, she knew he wanted her just as badly. The forcefulness of his touch, the deepening kisses, all made Maggie's breathing quicken. How she loved this man. How she needed him. She wanted to lose herself to him.

Sam pulled back. Taking her hand, he led her to the bed. "Don't you move." he whispered, smiling. He kissed her one more time before walking towards the chair that sat in the corner of the room, unbuttoning his shirt as he did so.

Maggie couldn't help but watch as he removed his clothes. She knew every inch of him. His chest that she loved resting her head on, his strong arms, his toned and muscular body, the three tiny moles at the base of his neck that formed a perfect little triangle, down to the small scar by his right elbow. She knew how it felt to touch him. Knew what his touch did to her. Her heartbeat quickened at the anticipation of him.

4

Rebecca had to remind herself to breathe. Her heart felt like it was going to explode. Luckily, the clouds had parted just enough as to allow moonlight to come through the windows. Even though they would still need their flashlights, at least they were no longer in total darkness. Rebecca glanced at Deputy Moyer, nodded and with her gun ready, carefully made her way towards the kitchen.

Again she checked every room and behind every door. They had already done this once, but until they knew why the music had stopped, it had to be done again. It was slow going but she knew if she made a mistake, it could be her last. Keeping her back against the wall, she covered every inch of the ground floor as she made her way back to the kitchen. There, on the table, sat the CD player looking unremarkable. She couldn't tell why the CD had stopped so abruptly, but she certainly wasn't going to touch it and possibly destroy any fingerprints. Until they found Mary Haskins safe and sound, they really didn't know what they were dealing with. But of course they'd find Ms. Haskins. She probably went to visit a neighbor and had no idea everyone was looking for her. After all ... this was Rosedale. Rebecca went to the basement door. It was locked from the kitchen side.

With no one around and no sign of anything disturbed, she returned to Deputy Moyer who was still standing on the staircase, his gaze focused on the top landing. He glanced down as Rebecca walked back to the foyer and resumed her position on the stairs behind him. She shook her head and motioned to the second floor.

Slowly they started their ascent. With each step Rebecca held her breath, somehow making herself believe that it would prevent the stairs from creaking under her weight. Finally they reached the top of the landing. They stood motionless waiting to see if they could hear anything. But other than the ticking of a grandfather clock that stood on the landing, they heard nothing.

"Ms. Haskins can you hear me?" called out Deputy Moyer yet again. "Sheriff's Office. Just checking to make sure you're okay."

Nothing.

Rebecca found herself wishing that Frank hadn't stopped singing. At least another rendition of Fly Me To The Moon would help cover the sound of her breathing, which now seemed unnaturally loud.

Meticulously they covered the second floor, going from room to room. Bursts of light from their flashlights and then back to dark. Over and over again. Miss Haskins wasn't there, but then, no one else was either. After being satisfied that they had covered every inch of the second floor, they proceeded to the third floor. The attic.

The stairs were much more narrow and confining. They turned off their flashlights, preferring not to announce their arrival to the attic. Rebecca worried that someone could be waiting for them as they reached the top. They would be trapped. They had heard foot steps. Who made them? She seriously doubted Ms. Haskins would be up in the attic - or perhaps she was. Perhaps she had gone up to the attic and had fallen. Or maybe someone else was waiting to ambush them in the attic. Rebecca knew she had to get her thoughts under control. Be calm and be aware.

They moved slowly. Guns ready. Rebecca's eyes darted from side to side and periodically behind them, confident her partner was trained on what was ahead. She was grateful her eyes had grown accustomed to the dark.

Deputy Moyer's breathing had quickened. He didn't want Rebecca to see how tense he was. He was hoping that she couldn't see the sweat that had started to build on the back of his neck and on his brow. The third floor was warmer than the rest of the house which wasn't helping. Suddenly Deputy Moyer regretted that he had never married. Why on earth did that thought enter his head? Now of all times? 'Focus. Focus. Focus. Don't let Rebecca see how nervous I am.' he thought to himself. That's when he noticed his hand was shaking ever so slightly.

He quickly wiped the sweat from his brow that was threatening to enter his eyes and impair his vision. They were almost at the top. Almost on the third floor.

With just a few more steps to go, Deputy Moyer stopped and looked at Rebecca. He motioned to the top of the staircase. She nodded. She knew what he wanted her to do. She was ready. 'Is this really happening?' she thought to herself.

They resumed their careful and quiet walk up the remaining steps. Three, two, one. And in a single burst, the beams of light from their flashlights exploded into the attic. In a second they had covered the entire space. They saw no one. Nothing. No one was waiting for them. It was quiet.

The attic was nothing more than one large room. The walls followed the slope of the house. Windows, tucked into dormers, lined both sides. The room contained the usual attic fair. Pieces of furniture, some covered with sheets, some sitting unprotected, collecting dust. Boxes stacked in various areas, a dusty old mirror, paintings that apparently no one liked any longer had been abandoned here, never to be admired again. An old rocking chair sat off in the farthest corner.

Something about that rocking chair caught Rebecca's attention. She couldn't quite make it out. She trained her flashlight on the chair and slowly started walking towards that corner of the room.

Deputy Moyer was busy making sure no one was hiding behind any of the boxes. He knew they had heard footsteps on the second floor. He was grateful Rebecca had heard them too. If not, he would be questioning his sanity at this point. He pulled aside some of the sheets covering the furniture, to make sure all was clear. He hadn't noticed Rebecca walking slowly to the corner of the room.

Clothes. There were clothes piled on the chair. Rebecca moved closer. No, not clothes. Something else. It was as though her brain was trying to make sense of what her eyes were seeing, but without success. If only there was an overhead light. There probably was, but she didn't want to take the time to look for it. The light from the flashlight played games with her eyes. Turned everything into a fun-house. Yes, clothes. Maybe Halloween decorations. But they didn't look right. Something was off. Something was wrong.

Rebecca moved her flashlight up towards the back of the chair. She stopped. Everything stopped, except for the screaming that had started in her head. There, in front of her, sitting in the chair, was the body of Mary Haskins. Her eyes opened wide, locked in a permanent look of horror.

Mary Haskins had been an attractive woman in her 50s, but there was nothing attractive about what Rebecca was now staring at. So much blood. Her mouth had been cut from the corners to her ears. Her hair was matted with blood. It was apparent she had suffered a horrible beating.

As Rebecca's eyes moved down, she saw that Mary Haskins had been cut down the middle. What Rebecca thought was a Halloween decoration was actually Mary Haskins' intestines that now lay on her lap. Rebecca looked back up at her face. Her eyes. Her eyes frozen in terror staring wildly at Rebecca. Her eyes that begged Rebecca to do something. Please do something. Please stop this. Please help me.

Suddenly Rebecca heard a woman's voice yelling to Deputy Moyer. Then she realized, it was her own.

"Oh my God." murmured Deputy Moyer as he walked up behind Rebecca. He wiped the sweat from his face. Suddenly he wasn't feeling well.

"We have to get Sam here." whispered Rebecca, unable to take her eyes off the horror that lay before her.

"You go down to the patrol car. Get in touch with Bernice and have her call the Sheriff. I'll wait up here. Don't tell her what we found. Just get Sam here. I'll look around a bit more. Maybe we missed something."

"Yeah okay." replied Rebecca, as she started walking towards the stairs.

"Don't let your guard down. Whoever did this ..."

Rebecca understood. She started down the stairs, her gun still in her hand. Her eyes darted in every direction. She was ready. It was doubtful the perpetrator was still in the house, but she couldn't take any chances. Anyone capable of doing what she just saw, was capable of anything. But nothing ever happened in Rosedale. This made no sense. Why? Who would do such a thing? These things happened in big cities, not places like this.

She made her way out the front door. The cool night air hit her face. For a moment the nausea she was feeling seemed to subside. She felt grateful to be out of the house. Away from what she had just seen. Briskly she walked to her patrol car. A perfect night ... the gentle breeze, the full moon. Nothing to hint of the horror that had played out in the beautiful doll house. Still not allowing herself to relax, she got into her patrol car and radioed Bernice.

"Go for Bernice."

"Bernice, call Sam. We need him here right away."

"What's happened?" asked Bernice

"Just call Sam. Now!"

Before Bernice could ask another question, Rebecca disconnected and replaced the radio. She sat there for a moment, staring out the windshield, wishing she could wipe the image from her mind. Although the night air was cool, she was starting to sweat. She was feeling dizzy and suddenly clammy. Quickly she opened the car door, managed to get her body half way out and threw up onto the pavement.

It felt like hours. Hours of sitting in the patrol car, staring out the windshield. Trying to forget. Rebecca stopped throwing up - mainly because there was nothing left. The chills and the sweats had also stopped. Now if only she could get her mind to stop replaying what she had seen in the attic. Where was Sam? She glanced at her watch. It hadn't been that long since she radioed Bernice.

Maybe only 10 minutes. Why did it feel so much longer?

She tilted the rear view mirror in her direction so that she could take a look at herself. The color had drained from her face. She looked grey. She looked ill. Her pony tail was still damp from sweat and strands that had escaped the elastic band were sticking to the sides of her face. She reached over to the glove compartment and took out a tissue. Again, back to the mirror as she started to wipe the moisture from her forehead and then, with her fingers, tried to make sense of her hair.

She couldn't let Sam see her like this. It was unprofessional. She had to do better. She had to keep it together. It was her job. But how do you prepare yourself for something like this? Will it get easier? Will she ever see anything like this again?

As she sat there, trying to fix her hair, thinking through the endless questions that raced through her head, her mind suddenly revisited the scene in the attic and she felt the now familiar flip of her stomach. 'No!' she thought to herself. 'That is not going to happen.'

She shut her eyes and focused until the feeling passed. She had to get herself together. She took one last look into the rear view mirror. Sam would still be able to tell if he really looked at her, but it was the best she could do. With a sigh, she tapped the mirror back into position.

She looked down the street. It was dark and quiet. There was no movement at all. No sounds. Maybe three darkened cars parked along the street, but other than that, nothing. Most of the houses on the street were now also shrouded in darkness. Everyone peacefully sleeping in their homes with no idea of the horror that had played out so near to them. 'I wonder if he's out there.' she asked herself. Suddenly she had the feeling she was being watched. The hair on the back of her neck stood up and her breathing became shallow. "Stop that Becca!" she pleaded with her-self. "That's ridiculous. He's long gone. Probably already left town. Stay professional."

Finally off in the distance, she saw the glow of headlights coming towards her. She let out a sigh of relief. Sam. She got out of her car and slowly started to walk in the direc-tion of the approaching vehicle. Briefly the blinding headlights washed over her, making it impossible for her to see anything but the white glaring light. For a moment she pan-icked. What if this wasn't Sam? What if it was HIM? She should have stayed in her car until she was sure. But as the car pulled over to the side of the road, she could make out the Sheriff's Department logo and her heart-beat returned to normal. The headlights went to black and the car was turned off. Sam got out of the patrol car. He hadn't bothered putting on his uniform, but instead he had thrown on jeans and a shirt.

"What's going on?" he asked Rebecca as he walked over to her. "All Bernice would say was that there was issue at this address and you needed me here, but nothing more."

"That's because we didn't tell her."

"Tell her what?" asked Sam.   As he looked at Rebecca waiting for her reply, he could tell something was wrong.   "Deputy Sanchez?"

"Yes, Sheriff.   It looks like we have a homicide. It's bad. Really bad. Mary Haskins. She's ... her body is in the attic."

"Where's Jason?"

"Still in the house ... with ... the body. No sign of the perpetrator.   We checked the house. I'm guessing he's long gone."

After a beat, Sam turned away and walked back to his patrol car. Getting inside, he reached over to his glove compartment and as he exited the car, Rebecca saw that he was strapping on his gun.

"What do you want me to do?" she asked Sam. She had never faced anything like this before during her short career in law enforcement. This was Rosedale after all. She felt totally unprepared.

"I want you to radio Bernice. Ask her to contact Doc Simpson. Let him know there's a body. He'll have to call the death and perform an autopsy. Make sure he brings a transport vehicle. When you're done with that, come back to the house. Do you have your finger-print kit?"

"In my trunk."

"Good. Bring it with you."

Rebecca nodded and turned to walk to her car. Sam watched her for a moment and then turned and began his walk to the scene of the crime. Rebecca looked devastated. He had never seen her like this before. But for that matter, there had never been a murder in Rosedale for as long as he could remember. This was going to be new for everyone. He couldn't let her know he was as unnerved by this as she was. 'Guess you're never prepared for your first homicide.' he thought to himself. He wondered if he should reach out and get a detective on board to help with the investigation. Exhaling a cleansing breath, he decided he would make that decision later.

He noticed the coolness in the night air. Everything seemed strangely silent except for the sound his boots made as he walked on the pavement. As he approached the house, part of him just wanted to turn around and go back home. Back to Maggie's arms, back to his blissful, uncomplicated life. But he was the Sheriff. He was in charge. There had been a murder in Rosedale. He just kept trying to convince himself that what he was about to see, wasn't as bad as Rebecca made it seem.

But it was. It was worse. Far worse.

Doc Simpson had arrived quickly. He watched the body of Mary Haskins being zipped into the black body bag and removed from the attic by two of his employees. Deputies Sanchez and Moyer scoured the house - collecting anything that might lead them to discover who had done this. Photographs were being taken of every square inch of the beautiful dollhouse.

Sam exhaled deeply and glanced over at Doc Simpson. Dr. Arlen Simpson. Respected citizen of Rosedale. He had been the town doctor for as long as Sam could remember. As much as Sam tried to tell himself it was impossible, Arlen Simpson never seemed to age. He had to be in his 70s by now, Sam guessed.

He was the town's only doctor and also the coroner. He stood next to Sam. The dark skin on his face etched with only a trace of fine lines and the odd wisp of white blending into his dark hair. His brow was furrowed. He looked tired and concerned.

"Never seen nothing like this before. Certainly not around here."

"Can you tell the cause of death?" asked Sam.

"I'll have that answer for you after the autopsy. But I can tell you one thing - it wasn't an easy death. That poor woman suffered. Jesus Christ Sam - what kind of monster would do that to another human being ... and why? Miss Haskins was a nice lady. I don't think she had an enemy her whole life. Too young to die. Too too young."

Just then Deputy Moyer approached them. "Sheriff, there's a window on the second floor that was partially open. I'm thinking maybe that's how he got out of the house without us seeing him? We dusted for prints. Pulled a few but I don't know if they're going to help us. There's a tree close enough to that window - he could have grabbed ahold of it and climbed down."

"Make sure you dust for fingerprints on the outside of that window as well. I want to see if that's how he got in."

"Yes sir." responded Jason Moyer. "And uh, we found blood. A lot of blood in the basement. Looks like that's where he killed her and then brought her up here."

Sam nodded. "Anything else?"

"Not right now Sheriff. I'll let you know if there is." Jason turned and headed back down the stairs.

"I'm guessing she was a patient of yours?" asked Sam as he turned back to Doc Simpson.

Doc Simpson nodded.

"She have any relatives you know of? Someone who should be notified?"

Doc Simpson shook his head. "As far as I know there wasn't anyone. I hope you find the son-of-a-bitch."

"Me too."

"Well...," said Doc Simpson, rubbing his neck, "I'm going to get on home now. I'll start the autopsy first thing in the morning. I'll let you know what I find. How about you? You staying here?"

"Yeah. We still have work to do. But I'll be in the office early, so if you need to reach me, doesn't matter when, just call."

"Yes sir Sheriff." replied Doc Simpson as he turned to make his way down the stairs.

"You be careful. And say hi to Maggie for me. How's she doing? Haven't seen her in a while."

"She's good. I'll tell her you were asking."

Arlen Simpson nodded, turned and started to make his way down the narrow staircase, leaving Sam in the attic.

From the street, the house on Lincoln Way was lit up like a Christmas tree. A few of the neighboring houses were now lit up as well. The residents were curious to find out what was going on in their neighborhood.

Already the gossip had started. A real life mystery. This was the most excitement Rosedale had ever seen. Some of the neighbors had decided to camp out on the street, just outside the police tape that sectioned off the house. Lawn chairs were placed so as to offer the best view of the activity. Thermoses of lemonade and hot coffee were being passed around so that people could fill their paper cups.

Conversation halted though as the body of Mary Haskins was wheeled out and loaded into the transport vehicle. Deputy Sanchez was busy interviewing neighbors to see if anyone had seen or heard anything out of the ordinary. Brown bags filled with possible evidence were being removed from the house by Deputy Sanchez and loaded into her vehicle.

Doc Simpson weaved his way through the crowd and finally got to his car. He was exhausted but somehow not tired, if that made any sense at all. He decided that he would start the autopsy right away. No point in waiting until morning. He wasn't going to be able to sleep anyway.

With all the activity going on, it wasn't a surprise that no one noticed the man sitting quietly in one of the darkened cars parked on the street, just a few houses down from the house where Mary Haskins had lived - and died. A man wearing all black. He watched as the lifeless body of Mary Haskins was being wheeled out of the house. He couldn't help but giggle at the sight. Such memories.

He brought his fingers up to his nose and inhaled deeply. The smell of blood. He shut his eyes to better focus on the unique smell. Her blood. It had been perfect. Orgasmic in fact.

How lucky he felt. Just by a twist of fate, he ended up here, in Rosedale. His new hunting ground. The beauty was, no one seemed to know the things he knew, so he was free to do as he wanted. Free to hunt. A grin spread across his face. Life was going to be very good here in Rosedale.

5

Maggie stretched her arms above her head taking in a slow, deep breath. She opened her eyes. The early morning sun streamed through the windows. She would have to get up and get breakfast ready. Jordan had to get to school. She turned her head towards Sam and for a moment she panicked. He wasn't there. And then she remembered. He had called her late the night before to tell her he wouldn't be home. Apparently there had been a murder in Rosedale and he was going to grab a couple hours of sleep at the office. They had made arrangements to meet at Pop's Diner after she got Jordan off to school.

Quickly she took a shower and threw on her jeans and a comfortable top and was in the kitchen by the time Jordan made her way down.

"Aren't you having breakfast?" asked Jordan as she settled down in front of her plate of pancakes.

"No. Just coffee. I'm meeting your Dad at Pop's Diner this morning."

"He sure left early." commented Jordan as she drowned her pancakes in maple syrup.

"Yeah well, he's busy."   There was no point in telling Jordan about the murder. She didn't want her daughter to worry and be-sides, she didn't need to know any details. But for that matter, even Maggie didn't know any details. Sam didn't say very much when he called, but Maggie could tell he was stressed. Whatever it was, she had a feeling it was going to be a pivotal event for Rosedale.

She honestly couldn't remember there ever having been a murder in Rosedale.

She poured herself a cup of coffee. What was it about coffee in the morning? As she stood there, leaning against the counter, she looked around at her kitchen. She never realized it before, but it reminded her of her grandmother's kitchen. As a child she loved sitting at the kitchen table watching her grandmother cook. It always felt like such a warm, safe place. The thought made Maggie smile.

Now here she was in her own kitchen, with its farmhouse sink, glass front white cabinets, fresh flowers in a vase on the table. She watched as Jordan downed her pancakes and orange juice. She hoped Jordan would grow up with the same fond memories of her own kitchen. Maggie sighed and took her coffee to the table to join her daughter.

"This is super good." smiled Jordan as she was sopping up the last bit of syrup with her last bite of pancake.

"Honestly I don't know where you put it!" laughed Maggie.

"Mom, since this is Friday, would it be okay if I spent the night at Susan's? I was thinking I could just go straight to her place after school."

"Are her parents going to be there?"

"Yup! And you know her mother's even stricter than you are!" laughed Jordan. "I'll be fine."

"How is Susan? You know I haven't seen her in ages. Why don't you invite her here the next time."

"Yeah I'll do that. So can I go?"

"Yes you can go. But, I want you back here tomorrow morning. I need to take you shopping. You really need some new clothes."

"Deal. I'll be home by ten." Jordan looked at the large clock on the wall. "I've got to get going if I'm going to get to class on time."

"Do you want me to take you?"

"Nah, I'll be fine." said Jordan as she was collecting her things. I'll walk. I can take some short cuts and be there in no time."

"Okay, well, be careful." responded Maggie as she watched her daughter bolt out the front door.

"Will do!"

"See you tomorrow ... don't forget - no later than ten!" shouted Maggie from her front porch. She watched as Jordan swung around, giving her a thumbs up and then hurried down the street and out of view. Maggie couldn't help but smile.

But as she turned to go back into the house, she was hit with a sudden and overwhelming feeling that someone was watching her. She spun around, half expecting to see a person standing on her front yard, but there was no one. She looked in every direction but again, saw no one. The hair was standing up on her arms and on the back of her neck as she felt something like an electrical charge run through her body. What was happening?

And then as quickly as the feeling came over her, it was gone.

Thoughts of calling Dr. Simpson for an appointment stayed in Maggie's mind as she cleaned the kitchen. This was twice now that she experienced something she couldn't explain. Even though somehow the two incidents felt different from each other, something was definitely going on.

She put the last of the dishes away before adding the final touches to her makeup and then sending a text to Sam, letting him know she was on her way to the diner. Maggie grabbed her car keys and her purse and headed out the front door. Closing the door behind her, she had just started down the front steps when she stopped. There had been a murder in Rosedale. She didn't know any details yet, but someone had been killed. She turned back to her front door, selected her house key from the metal loop and locked it.

She had never locked her front door during the day before. Perhaps she should start now, if only for the time being. Trying to convince herself that this was only a temporary situation, she got into her car, backed out of the driveway and headed into downtown Rosedale.

She had only gotten to the end of the block before her cell phone chimed with a message. It was from Sam, letting her know he would meet her at the diner as soon as he could.

She stopped at the stop sign before making the left turn that would eventually take her downtown. Everything looked so normal. The sun was shining, she saw residents walking their dogs or riding their bikes. Picture perfect. But she couldn't help but wonder who had been killed. Was it someone she knew? Who had done such a horrible thing? She guessed Sam would fill her in on the details when she saw him. Hopefully he'd tell her there was no reason to worry.

Before she knew it, she was approaching Pop's Diner. There weren't many restaurants in Rosedale. Pop's Diner was everyone's casual favorite. Luckily there was an open parking spot right in front. As she walked through the door of the diner she was immediately hit by the strong aroma of coffee and bacon and the sound of loud conversations. The restaurant was bustling with customers. She didn't think she was hungry, but apparently she was wrong.

"Mrs. Cooper!"

Maggie turned to see Emily Patterson standing next to her, smiling. Emily had been a waitress at Pop's Diner for a while now. From what Maggie could gather, Emily's life had been difficult at times, but recently things had turned around for her. She met the love of her life - Steve - who worked at the local gas station as a mechanic and 22 year old Emily couldn't have been happier.

"You joining us for breakfast this morning?"

"Yes I am and I'm expecting my husband as well." replied Maggie, smiling. "So I'll wait to order until he gets here. Do you think we could have a booth with a bit of privacy?"

"Yes I can do that for you! This way..."

Maggie followed Emily to the back corner of the restaurant. "Will this be okay?"

"This is fine. Thanks Emily. How are you and Steve doing these days?" asked Maggie as she settled into the booth.

Emily's smile broadened as she put the menus on the table and straightened out the silverware. "Oh he's great! Everything's great! See?"

Emily pointed to a photo that was up on the wall. It was a framed photo of her and under the picture was written "Employee of the Month".

"Congratulations!" exclaimed Maggie

"Thanks." smiled Emily. "It doesn't mean a raise or nothing, but if I keep doing a good job, maybe they'll make me a manager one day. Anyway ... can I get you a cup of coffee while you wait?"

"That would be great, thank you."

And with that, Emily flashed her smile one more time and left to go get a pot of coffee as Maggie nervously fidgeted with the silverware. At least she had a clear view of the door so she could see Sam as soon as he arrived. She found herself smiling as she thought about what it had been like making love to him the night before.

"Happy thoughts?" a man asked.

Startled, Maggie looked up and was glad to see the familiar face. "Wyndham! Please join me! I'm waiting for Sam but I'm afraid he might be a while."

"Why Mrs. Cooper I would be honored to sit with you."

As Wyndham made himself comfortable, Maggie couldn't help but laugh. "Wyndham, you and I have known each other for ages ... are you ever going to call me Maggie?"

"Probably not." replied Wyndham, after reflecting for a moment. "Proper etiquette you know. You're very kind to imply that I have the right to refer to you by your given name, but I feel more comfortable addressing a lovely lady such as yourself by the more formal, 'Mrs. Cooper'."

"Well suit yourself Wyndham." replied Maggie warmly. "But if you ever change your mind, know that I would be fine with it."

"Thank you. That's very kind of you. Personally I think the world would be a better place if more people followed the simple rules of etiquette. Bad toilet training is what I call it. Bad toilet training. And now, a murder in Rosedale! Bad toilet training I tell you."

Maggie couldn't help but smile. Wyndham was one of a kind. At a mere 5'5" tall and very slender, he was not an imposing figure, but he was definitely one of a kind and truly memorable. He had been a banker in New York before coming to Rosedale. She suspected he had grown up in a rather well to do family, although she never thought it proper to ask him.

He spent his days walking the local nine hole golf course, reading extensively and painting - landscapes in oil. He was one of those people who's age was elusive. Perhaps he was in his 60s or maybe his 70s or for that matter, perhaps even his 80's. But his age was unimportant. He was one of a kind and Maggie always felt a little flattered that he fussed over her as he did.

"So obviously you heard about the murder." responded Maggie.

"Oh my yes. I think everyone has. She was a lovely lady you know. Mary Haskins. Of course none of us know the details but the rumors are 'a flyin'. I think it was probably an old long lost boyfriend. It's always the boyfriend. Just remember that Mrs. Cooper."

Maggie found herself laughing as Emily returned to the table with a pot of coffee.

"I'm sorry it took so long but I brewed a fresh pot." commented Emily as she poured the steaming coffee into Maggie's cup. "Would you like a coffee as well?" she asked Wyndham.

"Oh my no. I must be on my way but I thought I'd just say hello to my dear friend."

Emily smiled and walked away.

"Well I will remember - the boyfriend." grinned Maggie. "Luckily for me, I have a husband instead."

"Yes you do. And a fine husband he is. And I think the fact that he is the Sheriff, he might well be the exception to the rule anyway."

"One can only hope." laughed Maggie.

"Here here!" grinned Wyndham "Oh I do so enjoy your company Mrs. Cooper, but I really must be off. Perhaps we could play a bit of golf soon? It would be such fun."

"I would love that." replied Maggie. "You take care of yourself and it was wonderful seeing you!"

Standing next to the booth, Wyndham smiled at Maggie. "Always a pleasure seeing you Mrs. Cooper. We shall talk again soon." And with that, he nodded his head, gave an ever so slight bow and walked off.

As Maggie watched Wyndham leave, she saw that Sam was holding the door for him. She watched as they exchanged a few words and then she saw Sam flash his smile. God she loved that smile. After Wyndham left she saw Sam quickly look around the restaurant. She waved and he hurried to her.

"Hey Babe." he said as he bent down to give her a quick kiss before sitting down.

"Hey Babe yourself." replied Maggie. "You look exhausted."

"I am exhausted. Don't think I ended up sleeping at all last night."

"Hi Sheriff!" said Emily as she approached the table holding a pot of coffee. "Coffee?"

"Yeah please. Thanks Emily. Just keep it coming."

"No problem." replied Emily as she filled his cup.

"You and Steve doing okay?" Sam asked, smiling.

Emily grinned. "Yeah we're great! Thanks for asking! Do ya'll know what you'd like or do you need a minute?"

Maggie glanced at Sam. He nodded for her to order if she was ready.

"I'll have two eggs, sunny side up, bacon crisp and a side of rye toast." responded Maggie.

"And for you Sheriff?"

"Make mine the same, Emily. Thanks." smiled Sam. After jotting down their orders, Emily vanished back into the kitchen.

"So tell me ... what's happening?" asked Maggie, making sure to keep her voice down. Sam lowered his head and moved in closer to her.

"Mary Haskins. I don't know if you ever met her..."

Maggie shook her head. "No I didn't know her."

"Nice lady. Quiet. Lived alone in that big Victorian House on Lincoln Way."

"That big one with the roses out front?"

Sam nodded. "Found her in a chair in the attic. It was bad Maggie. Really bad. Looks like she was tortured before he finally killed her."

"Oh my God... So do you have any leads? Wyndham thinks you should look for an old boyfriend. He says it's always the boyfriend."

"No boyfriends - old or new, no family, no enemies. Nothing."

"So what are you thinking?"

Sam took a deep breath. "I just have this feeling I can't shake. It wasn't a robbery - her purse was there with her wallet. All of that was untouched. Jewelry still in the case - heck she was wearing an expensive ring that he didn't bother taking."

Sam paused to take a deep breath and consider what he was about to say. Maggie waited patiently for him to continue.

"According to Doc Simpson, as far as he can tell after his preliminary examination, there was no sexual assault. Everyone we spoke to thought very highly of her - so, no enemies.

Nice person. We're looking into her finances to see if there's anything there ... bad business deal - something. But I doubt it. She sang in the Church choir for Christ sake."

"So what are you thinking?" asked Maggie quietly.

"I could be wrong - but I don't think we'll find anything. It feels random. I can't find any motive for anyone to have done what they did - except for one ..."

"Which is?"

Sam sighed. "For the fun of it."

"What?" exclaimed Maggie, a bit too loudly as a few restaurant patrons glanced in her direction. She lowered her voice again. "What do you mean for the fun of it?"

"Someone who likes inflicting pain. Enjoys the feeling of power. Someone who simply likes to kill, likes to create fear. Something about Mary Haskins caught his attention and who knows what that was."

Maggie sipped her coffee as she considered what Sam had just said. "So you don't think it was ... personal?" asked Maggie.

Sam shook his head, wrapping his hands around his coffee cup. "No... but I could be wrong. I hope I'm wrong." He took a sip of his coffee as he considered what he was going to say. "Maybe we overlooked something. I'm meeting with Doc Simpson, Jason and Rebecca this afternoon ... and I'm going back to the Haskins house myself to look around."

"But if you're not wrong - if it was random, just for the fun of it, as you say..." Maggie stopped mid-sentence.

"He's probably moved on by now, Babe. Can't see him hanging around risking getting caught."

"But if it was for the fun of it," pressed Maggie, "and you think he likes inflicting pain - likes to create fear, then that could mean..."

"That could mean he'll strike again, here in Rosedale where everyone is already nervous..."

"Oh my God Sam…"

Sam reached to Maggie and took her hand in his. "Listen to me." Sam looked deep into Maggie's eyes. "I'm probably wrong. We've just started investigating and who knows, maybe it will turn out to be some old boyfriend with a grudge - in which case Wyndham was right and we all get to sleep at night.

But until I know for sure, I want you and Jordan to be very cautious. That means locking the doors to the house - even if you're inside. Check the windows and make sure they're all locked. I want you to be aware of everything and everyone around you. And do not open the door to anyone you don't know."

"Unless the killer is someone we DO know!" Maggie shook her head. "Is this really happening? Here in Rosedale?" Then she remembered, "Jordan! Jordan wanted to go to Susan's after school and spend the night. I told her it was okay. Should I call her and tell her to come home instead?"

Sam thought for a minute. "No. I don't want to frighten her. I'll call Susan's mother and tell her to be careful and not let the girls go anywhere alone. But after tonight, let's have her stay close to home. She can have her friends over to our place."

"Okay."

"Listen, " Sam said quietly. "I'm probably being overly cautious. There's a very good chance whoever did this is long gone and I'm wrong about the motive. I don't want to scare you, but until I have a better handle on what's going on, I just want you to be aware, that's all. I couldn't stand it if anything happened to you or Jordan."

Maggie nodded. She was about to say something when she spied Emily coming towards them with two plates heaped with food. She made sure to make herself smile as Emily approached. Sam did the same.

"Okay, here you go!" grinned Emily as she placed the dishes on the table. "Can I get you anything else?"

"No this is great.   Thanks Emily." responded Maggie.

"If you need anything just let me know!"

Maggie watched as Emily disappeared back into the kitchen.   Suddenly everything felt just a little off. How could this be happening — in Rosedale of all places. Maggie looked around at the other customers in the restaurant. Suddenly they seemed like strangers to her. Could one of them be the person who did this? What secrets were they keeping? Were these the same people she passed every day? Is it possible she knew the killer?   Rosedale wasn't very big. He could be in this restaurant right now and no one would know.

She looked around the restaurant as Sam was busy eating. Almost every table was taken and there was a line of customers waiting to be seated. Her eyes took in the faces. But there was one, a man, brown hair, glasses ... he was looking at her. Why was he looking at her like that? He was staring at her. Suddenly a chill ran down her spine.

"Sam..."

Sam looked up. "What?"

She looked into his eyes and spoke in a low yet firm voice. "There's a man standing in line waiting to be seated. Plaid shirt, brown hair, glasses. I've never seen him before and he's staring at me. Something's not right..."

Sam turned around to get a look at the line of customers. "I don't see anyone in a plaid shirt..."

"He's right there!" said Maggie in a frustrated voice. But as she looked over to the line, she no longer saw him. Quickly she scanned the restaurant, but didn't see him anywhere. "He's gone. He was standing right there, behind the woman in the blue dress."

Sam put down his fork and once again took Maggie's hand in his. "Look at me."

Maggie looked deep into those blue eyes of his. She saw worry and concern, but she also saw exhaustion. She knew he didn't need her being hysterical at this point.

"I don't want you afraid." said Sam softly. "I love you. I just want you to be careful. I don't want you to panic. Okay?"

She nodded. "I love you too. More than you'll ever know. I'll be okay. It's just the shock I guess. Who would think something like this could happen. You don't have to worry about me - or Jordan. You do what you have to do ... but promise me something?"

"Anything." responded Sam softly.

"Just promise me you'll be careful. I couldn't bear anything happening to you either."

Sam smiled and kissed her hand.

6

Doc Simpson sighed. "It wasn't an easy death, I'll tell you that. Evidence of torture - a severe beating about the head, I would say with a fairly heavy object, wooden - judging from the splinters I found embedded in the wounds; burns to her arms and legs. Looks like he strangled her to a point and then would back off. I see numerous strangulation attempts. Best I can tell she died from the knife wound to her neck. The jugular was severed. The cut into the abdomen was done post mortem, thank God. He's one crazy son-of-a-bitch."

Sam rubbed his forehead. He hadn't had a migraine for as long as he could remember, but it felt like he was getting one now. He sat at his desk. Doc Simpson sat in the old leather chair facing him, with his notes resting on Sam's desk, while Deputies Moyer and Sanchez sat on the worn sofa that backed up against the back wall.

Sam had made sure to close his office door so that Bernice wouldn't hear the details of what they were discussing, but he figured she was probably standing on the other side of the door trying to listen anyway. As the light poured through the windows behind him, he was reminded of how dingy his office looked. He glanced over at Rebecca.

"I spoke with the neighbors," added Rebecca, sensing it was her turn to speak. "No one saw anyone unusual - not on the block or around the Haskins house. I spoke with a few women who were her close friends. She never confided in them that there was anything going on in her life she was concerned about. No problems at all. No talk of anyone showing up from her past. As far as they knew, everything was perfectly normal. Nothing to indicate she was having issues with anyone. In fact everyone I spoke to had nothing but kind words for her. Everybody loved her."

"Well obviously not everybody." responded Sam. "No one heard anything during the evening hours?"

Rebecca shook her head.

Jason looking a little awkward, slightly raised his hand as though getting permission to speak. Sam nodded at him. "Well," started Jason, reading from his notes, "judging from the blood in the basement, that's where the murder took place - and the torture. There was a bloody piece of two by four, rope, that sort of thing. We photographed everything and bagged and tagged it all.

There was a lot of blood. It would make sense that no one heard anything. You could scream bloody murder in that basement and no one would hear you." Jason suddenly looked uncomfortable and apologetic. "Sorry about the poor choice of words there..."

Sam waved it off. "That's okay. Any sign of forced entry? What about that window?"

"Nothing." continued Jason. "No sign of forced entry anywhere and the only finger-prints on that window upstairs, were Mary Haskins'. So all I can figure is that he must have been wearing gloves. Or maybe she just let him in. Sheriff you know as well as I do that nobody locks their doors around here. And until now, nobody's ever been worried about opening the door to anybody! This is Rosedale not some big city. But Deputy Sanchez and I heard him running upstairs. He had to have at least exited out that window.

Honestly Sheriff, we looked all over that house. It's as if he just showed up, killed her and then disappeared into thin air. There's just no trace of him anywhere. It's going to take a while before we get the results of the blood samples taken from the basement. It's not unusual for a perpetrator to cut himself while using a knife on his victim so I'm thinking some of his blood has to be in that basement too. We just have to find it."

Sam's head was really beginning to throb. He opened his desk drawer hoping to see a bottle of aspirin but of course there wasn't any. Everyone was waiting for him to tell them what to do. If only he knew. In his entire career he had never had to deal with a murder, much less one like this.

He took a deep breath. If only the pounding would stop he would be able to think more clearly.

"Oh and there was evidence of scraping on her wrists - indicative of handcuffs and I found adhesive residue on her mouth." added Doc Simpson as he read from his notes.

"Okay then," began Sam. "so she either invited him in or he let himself in somehow. Taped her mouth, put cuffs on her and took her to the basement where he proceeded to torture and eventually kill her. At this point I don't know if the music was to cover any noise, or it was for dramatic purposes. The son-of-a-bitch is having fun." He turned to Jason. "No evidence on the CD or the player?"

Jason shook his head. "Nothing. It was clean. Just that one song recorded over and over again - until it stopped when it did."

Sam sighed. "Well, he obviously enjoyed what he was doing and enjoys showing off his work. But why stage in the attic? Why take her through the house and put her in the attic?"

Jason cleared his throat. "Well, it took us longer to find her. Maybe that gave him time to make sure he got out of the house."

"Or ..." began Rebecca.

Sam looked at her. "Or what?"

Rebecca looked a little uncomfortable. "Well this is going to sound stupid."

Sam shrugged. "Under the circumstances I wouldn't worry about that. We're just floating ideas at this point. So ... or what?"

"Well just that the attic is a place where you put things that you're done with. Maybe he just felt like it. He was done with her ... nothing more..."

The pounding in Sam's head had intensified. "Bernice?" There was no response. "Bernice I know you're on the other side of that door."

All four watched as Sam's office door slowly opened. Bernice looked a little uncomfortable at being caught eavesdropping.

"Bernice," continued Sam, "I need you to run to the pharmacy for me and get me some aspirin or whatever they suggest for a whopper of a migraine. Take the money out of petty cash."

"Yes Sheriff." replied Bernice. He watched her as she headed out of the office and onto the street. Maybe once he got rid of his headache he could think a little more clearly. Then it would be time for him to make a stop by the Haskins house and look around. It was going to be a long day.

*   *   *

Maggie slowly pushed the cart through the grocery store. After leaving the diner, she thought she might as well get some of the groceries she needed. However, with her mind constantly replaying what Sam had told her, she was finding it difficult to concentrate on mundane things like laundry detergent and milk. But there was something comforting about the familiar process of slowly walking around the store, looking at the products as she strolled by.

The look in Sam's eyes had scared her. She had never seen him like this. But then, nothing like this had ever happened in Rosedale. Could this be real? Suddenly the people she passed in the aisles looked different to her. Every man was a suspect. Every man was someone to be feared. Every woman was perhaps someone who wasn't going to live through this.

She had never felt like this before. She knew though that she had to get a grip on things or she'd end up scaring Jordan - and that was the last thing she wanted to do.

Sam was right - it made more sense that whoever it was had long since left Rosedale. After all, he must have known that the residents would be much more careful now that they were on the alert. It wouldn't be as easy for him to do this again.

She smiled to herself. Yes - he was most likely gone. All the same, she knew they still had to be cautious until Sam was sure all had returned to normal.

She looked down at her cart. Without paying much attention to what she was doing, she had managed to gather up quite a bit of groceries. All she had still to get was coffee and then she'd be done. Slowly she pushed the cart towards the coffee aisle. The peaceful piped in music helped to calm her nerves. Captain and Tennille's Muskrat Love played softly in the background as though nothing could possibly be wrong.

Hugh's Grocery. It still had wooden floors and a manager who knew your name and more than he should about your personal life. It wasn't a large store like some of the chains, but what it lacked in size, it made up for in service.

'Steaks!' she thought to herself. 'I think I'll get a few steaks and we can put them on the grill when Sam gets home.'

She quickly made a sharp u-turn and headed to the meat counter.

"Mrs. Cooper! Nice to see you this morning!" exclaimed George Baxter, Hugh's Grocery's long time butcher.

"I'm doing good George. How about you?"

"Oh can't complain." smiled George. "And even if I could, no one would listen."

"Isn't that the truth?" smiled Maggie.

"So what will it be today Mrs. Cooper?"

"I was thinking about some rib-eyes. Three. Do you have any with some good marbling?"

"How about this?" asked George as he gathered one of the steaks onto a sheet of paper and presented it to Maggie.

"That looks perfect. Could I have three please?"

"Yes Ma'am!" responded George as he began putting the order together. "Terrible about Mary Haskins isn't it? She was just in here the other day. Nice lady. Guess you never know... One day you're here and the next..." His voice trailed off.

Maggie said nothing. There was nothing to say. She didn't want to get into a conversation with him about it. The thought of what had happened still scared her and she certainly didn't want to accidentally divulge anything that Sam had told her over breakfast. She watched as George wrapped the last of the steaks and applied the price stickers to the packaging. Smiling, he handed her the parcel.

"Here you go Mrs. Cooper. Enjoy. And be careful."

"Thank you George. And you be careful too." smiled Maggie. She put the package in her cart and headed towards the coffee aisle.

As she slowly pushed the cart, letting the soft music calm her nerves - an instrumental version of Rainy Days and Mondays had started to play - she had a disturbing thought. How well did she really know George? He was a butcher. He worked with knives. He must be in his 50s ... maybe 60s even. Did he have family? She didn't know. She really didn't know him at all. For all she knew...

'Stop that!' she scolded herself. She knew she was letting her imagination get the better of her. Even still, she found it virtually impossible to stop watching the other customers as she passed them. She finally reached her destination and after putting a large container of ground coffee in her cart, she headed towards the registers.

Luckily the store wasn't very busy at that hour in the morning, so at least she wouldn't have to wait in line. As she approached, she saw an unfamiliar face manning the register. It was a young man, maybe twenty something. Thin build with his medium length hair tied back in the all too familiar "man bun" that Maggie simply hated. Maggie couldn't figure out if the look on his face was one of sheer boredom or perhaps anger at finding himself working at a grocery store.

"Did you find everything you were looking for?" asked the young man as he started to scan her groceries.

"Yes I did." replied Maggie, even though she knew he wasn't really waiting for her answer. She glanced down at his name tag. "Kenny, I've never seen you here before. I'm used to seeing Ruth. Is she off today?" asked Maggie as she piled even more groceries up onto the belt.

"Ruth?" questioned Kenny. He stopped for a moment as if trying to recollect the name.

"Yeah, you know ... red hair, always telling jokes... Then again you're new here so maybe you don't know who I'm talking about."

The young man shook his head and resumed scanning items.

"Actually I've been here forever and I don't recall a Ruth."

Maggie was starting to feel annoyed. There was a certain rudeness to his response that she thought unnecessary. He certainly hadn't been here forever. She had never seen him before. Unless of course he had been working in some other area and just started at the registers. That was probably it.

"If you'd like, I could ask Mike the manager."

"No," Maggie shook her head. "It's not important. It doesn't matter."

"That comes to $97.32."

Maggie reached in her purse to retrieve some cash. She was still feeling a little annoyed as she handed over $100 and waited for her change. He seemed so sure of himself. Almost cocky. But, thought Maggie, maybe there was some kind of store policy about giving out information on employees. That was probably it.

*   *   *

His headache finally gone, Sam pulled up to the Haskins house. The only clue that something horrific had happened was the yellow police tape still surrounding the house. That, and Bill Campbell who Sam had deputized and posted at the front door of the house, in order to make sure no one disturbed the scene. Inside he knew he would find the forensic's team still collecting evidence.

He turned off his car and sat, staring at the house. The picture of what he had seen in the attic was still clear in his head. He had the feeling it would always be that way. What was it about Mary Haskins he wondered. Why her? Why her house? Why this street?

He thought about his breakfast with Maggie. The look in her eyes as he told her about what had happened. It killed him to see her so afraid. All he could do now though was hope whoever was responsible had indeed left the vicinity. If it was a stranger to Mary Haskins and if fingerprints could not be found and matched, there was a very good chance they would never be able to solve this murder.

He reflected on the fact though that since Mary had no family, he would never have to deal with a tearful loved one begging for answers. He didn't have any and for some reason, believed he may never.

He couldn't help but feel sorry for Mary Haskins. All alone. No one fighting for her. No family. No one. He couldn't imagine what he would do without Maggie and Jordan. What a sad life and death for Mary Haskins. The woman everyone liked but was still alone.

He would do his best to find who had done this. He would be Mary's family.

With that, Sam exhaled deeply and exited his car. He walked slowly towards the Haskins house. He imagined Mary Haskins standing on her front porch. A smile on her face as she greeted one of her friends. Sam wondered if maybe one of those friends could have done this to her. Maybe it was someone she knew, or at least thought she knew. Sam continued walking slowly on the sidewalk, staring at the Haskins house across the street. If only the house could talk. It knew. It had seen it.

Sam glanced down the road to make sure there was no traffic and then crossed the street. He didn't exactly know what he was hoping to find inside the house. But he knew he could feel Mary Haskins in his very soul. He had to do what he could. And he had to make sure no one else would be hurt.

Sitting in his car, a safe distance away, the man watched Sheriff Cooper cross the street towards the Haskins house. Some idiot, whoever he was, had been standing guard on the porch the entire day, which meant there had been no way of getting back into the house. That made him angry. Going back was half the fun.

As he bit down on his hamburger a bit of ketchup collected in the corner of his mouth. Chewing slowly, he reached for the napkin that sat on the passenger seat and wiped his mouth, never for an instant diverting his gaze. This was the best entertainment he could have hoped for. He had to smile though. He knew they would find nothing. He was smart. Smarter than they were.

He remembered Mary Haskins begging him for her life. It was a good memory. Another bite of his hamburger as he watched Sam begin to climb the front stairs of the house.

He had seen the Sheriff around town. Had a pretty wife and an even prettier daughter. He smiled as he chewed. Maybe in a little while he'd have to pay them a visit. Especially the daughter. Especially the daughter.

He shoved the remainder of the hamburger into his mouth as bits of bread landed on his shirt. He would sit there a while longer and watch the entertainment. And then perhaps a drive. Yeah ... a drive.

7

"I honestly don't know what's wrong with me. I'm not sleeping. I'm having these weird dreams almost every night."

Patty studied her friend for a moment. She and Maggie were at the local gym, side by side on stationary bikes. "Well maybe you should get ahold of Dr. Simpson. Maybe he could give you something to help you sleep."

Maggie sighed and wiped the back of her neck with her towel as she continued to pedal. "Yeah I suppose that's not a bad idea. But, I just hate going to the doctor, you know? ...

I've been having these strange panic attacks too - at least that's the only way I can describe them."

"Panic attacks?" exclaimed her friend. "That's weird. But maybe it's because you're not sleeping. Sleep deprivation can do a lot of strange things to you."

"I suppose you're right."

"Aren't I always?" laughed Patty. "How's Sam doing?"

Maggie sighed. "As good as can be expected. I think he's frustrated that they aren't any closer to figuring out who killed the Haskins woman."

"Well, luckily it's been a couple of weeks and everything's been quiet. Maybe Sam was right and the guy moved on."

"I hope so."

"I wonder when they're going to put the house up for sale."

Maggie stopped pedaling and looked at her friend in shock.

"Don't look at me that way! It's a nice house! I was just curious that's all. You can't be a successful real estate agent without a house to sell!"

Maggie continued to stare at her.

"Okay! Let's just forget I asked."

"I'm trying to." responded Maggie as she resumed pedaling. She looked around the gym trying to take her mind off her now burning legs. The sound of weights clanking, music playing through the sound system designed to motivate, body builders admiring their biceps in the mirrors that lined the walls of the gym.

Slowly her gaze moved towards the front doors. It took a second before her brain made sense of what she was seeing, but there, just inside of the gym, still on the other side of the check-in desk, stood the man she had seen at the restaurant a couple of weeks earlier - shaggy brown hair, dark rimmed glasses. Again, as before, he was just standing there, staring at her. Maggie could feel the panic rise up inside of her. There was no emotion in his gaze - but it was intense.

Gym patrons walked passed him without seeming to notice the strange man who appeared quite out of place. Fear was starting to overtake Maggie. She stopped pedaling. She felt drawn to him. She could feel herself falling into some sort of abyss. She had to pull herself out. She had to tell Patty. She needed her to confirm what she was seeing. She forced herself to look away. She turned to look at her friend.

Patty, now with her eyes shut, was still pedaling her bike, oblivious to the sudden change in Maggie. However, just as Maggie was about to speak, she turned her gaze back to the doors of the gym, back to the stranger, but he was gone. Wildly she looked around, hoping to see him - but it was to no avail. He had vanished. Just as before.

Maggie started pedaling again. Was he even there to begin with, or was it possible she was imagining this person? Or could it be this was the man who killed Mary Haskins and was now watching her? Panic was overtaking her thoughts. Until someone else saw him, she couldn't be sure of anything. She was happy she hadn't said anything to Patty. Patty would have thought she had lost her mind. Maybe she had.

The dreams, the panic attacks, her inability to sleep and now this strange vision of a man who just stands off in the distance and does nothing more than stare at her ... maybe seeing a doctor was a good idea.

By the time they finished another 20 minutes on the stationary bikes, followed by 30 minutes of weights, they were ready to be done and head to the diner for their usual lunch.

"What do you say we walk?" asked Patty as she held the door open for her friend. "Sun is shining, birds are singing and we both need some fresh air."

"Yeah," replied Maggie, tying her jacket around her waist. That sounds good. Guess we can leave our cars here."

They started walking but it didn't take long for Patty to notice something had changed. Maggie seemed distracted. "Look I'm sorry if me asking about the house was insensitive. I didn't mean for it to come out the way it did."

"It's not that." Maggie stopped walking and turned to her friend. "I'm just not feeling really well all of a sudden. Do you think I could have a raincheck for lunch? I really think I need to go home."

Patty looked concerned. "Sure. No problem. Are you going to be okay driving?"

Maggie nodded. "Yeah. I just think I need to lie down for a few."

With that, Maggie left Patty standing on the sidewalk as she headed for her car.

"Okay, well, call me later!" Patty called to her from across the parking lot.

Maggie couldn't get to her car fast enough. Another panic attack was starting. She could feel it. Fumbling in her purse, she finally grabbed her keys and managed to get safely inside her car before it got any worse. She sat with her hands on the steering wheel, trying to regulate her breathing.

She shut her eyes for a moment but when she opened them, she wasn't prepared for what she saw. The hands on the steering wheel - they weren't hers. They belonged to a man. She looked around the inside of the car but it wasn't her car. Nothing was right.

Her breathing quickened and she could feel her heart pounding in her chest. What was going on? Why was she hallucinating? She shut her eyes once more and again, tried to calm herself and slow her breathing.

But this time, when she slowly opened her eyes, they were her hands on the steering wheel and she was back in her own car. She sat there dazed and confused. She would make that appointment with Dr. Simpson.

What was wrong with her? All the possibilities ran through her head. She needed to get home. Now. Before anything else happened.

*   *   *

Father McNeal was walking back from the grocery store and thought he had seen Mrs. Cooper leaving the gym. But, after finally crossing the street in order to talk to her, she seemed to have vanished.

'Oh well', he thought to himself. 'I'll probably see her at Mass tomorrow.'

He turned away from the parking lot and resumed his walk back to the rectory - a plastic bag of groceries swinging from his right hand.

He had wanted to thank her for coming to Mary Haskins' funeral service. Without family, it would have been a sad day indeed if Mrs. Cooper hadn't been there and hadn't been so kind as to round up others from Rosedale to attend as well. She made sure that if Ms. Haskins was looking down from above, she would see that she was loved and would be missed.   Seeing Maggie Cooper started him thinking again about the Haskins woman.

Father McNeal had wanted to be a priest for as far back as he could remember. How lucky he was that he was given the Parish in Rosedale to call his own. He knew his superiors in the Church could relocate him at any time but he tried not to even consider that possibility. Rosedale was his home. Rosedale was perfect. Something about it reminded him of his childhood - the innocence of it all. Riding his bike down the street, playing baseball with his friends. And here he was now - a man barely in his 30s getting to live the life he had always wanted - serving God and the community.

He had met Mary Haskins a number of times. Lovely woman. He would always remember her smile as she walked up to him holding another of her wonderful pies for the Church's bake sale. She said her secret to her pies was that she always listened to big band music while she baked. Claimed it made her crust a little flakier. She had even surprised him a few times by bringing him one of her blueberry pies without any reason whatsoever. She would always joke that she was hoping to get a good seat in Heaven.

He caught himself smiling at the memory, but then a few seconds later, stopped, when he remembered her terrible end. "I'm so sorry, Mary." he said aloud softly "I hope you're front row center up there. You will be missed."

He walked the remaining few blocks trying not to think of Mary for the time being. He liked the feel of the sun on his face and the smell of flowers planted in gardens along the way. What a glorious day it was. He would put his groceries away, perhaps make some tea and then work on his sermon for tomorrow. He thought a sermon about forgiveness would be a good choice for the upcoming Mass, especially as everyone was dealing with the murder.

It wasn't long before he saw the old stone Church standing proud at the top of the hill. Next to it was the small but equally impressive stone rectory. His home. He looked forward to settling down and writing. He felt inspired.

He followed the path to his front door, pulling out his keys from his pocket. Ever since the murder of Mary Haskins, he started locking the rectory door when he wasn't there. His belief in God was strong and he knew he could always count on Him for assistance, but he saw nothing wrong with making God's job a little easier when he could.

Turning the key in the lock, he heard the familiar clunk of the dead bolt as it opened. Returning the keys to his pocket, he walked into the rectory, shutting the door behind him.

The interior of the rectory was old and a little worn, but it was home and always made him feel welcomed. He would have his tea out on the back porch. Yes, that would be nice.

He made his way straight back from the front door into the kitchen with its antique enamel fridge and stove. The large window over the sink helped bathe the kitchen in sunlight. It was beautiful.

He put away his groceries, put the kettle on the stove, retrieved a tea bag from the pantry and put it in his favorite mug. He was just about to reach back into the pantry for a few cookies to go with his tea, when he heard a knock at his front door.

Turning off the kettle, he made his way back down the hall. Peering through the peep hole, he could only make out the figure of a man who seemed to be looking out towards the street. Curious, Father McNeal opened the door. As he did, the man turned and looked at him. A stranger. At least Father McNeal had never seen him before - or at least he didn't remember seeing him.

"Yes? Hello?" asked Father McNeal politely

From what Father McNeal could surmise, the man must have been in his 20s or maybe even 30s with dark brown hair. Nothing in particular stood out about him, except for maybe his eyes. There was something about his eyes. That and the fact he was a rather imposing figure.

"Yeah Father... I'm new here in town and uh... I was thinking about joining your Church." he spoke slowly.

Father McNeal was a little surprised by the sound of the man's voice. It was much deeper than he expected it to be and oddly flat. The man's mannerisms and shy demeanor however, made Father McNeal think of a child.

Father McNeal smiled at him. "Well, perhaps you could visit me in my office on Monday and we could chat then? Truthfully I was just about to start working on my sermon for tomorrow. You would however be more than welcome to attend our 9:00 a.m. service tomorrow and meet our parishioners".

"Okay," the man mumbled with his deep voice, "I was kinda hoping to be able to talk to you today, being I don't know anyone in town. But I guess even a priest needs to leave work sometime."

The man nodded his head and turned to leave. Suddenly Father McNeal felt selfish and guilty at the thought of turning him away.

"Wait! ' I suppose that's not very neighborly of me, to say the very least. Perhaps instead of writing my sermon on forgiveness, I should write it on the importance of fellowship. By all means I'd be happy to talk with you. And may I say welcome to Rosedale." Father McNeal extended his hand to the man who, after a brief hesitation, accepted the display of friendship.

"Robert Kraus. You can just call me Robert."

Father McNeal smiled broadly. "Well Robert, I'm Father McNeal. Father David McNeal. Please won't you come in? I was just about to make myself some tea. Perhaps you'd care to join me and we could sit outside on the porch and have a chat. I can't talk very long since I do need to get my sermon done, but I'm happy to spend a few minutes chatting."

Robert entered the rectory and stood in the foyer looking a little uncomfortable and strangely awkward, with his hands shoved into the pockets of his pants. Father McNeal shut the door behind him and then led him into the comfortable kitchen. He motioned to Robert to have a seat at the table. He put the kettle back on the stove and reached up to the cabinet to retrieve a cup for his guest.

"How do you take your tea? Do you like it with milk or —"

*   *   *

"I don't know why you won't let me go!" complained a frustrated Jordan.

Maggie, looking exhausted from arguing, sighed. "You know why. Until your father gives the all clear, you're staying close to home. We aren't taking any chances and especially not with you!"

"Oh this is just stupid!"

"Jordan!"

"Seriously Mom! I'm sorry that lady got killed, but it's been two weeks and nothing else has happened! What are you going to do? Keep me on house arrest for the rest of my life?"

"You know that's not a bad idea!"

"Mom!"

"Look I'm sorry but you cannot go to the party. That's final. If you want to get together with your friends, you can invite them here. I've got no problem with that. But there's no point in continuing this conversation. We're not changing our minds. That's it."

Jordan stared at her mother in disbelief and then, with a huff, turned and stomped up the stairs. A few seconds later, Maggie heard the door to her bedroom slam shut.

"That went well." Maggie mumbled to herself. She glanced at the clock on the wall in the kitchen. Sam would be home soon, thank God. Between seeing the mystery man staring at her at the gym, the weird experience she had in the car and now the argument with Jordan - it was becoming just a bit too much.

Why did it feel as though everything was unraveling? Who was that man she kept seeing? Was he even real? The headaches, the lack of sleep, the panic attacks ... maybe he was some sort of hallucination ... like when she was in the car.

Coffee. When in doubt, have a cup of coffee. Maggie let herself smile as she poured water into the coffee maker, added four heaping spoons of ground coffee and pressed the brew button. Coffee might clear her mind a bit. Even the smell of it brewing was strangely comforting.

Sam was bringing dinner home so at least she didn't have to cook. Have a cup of coffee, curl up on the sofa and relax. She was probably just stressed out about this whole Mary Haskins thing.

But Jordan was right. It had been a couple of weeks and nothing out of the ordinary had happened in Rosedale. Hopefully everything could get back to normal soon. Well, at least normal for everyone except for Mary Haskins.

Maggie rubbed her forehead. 'I need to get those thoughts out of my mind.' she scolded herself. With the coffee brewing, she took the half and half creamer out of the fridge and put it on the counter.

She reached up to the cabinet to get her favorite mug, but the second she grabbed ahold of it, a feeling swept through her body with the sudden impact of a strong wave. She felt it hit her head and then wash completely over her body. In a flash it felt as though she was deep underwater.

Maggie was no longer in the kitchen, but rather she was outside. Outside walking in a neighborhood that didn't look familiar; hearing sounds she couldn't identify. Slowly she looked at her hand, expecting to see herself gripping a coffee mug, but she didn't see a mug, nor did she see her hand. Once again, she was staring down at the hands of a man. In disbelief she started to look up. She could hear something familiar. What was that? What was that sound? She shut her eyes. She didn't want to see any more. What was that sound?

"Maggie! Maggie!"

She opened her eyes. She was staring at a man's face. For a second she felt she needed to fight him, but then as her senses began to return, she realized it was Sam. Her Sam. He was holding her.

She was on the floor back in her own kitchen. Pieces of the shattered coffee mug were scattered everywhere. Maggie shifted her gaze and saw Jordan in the corner of the kitchen, obviously upset. Sam, realizing that Maggie was coming to, picked her up and carried her to the sofa in the living room.

"Jordan get me a glass of water please."

"What happened?" mumbled Maggie, looking confused.

Jordan came back into the living room, holding the glass of water. She handed it to her father.

"Here, drink this." instructed Sam as he held the glass to her lips. After a couple of sips, Maggie backed away and nodded.

"I'm okay. What happened?"

"I don't know babe." replied Sam. I walked into the kitchen and you were passed out on the floor."

"It's probably my fault!" lamented Jordan. "Mom and I were arguing. I'm sorry for being so horrible Mom."

Maggie smiled. "This was not your fault Jordan. It wasn't. Whatever happened it had absolutely nothing to do with you. But I'm feeling better now. Maybe I just lost my balance when I reached up to get a mug."

"Are you sure you're okay?" asked Jordan quietly.

"Positive. But would you mind picking up the broken mug? I don't want anyone stepping on a piece."

Jordan nodded and retreated to the kitchen. Sam and Maggie stared at each other.

"Okay ... so what happened Maggie?"

Maggie sighed. "Honestly Sam I don't know. One minute I was getting a coffee mug out of the cupboard and the next minute I was looking into your face."

Maggie had decided she wasn't ready to tell Sam about the vision - or whatever it was. There was no point in bringing that up until she could offer some sort of rational explanation. "But I promise, come Monday morning, I'll call Dr. Simpson and get an appointment. Get everything checked out and make sure nothing is wrong. It's probably just something stupid. But I will call him Monday morning."

"That's a good idea. But an even better idea is that I call Doc Simpson right now at home and get you an appointment for Monday morning. How's that?" Sam smiled and kissed her on her forehead.

Maggie smiled back. How she loved him. "If you say so, Sheriff." she replied.

"I brought chicken for dinner. Do you feel like eating or do you want to just lie here for a bit?"

"No really I'm fine!" replied Maggie. "Whatever it was, it's passed. And I'm starved. Lead me to the chicken!"

Maggie put her arm around Sam's waist and they walked together into the kitchen. It had been a long day.

8

Sunday morning was beautiful. The temperature was perfect and the only clouds in the sky were white, fluffy and drifting lazily off in the horizon. It was a perfect morning in Rosedale. But then, it always seemed to be a perfect morning in Rosedale.

Sam had to work, so Maggie and Jordan were on their way to Church without him. It was one of the few times Maggie could get her daughter to wear a dress, so that was always something to look forward to.

Maggie couldn't help but notice how much Jordan had grown up. Soon she would be out on her own, but that was a thought Maggie wasn't prepared to deal with today. Not today.

There was such a strong sense of community in Rosedale. Going to Church was as much about the sermon and the connection to God as it was catching up with the other residents of the town. She had seen the same play out in front of the other places of worship throughout Rosedale. It seemed everyone simply enjoyed being social and perhaps gossiping just a little.

Jordan was no longer upset about not being able to go out, which was something Maggie was grateful for. She would talk with Sam later that evening to see if perhaps they could loosen the reins a bit on their daughter. It really didn't seem fair to continue to restrict her as they had. With such a beautiful day unfolding, it was hard to believe anything bad had ever happened in this wonderful town.

Sam had called Dr. Simpson and set up an appointment for Maggie at 10:00 Monday morning. She was a little nervous about the thought of telling the good doctor that she had been having hallucinations, but she had to get to the bottom of what was going on. It might be serious.

She didn't let on to Sam or Jordan how nervous she felt about it - she didn't want them to worry. But she hoped it would turn out to be nothing that couldn't be cured with a couple sleeping pills.

Maggie parked the car and she and Jordan walked towards the steps leading up to the impressive looking Church. As usual, people had gathered outside before going in, so as to talk and laugh with friends they hadn't seen since the previous Sunday.

The town was small enough that Father McNeal only had one service on Sunday - that was at 9:00 a.m. He had tried having a few services throughout the day, but attendance was sparse. So, one service on Sunday morning seemed to suit everyone.

As Maggie and Jordan approached, Maggie noticed Wyndham was in the crowd, smiling and waving to her. She waved back and they made their way to him.

"Mrs. Cooper! Lovely to see you!" bubbled Wyndham. "And you, Miss Cooper," Wyndham turned his gaze to Jordan, "you are more stunning every time I see you!"

Jordan smiled back, obviously a little embarrassed.

"May I join the two of you inside the Church?"

"Of course!" responded Maggie. "But it's almost a shame we have to go inside - it's so beautiful out here."

"It is indeed!" answered Wyndham as he checked his watch. "However, taking note of the time, I'm thinking we really should consider moving inside. The Mass will be starting in about ten minutes. Maybe after, the three of us could go to the diner? They have a wonderful Sunday brunch as I'm sure you know!"

"That sounds perfect." agreed Maggie, smiling. "Sam is working so there's no reason for us to hurry home."

She glanced around at the crowd that had gathered outside the Church. There were some familiar faces and as usual, some not familiar. One of the faces she recognized was Deputy Sanchez.

Rebecca was surrounded by a small group of women who were all chatting and laughing. When she looked up and saw Maggie, she waved and smiled before turning her attention back to her friends. Maggie liked Rebecca Sanchez. She was a good addition to the Sheriff's office and Sam spoke highly of her.

It was so nice to see life returning to normal. Maggie smiled at the thought, but then remembered her appointment in the morning.

It was at that precise moment blood curdling screams were heard coming from inside the Church.

Immediately all conversations stopped. Everyone froze and looked up the steps to the Church. Maggie and Deputy Sanchez made eye contact. Deputy Sanchez nodded.

"Wyndham keep Jordan here!"

Without waiting for a response, Maggie and Deputy Sanchez ran up the stone steps and into the Church.

Upon entering, it took a second for their eyes to adjust to the dim lighting. They looked straight ahead and saw four people. Three women were huddled on the floor behind the pews. One was crying hysterically. The forth, a man, turned to them as they approached.

As Maggie became more and more accustomed to the Church lighting, she saw other small groups of people comforting each other, some crying. Two men were on their knees trying to revive someone who had obviously passed out. Others running from the Church, bumping into Maggie and Rebecca, almost knocking them over, as though they weren't even aware anyone stood in front of them.

The two women stared at each other, shaking their heads. What had gone on here? Why was everyone upset? They quickly looked around the Church, but saw nothing that should have triggered this reaction.

The man who saw them enter the Church slowly approached. He was probably in his 70s and in obvious distress. He was shaking. Maggie was afraid he was going to pass out before getting to them. He walked directly up to Deputy Sanchez and stared deep into her eyes. "What's happening?" he implored. "What's happening to Rosedale?"

Deputy Sanchez stared at him, confused. He slowly started to stumble out of the Church.

"Wait!" called Rebecca. "What happened in here?"

The man stopped and slowly turned to face her. "Father O'Neal. God help us. God help us all." he mumbled and continued to exit the Church.

Rebecca and Maggie looked at each other, completely at a loss as to what had happened. They entered the main part of the Church and saw even more parishioners in obvious distress but still no idea why. A woman was quickly exiting the Church and as she did so, bumped into Rebecca, who this time grabbed her before she could get away.

"What happened in here?" demanded Rebecca.

The woman stopped and stared at her and then slowly, raised her hand and pointed towards the alter at the front of the Church. Both Rebecca and Maggie turned their gaze to where the woman pointed. As soon as Rebecca released her hold, the woman ran from the Church, leaving the two of them standing staring at the alter.

"I don't see anything!" whispered Maggie.

"Neither do I ..."

"I see the pulpit, the altar, the ..." Maggie stopped speaking and froze.

"Maggie what is it? What?"

Strangely, Maggie felt as though the room had suddenly disappeared. For a few brief seconds, all she could hear was the sound of her own heart beat. All she could see, was the monstrosity in front of her. After what felt like an eternity, she gathered herself enough to answer Rebecca's question. "The cross. Look at the cross." she whispered.

Slowly, Rebecca shifted her gaze from Maggie, to the altar and then up to the large cross that hung above. It took a few moments, but then she saw it.

"Oh my God." said Rebecca softly with a look of disbelief and horror on her face. "Father McNeal."

There, attached to the large cross that hung from the ceiling, was Father McNeal.

His body laying over top of the image of Jesus. His hands and feet nailed in place. Again, it looked as though he had been cut down the middle, as Mary Haskins had been - covered in blood and with the same look of terror and agony on his face as Mary Haskins had on hers.

Rebecca inhaled sharply which seemed to shake her out of the trance she was in. Turning suddenly away from the altar, she focused her attention on the people still in the Church.

"Everybody out! Now!" She saw a young man standing by the doors who appeared to be less affected than the others. Rebecca turned to him. "I want you to stand right here until I tell you otherwise. No one enters this Church unless they're with the Sheriff's Office - got it?"

The young man nervously nodded as the remaining parishioners quickly filed out of the Church. Maggie came up behind her.

"I'll call Sam. You handle what you have to here."

Rebecca mumbled a quick thanks and then exited the Church in order to address the crowd standing outside. There was nothing she could do to stop the panic she knew would overtake the citizens of Rosedale, but she had to get them away from the Church. It was now a crime scene.

Maggie followed Rebecca out and as Rebecca spoke to the crowd that surrounded her, Maggie was already on her cell phone speaking with Sam. She hurried straight to Wyndham and her daughter, disconnecting the call just before getting to them.

"Oh my Mrs. Cooper! This is just terrible. Poor Father McNeal. This town will never be the same I tell you. Never the same."

"Wyndham would you please do me a favor?"

"Why of course!"

"Would you please take Jordan to the diner and wait for me there? I'll be over as soon as I have a chance to talk to Sam. He should be here soon."

"Mom why can't I just wait here with you?" complained Jordan.

"Oh Jordan," began Wyndham, cutting off Maggie before she had a chance to reply, "when a woman has a look on her face like your mother has on hers, it's best not to argue. Come with me child ... let me buy you some delicious pancakes."

Maggie nodded at Wyndham, mouthing the words thank you, as he turned to walk to the diner - Jordan in tow. She watched as they crossed the street before turning her attention back to the Church. Rebecca had managed to convince most of the crowd to disburse and was in the process of blocking the Church off with yellow tape she had retrieved from her car, when Dr. Simpson arrived followed closely by Sam. Maggie hurried over to him, getting to his car just as he was stepping out.

"Sam." Maggie threw her arms around him. "It's just awful."

"Where's Jordan?"

"She's with Wyndham at the diner. She's safe."

Sam let out a sigh. "No one's safe."

"What do you mean? What are you talking about?"

Sam looked deep into her eyes. "We'll talk about this later. In the meantime, I want you to go to the diner and meet up with Wyndham and Jordan. From this point forward, Jordan isn't allowed to go anywhere without an adult by her side. I need to get inside. I'll see you at home later. Okay?"

Maggie nodded and started to turn away.

"Hey babe."

Maggie turned to look at Sam.

"Be careful... not afraid, but careful. Got it?"

Maggie nodded once more. "We'll be fine. I'll see you when you get home. You be careful too."

Sam stared deep into her eyes once more, brushed her cheek with a kiss and then hurried over to Dr. Simpson before the two of them vanished into the doors of St. Boniface Church.

Maggie stood there on the street for a few moments. The day had started out with so much promise. How could something that started out so beautifully suddenly turn so ugly.

The sight of Father McNeal played over and over in her head. Would she ever be able to forget? She doubted it. Taking a deep breath she started walking towards her car when suddenly the feeling of being watched over took her. She spun around but saw no one looking at her. She didn't know what she expected to see. Maybe the mystery man with the brown hair and glasses? Was he the killer? Or... was he just the product of an overactive imagination?

"What's wrong with me?" she quietly asked herself. She quickened her pace. Suddenly she didn't feel safe nor did she feel alone.

Sam and Doc Simpson entered the Church. The lighting was subdued and the air felt chilled. Or maybe the chill that Sam felt was coming from inside of him. He dreaded having to bear witness to another murder victim, but apparently it had become his job. He and Doc Simpson walked silently up the center aisle of the Church, towards the altar. Deputy Sanchez was waiting for them there.

"God help us." Doc Simpson said quietly when he reached the altar and looked up at the cross that carried not only Jesus, but now Father McNeal as well. Despite the coolness in the air, he took a white handkerchief from his pocket and wiped the sweat off his face.

"Jason will be here in a minute." Sam said to Rebecca.

"We'll have to get the body down before I can declare time of death. So I'll just wait until you're done before we do that." said Doc Simpson to Sam.

"How the hell did he get him up there?" questioned Sam as he stared at the cross. "How did he get him up there and manage to nail his hands and feet?"

"Maybe there's more than one of them. Maybe he has help?" offered Rebecca.

"That's a thought. And I hope you're wrong."

They heard conversation at the doors to the Church and turned to see what was happening. Two men were trying to get in but the young man Rebecca had asked to control the doors, wasn't having it.

"You can let them in!" called Doc Simpson. "They're with me." He turned his gaze back to Sam. "They'll get the body down and transport it for me."

The young man backed away and the two entered the Church, walking directly to Doc Simpson.

"Holy shit." exclaimed one of the men as he looked up at the cross. Immediately regretting his comment, he looked at Deputy

Sanchez. "Sorry Ma'am. I'm just surprised, that's all. Never saw anything like this before."

"Welcome to the club." replied Sam. "Can you see if you can find a ladder? We're going to need it to get him down anyway, but I want to take a closer look before we do."

The men turned and headed back out the Church, talking to each other about where they might find a ladder.

"Deputy Sanchez, would you go get your camera and fingerprint kit?"

"Yes sir." replied Rebecca as she headed out. Just as she exited the Church, Deputy Moyer entered and walked up to Sam and Doc Simpson.

As he approached and looked up at the cross, he let out a slow whistle.

"Good Lord."

"According to Maggie, at least a third of the congregation saw this first hand. And by now, the other two thirds have heard all about it in great detail." said Sam quietly, not wanting his words to echo through the building.

"You're going to have a panic on your hands, you know that don't you?" commented Doc Simpson.

"Yup. I know. Going to have to figure out something to say to them and try to answer their questions. Just wish I could think of something to say that would put everyone's minds at ease. But then, maybe it's better they're afraid. Might make everyone more careful. At least we now know one thing we didn't know two weeks ago."

"What's that?" asked Doc Simpson

Sam looked at him and shook his head. "That everyone is at risk. There isn't a type he's going after ... it could be any one of us."

During this exchange Deputy Moyer continued staring up at Father McNeal, not sure of what he was seeing. "What's that around his neck?" he asked, pointing up to the body.

"What?" asked Sam. "What do you see?"

Deputy Moyer took out his flashlight and aimed it at Father McNeal's neck. "There. What is that?"

Sam stepped a little closer and looked from a different angle.

"Well I'll be damned!" quietly mumbled Sam

"What?" asked Doc Simpson as he moved to position himself behind Sam in the hopes of seeing whatever it was Sam was looking at.

"It is a rope. Jason give me the flashlight."

Deputy Moyer handed Sam his flashlight. Sam aimed it at Father McNeal's neck and then used the light to follow the rope.
"It's a noose ... and it goes up, wraps around the beam up there and then back down and then secured there - around that statue." The beam of Sam's flashlight rested on a large statue of Mother Mary, on which the rope was secured. "That's how he did it. He hoisted Father McNeal up using the rope, secured it

and then positioned the body for maximum effect."

"That was still a hell of a lot of work." commented Doc Simpson.

"He obviously takes his work seriously." Sam replied.

Just then the doors to the Church opened once more. They turned to see Doc Simpson's assistants walking in with a ladder, as well as Deputy Sanchez with her camera and fingerprint kit.

"Start taking photographs." he instructed Deputy Sanchez. He then directed his attention back to Doc Simpson, "When we've recorded everything - and I mean everything - you can have the body for your autopsy."

"I'll be on it."

"Once we're done here, Moyer, Sanchez and I will head over to the rectory. He wasn't killed here - not enough blood. Maybe it happened there."

*   *   *

By the time Maggie reached the restaurant and finally managed to get a parking spot, the diner was buzzing. Of course conversations were exclusively about Father Mc-Neal and his terrible demise. She looked around until she spied Wyndham waving to her from one of the booths. Apologizing, she pushed through the crowd still waiting to be seated and made her way to Wyndham and Jordan.

"This place is crazy." said Maggie as she settled into the booth.

Jordan was eating pancakes while Wyndham was nursing his coffee - his plate of eggs and bacon barely touched.

Maggie looked at her daughter. "Are you okay?"

"Yeah." replied Jordan softly, focusing on her plate of pancakes. But Maggie could see a tear welling up in her eye.

"It'll be okay Jordan. I promise."

Jordan nodded her head. "It's just that I really liked Father McNeal. He was really nice. And I just keep thinking how awful it must have been for him..." Jordan's voice trailed off but she continued to focus on her pancakes.

"We all liked that man. Wonderful man. So sad." added Wyndham.

But before Maggie could respond, she noticed a large woman pushing her way past the other customers, with the obvious intent of making her way directly to Maggie. Maggie cringed. It felt like a laser light was pointing right at her forehead. Alice Topper. Maggie couldn't stand the woman. Loud and obnoxious and, as far as Alice Topper was concerned, always right, regardless of the situation or the facts. Maggie took a deep breath and forced herself to smile at the approaching storm.

"Mrs. Topper! Lovely to see you." greeted Maggie as pleasantly as she could, under the circumstances.

"Well I wish I could say the same Mrs. Cooper."

"I see we're off to a great start. You re-member my daughter Jordan and my friend, Wyndham Hart?"

"Good morning Mrs. Topper!" gushed Wyndham. "My you're looking lovely today!"

Alice Topper grunted and returned her attention to Maggie. "I need to ask - since your husband IS the Sheriff around here - what is he doing to protect the citizens of Rosedale? Huh? Has he done anything to try to find out who's doing these horrible horrible things? Or maybe we need to start looking to find someone who is more experienced!"

Maggie could feel her ears starting to get hot. She looked at Alice Topper who was breathing much too heavily after only walking from the far side of the restaurant. Maggie determined some of the heavy breathing was probably brought on by anger. She couldn't ignore the similarities between Alice Topper and an angry bull and expected steam to come out of her nostrils at any moment.

"First of all," began Maggie, staring at Alice Topper with a look of steely determination, "I don't speak for my husband. If you have any questions concerning his investigation, I would highly recommend that you ask him directly. I'm sure he'd be happy to make an appointment for you.

Secondly, he was elected Sheriff because the majority of Rosedale citizens have the utmost respect for him and his abilities and if anyone can figure out who's behind this, it will be him.

And last but certainly not least, I DID point out that my daughter is sitting here with me and this is certainly not the time nor the place to have this conversation. Don't you agree?"

Alice Topper glared back at Maggie. But just as she was about to say something that everyone was going to regret, Wyndham chimed in.

"Isn't that the Mayor?" he asked looking at the far end of the diner.

Alice Topper stopped instantly and looked around. "Where?"

"There, by the doors ... I could have sworn I saw him sitting down at the booth by the doors."

"Well I'm going to go speak to him. Maybe HE will have some answers for me."

She looked at Maggie and Wyndham and nodded her head. "Mrs. Cooper ... Mr. Hart."

"Mrs. Topper." replied Wyndham, smiling as he slightly nodded in response.

And with that, Alice Topper left their table, slowly making her way once again through the crowd of customers towards the restaurant doors. Maggie and Wyndham watched her disappear into a sea of people.

"The Mayor isn't here is he?" Maggie casually asked, still watching Alice Topper push people out of her way as she rolled through the crowd.

"No." replied Wyndham.

Maggie couldn't help but smile. As she did so, an unfamiliar waitress walked up to the table. She was a woman, probably in her 30s maybe 40s with short jet black hair and bright red lipstick.

"Would you like to order?" she asked Maggie.

Maggie was a little startled to see this woman standing there, pencil and pad in hand. She had never seen her before and was so used to seeing Emily with her light brown shoulder length hair and scrubbed face, this was strangely jarring. "I don't think I've met you before..." started Maggie, looking at the waitress's name tag. "Robin, is it?"

"Yup that's me. But heck, I feel like I've been here forever! Guess I don't make much of an impression!" She chuckled as she spoke.

Maggie smiled at her. "Is Emily not working today?"

Robin looked confused. "Emily? Don't think I know an Emily."

"Of course you do! Emily Patterson ... twenties, light brown hair. In fact I don't think

I can remember a time when she wasn't here..."

"Actually Mrs. Cooper," interrupted a confused Wyndham, "to be quite honest, I don't know anyone named Emily either. I only remember Robin here. Maybe this Emily person works some place else, or perhaps the stress of the day, you know ..."

"No, it has nothing to do with the stress of the day Wyndham." replied Maggie, feeling a little annoyed. "Don't be silly. Remember the last time I saw you here, Emily was waiting on me and asked if you'd like a cup of coffee, but you told her you had to leave."

Wyndham's expression was totally blank as he slowly shook his head. Jordan had started to pay attention to the strange conversation and was starting to look a little bewildered herself.

"No Mom," said Jordan quietly. "I eat here all the time and it's always Robin who takes care of me. There's never been an Emily here."

Maggie looked blankly at the three of them. Why were they behaving this way? And then she remembered. "Alright then," said Maggie, feeling annoyed, "if there's never been an Emily Patterson working here, why did they make her employee of the month?" Keeping her focus on Wyndham and her daughter, Maggie pointed to a photo on the wall. But instead of the moment of realization she was expecting, she got no reaction from them at all.

Slowly she turned her head to look at the photo. It was hanging in the exact same spot, the exact same way, but it was different. Very different. It wasn't a photo of Emily Patterson, the twenty-something year old who was deeply in love with Steve. It was a photo of Robin Shelton, with her short black hair and bright red lipstick. Maggie froze. She felt the blood drain from her face.

*   *   *

He tried to stop himself from laughing out loud. People might take notice of him if he should burst out laughing while walking alone. The memory of Father McNeal begging for his life seemed strangely ironic.

He tried to point out the irony of the situation but Father McNeal wasn't understanding or maybe he was just too preoccupied with the pain he was feeling to really follow what was being said. He was disappointed in that, only because he thought it was in fact, a very interesting point that warranted discussion.

How odd that a man of the cloth, someone who preached eternal life and love alongside the Savior, be so afraid of leaving this earthly realm. Surely he as a priest, would have been guaranteed a ticket directly to Heaven. Or perhaps, he thought to himself, the good father wasn't totally convinced of the fairytale he tried to sell to his parishioners.

He kept his head down and watched the cracks in the sidewalk pass by under his feet. Left foot, right foot, left foot, right foot. At least with his head down, he could smile and no one would see. They wouldn't understand his jubilation.

Downtown Rosedale was unusually busy this Sunday morning. Residents had gathered in small groups everywhere, talking about the crazed killer who had made his way to perfect little Rosedale. This time he couldn't stop himself from giggling. He hadn't felt this happy, this content, this in control, for a very, very long time. In fact, for as far back as he could remember, he had never felt this powerful.

Another thought crossed his mind: he wondered if Father McNeal would be as willing to opt for forgiveness once it had become more than just an abstract thought - the subject of a sermon. Somehow he doubted it. When things got real, people changed.

That made him think of his mother. Strange she should enter his thoughts. He hadn't thought about her as far back as he could remember. Things had gotten real for her as well. She changed. How she liked to spew her favorite Bible verses. And when that made no impact, she reverted to simply screaming, "You're going to burn in Hell!". He smiled at the thought. She had failed to realize, that to him, that wasn't a threat. He welcomed the adventure and hoped it was true.

He stopped to look through the window of the book store, where a group of Rosedale residents stood, talking about the most recent murder. As he feigned interest in the books on display, he listened in on their panicked conversation. It thrilled him to no end. They were so afraid and yet, there he was, standing right beside them. He was so close he could smell their fear. The most powerful man in Rosedale and yet they had no clue. He sighed and continued walking.

Left foot, right foot, left foot, right foot - don't step on the cracks.

Memories of his mother flooded his thoughts. He wondered why. Why now? Although the memories did make him smile. The way her skull made that sound when the sledgehammer hit it. There was one brief moment when it looked as though her eyes focused on him. He wasn't sure. He hoped they had. He wanted her to know what was happening ... to know it was him. He wanted her to shut up.

Left foot, right foot, left foot, right foot.

When he recalled that night, he remembered the joy he felt. The laughter. And when that small bit of brain matter landed on his arm, it made him laugh even harder. He sighed.

He looked forward to finally getting home. He had taken some of the priest's belongings - a suit and his collar. Perhaps he'd try them on tonight. That would make him smile.

He had been watching the Church when his handiwork had been discovered. Such panic it caused. Watching the Sheriff arrive on the scene. The Sheriff's wife.

He had been watching her too after her husband left her standing on the street. All alone. For a moment, it looked as though she knew he was watching her. But that was impossible. It must have simply been his imagination. He was far enough away that she couldn't have seen him.

Again he smiled. He would be home soon. He looked forward to putting on Father McNeal's clothes. It would help him remember. He needed to remember...

9

Left foot, right foot, left foot, right foot. He kept his head down, focused on the sidewalk and thought - he always thought. He thought about how much he hated the kids at school. They made fun of the way he looked, the way he talked, the way he dressed. He was only eleven but already he thought about hurting them. Hurting them bad. That thought made him smile.

One day he'd show them. He wouldn't say anything - he would just do it. He wasn't much of a talker anyway. What was the point? His mother talked a lot and what good did it do? Nothing changed. Just talk.

An older brother who ignored him and a mother he wished did. He would wonder from time to time what had happened to his father. He figured he had to have had one at some point. It didn't bother him though. He never could quite figure out what a father was for anyway - unless it was his job to shut the mother up. He decided his father probably got fed up with how much talking his mother did and split.

'Yeah I bet my Dad would have shut the bitch up for real.' he thought to himself. That thought made him smile.

He turned off the sidewalk onto a path that cut through a large conservation area that which up to a number of houses. He preferred walking through the woods. He liked the feeling of solitude - the smell of the soil and decomposing leaves.

It also gave him the perfect vantage point to spy on people in the neighborhood. He chanced it once - sneaking right up to one of the houses. He was very careful. He hid in the bushes below a window and when the time felt right, slowly managed to look over the sill.

It was a bedroom but no one was home. At least there didn't seem to be anyone around. He decided though it was too much of a risk. It was much better just doing what he had always done before - wait until dark. Wait until his mother had gone to Church.

He had seen some interesting things at night in the neighborhood - behind those closed doors. Some things he saw he didn't understand and other things just disgusted him. People were filthy when they didn't think anyone was watching. His mother was filthy too.

Every time he saw people during his late night excursions, he would always try to picture them dead. That thought gave him peace. If only there was no one else around. How much nicer everything would be.

He continued walking through the woods, breathing deeply to clear his head. He hadn't been at home all day but just knew the second he walked through the front door, he would be in trouble for something. There was always something.

Seemed like she never yelled at his bother. No, Stephen was perfect. Stephen was her favorite. He hated her. One day he'd show her. He'd show his brother too.

10

Rebecca Sanchez stood in front of the Rectory door. Sam and Jason would be joining her shortly. She was grateful for that. The last thing she wanted to do was enter the building by herself. She couldn't begin to imagine what might be waiting inside.

She dusted the door handle for fingerprints, but only found one set - which would probably belong to Father McNeal. She couldn't get the thoughts out of her mind. Father McNeal. He had no way of knowing he'd never see Sunday. How he would never hold

Mass on that day or ever again. How fragile life suddenly seemed.

'One wrong move and it's over.' she thought to herself.

The breeze had started to pick up, as it often did late in the afternoon. But every time some leaves rustled or a branch swayed, she felt an uneasiness build inside of her. Never before had Rosedale scared her. But now, in the face of yet another murder, she was afraid.

She looked towards the front of the Church and saw that the body of Father Mc-Neal was finally being removed. The now familiar black bag was being wheeled towards the waiting van. Shortly after, she saw Sam and Deputy Moyer exit the Church. They were heading her way. She took a deep breath.

As they approached her, she could see the dread in their eyes. She guessed they as well didn't want to open the door to the rectory.

"Did you find any prints?" asked Sam.

"Just one set out here. Probably Father McNeal's. That was it. No sign of any forced entry anywhere. I walked around and checked all the windows and doors. Nothing."

"Well then," sighed Deputy Moyer, "I suppose it's safe to assume Father McNeal let him in."

"Maybe. Probably." responded Sam as he watched the van carrying Father McNeal's body pull away from the curb. "Probably thought like the rest of us - that he didn't fit the victim profile so he had nothing to be worried about.

Or maybe he just thought the guy was gone. We were all starting to feel a little too sure he had moved on."

Sam paused for a moment. Setting his jaw in resolve. "Do you have gloves in that case of yours?" he asked Rebecca, motioning towards her fingerprint case.

"Yeah, I do." she replied, crouching down in front of the case that sat on the stoop by the front doors to the rectory. She retrieved three pairs, keeping one and handing off the other two pairs to Sam and Jason.

"You know what we're probably facing in there." said Sam as he put on the gloves. "I want photos and fingerprints. And be careful not to disturb any evidence."

Sam flipped through the set of keys he retrieved from Father McNeal's pocket. Unlocking the door, he heard the thud of a dead bolt and felt the door give ever so slightly. He waited for a moment, and then, with a gloved hand, he slowly opened the front door to the rectory. As he did so, the hinges made a soft creaking sound that for some reason, reminded him of someone crying.

The air inside was cooler than he expected and seemed to rush up on him. Rebecca and Jason followed closely behind. There was a smell. It assaulted him. The smell of blood. But as he looked around, he didn't see anything that looked out of place.

The rectory was dimly lit and very old. At least that's how the front rooms looked.

Sam was suddenly struck by the realization that he had never been inside the rectory before. He regretted that. He regretted not having gotten to know Father McNeal better. He seemed like a good man. Certainly one who didn't deserve what had happened to him. But then, Sam thought to himself, no one would have deserved that.

Sam tried to think back. He couldn't remember another priest in Rosedale, other than Father McNeal. He must have been the pastor of St. Boniface for as long as Sam had been Sheriff - for as long as Sam had lived in Rosedale.

The living room lay to the left of the foyer. The furniture was dark in color and slightly worn. A lot of dark green velvet gave the room an oppressive feeling. A sofa and a chair faced the out of date television that sat silently in the corner. A heavy wood coffee table and a couple end tables holding gold colored lamps, completed the living room.

The dark pattern of leaves on the sofa with a row of fringe running along the bottom made Sam wonder why the Church had never updated anything inside the rectory. But then again, perhaps this is what Father McNeal liked. The room was meticulously kept and looked as though all the furnishings had come from an antique store.

They stood there silently as if honoring Father McNeal with a moment of silence as they stared at the room he would have enjoyed only a short time before. To their right was a steep staircase leading up to the second floor. Sam decided they would go upstairs after completely exploring the ground floor.

They continued walking down the hallway towards the back of the house. Farther down to their left, was the dining room. Again Sam paused and stared at the room with its dark mahogany table and chairs. Nothing appeared to be out of place. To the right of the table sat an intricately carved server with two candelabra positioned neatly on each side.

With every step they took, Sam's heart rate quickened. The smell seemed to be getting stronger as they approached the back of the house. He turned away from the dining room and continued down the hall. Ahead of him appeared to be the kitchen. He could see a few of the thickly painted white cabinet doors and a blue linoleum floor. There seemed to be a pattern on the cabinet doors. He knew what that pattern was.

By now his heart was racing. How he didn't want to walk any further. The smell of blood was making his stomach flip. He noticed Rebecca holding the back of her hand to her nose and mouth. He surmised she was having the same reaction.

He finally reached the entrance to the kitchen and stepped inside. Deputies Moyer and Sanchez followed. They all stood there, staring. There was blood. A lot of blood. Blood everywhere.

Sam's eyes trailed down from the blood splattered on the old stove, to the floor where it had pooled. He stopped breathing for a moment when he saw a shattered mug on the floor. He stared at it. He didn't know why it bothered him so, but it did. Deputy Moyer noticed the broken mug as well.

"I guess we found the scene of the crime." said Deputy Moyer rather matter of factly. "There's a mug on the counter too." he observed, being careful where he stepped. "A mug with a tea bag in it. Looks like maybe he was getting a second mug when he was attacked."

"He was going to make the bastard some tea." whispered Rebecca quietly.

"Oh shit," uttered Deputy Moyer.

"What?" asked Sam as he tore his gaze away from the broken mug. He looked at Deputy Moyer and noticed he was staring at the far wall of the kitchen. Sam followed his gaze and that's when he saw the words 'forgive me?' scrawled across the wall in blood.

"Forgive me?" mumbled Deputy Sanchez under her breath. "He wants us to forgive him?"

*   *   *

Maggie stared at herself in the bathroom mirror. She carefully studied her reflection - every curve, every line, every imperfection - hoping to notice something but not knowing what. After the embarrassing and uncomfortable brunch at the diner with Wyndham and her daughter, she dropped Jordan off at her friend's house for a visit. Sam would stop by Susan's on the way home and pick her up. In the meantime, Maggie had called Patty and asked her to come over. She didn't want to be alone. She needed to talk to someone. She needed to find out if she was losing her mind.

She ran the cold water for a while before splashing it on her face. As good as it felt, it didn't change anything. It certainly didn't take away the knot in her stomach. Nor did it help her to erase the memory of what she had seen. She patted her face dry, brushed her hair and made her way to the kitchen.

Why did the kitchen always make her feel better? Maybe because it really did remind her of her grandmother. It wasn't until recently that Maggie had noticed the similarity. Her grandmother had been gone for some time, but try as she could, she couldn't remember when exactly she had lost her. It felt like forever. Maggie was unnerved by the fact that she couldn't seem to remember the date of her grandmother's passing ... but then again, with everything going on, it was merely one more thing she couldn't seem to get her head around.

Patty would be by soon. She could always count on Patty for brutal honesty. She needed that. She would have to explain all of this and quite frankly, she didn't know how to do that without sounding insane. Maybe she was. Maybe she was losing it. Maybe Wyndham was right and it was the stress of dealing with the murders that was effecting her. Or maybe it was the lack of sleep. She still had her appointment with Dr. Simpson in the morning. She hoped he would have an answer for her.

She walked over to the coffee maker that sat on the counter. The sun was pouring into the kitchen. Everything looked so bright and welcoming it was hard to believe that she had witnessed the aftermath of a murder, or that she could be facing some horrible medical issue. She sighed and pulled the coffee pot out and started filling it with water when she thought better of it. She shut the water off, returned the pot to its place and instead, opened a cabinet and took down a couple of wine glasses. She retrieved an unopened bottle of white wine from the fridge and placed it on the counter as well. She was apparently losing her grip on reality. If that wasn't a good enough reason to have wine, she didn't know what would be.

She felt exhausted. Just as she started thinking about shutting her eyes for a few minutes, she heard a knock at the door. She walked out of the kitchen, through the dining room, towards the front door. She was about to swing it open, when she stopped herself. Even though she felt she was sure it was Patty, common sense told her to check.

Things had changed so much in Rosedale, nothing was a sure thing any more. Pulling her hand away from the door handle, she peered through the peep-hole. It was Patty. Feeling a little silly, she swung the door open.

"You look awful!" exclaimed Patty as she entered the house.

"Nice to see you too." replied Maggie with a weak smile, as she closed the front door and locked it.

"Oh I'm sorry. I didn't mean it like it sounded. You just look tired."

"No." corrected Maggie. "No you're right, I DO look awful. And I AM tired."

Maggie walked into her kitchen with Patty following behind. "Why don't you open the wine and I'll get some cheese and crackers to-gether." instructed Maggie, pointing to the wine bottle that sat on the counter. "The opener's in the first drawer underneath."

"Okay." started Patty as she retrieved the opener and started twisting it into the cork. "So what's up? Is everything alright with you and Sam? You know you can talk to me about anything."

"And that, is why I asked you over. Sam and I are fine so no it's not that."

"So what is it then? Is it Jordan?"

Maggie sighed as she shut the fridge door. She took a beat. "Let's get comfortable in the living room before I get into this, okay?" said Maggie as she carried the plate of cheese and crackers out of the kitchen. Patty followed behind with two glasses of wine, looking concerned. In truth, Maggie was try-ing to work up the courage to open up to her - trying to figure out the best way of starting the conversation.

They settled down on the white over-stuffed sofa. Patty placed the glasses on the coffee table and leaned back into the corner of the sofa, watching her friend nervously put the plate of cheese and crackers down between them.

"Alright. Out with it."

Maggie looked at her friend and saw that familiar look of determination and knew that she couldn't put it off any longer. If she was going to confide in Patty, it was now or never. "I have a doctor's appointment tomorrow."

She looked up at her friend, expecting a reaction, but got none. Instead, Patty was just looking at her waiting for her to continue.

"As you know, I haven't been sleeping. I've been having those panic attacks. But what you don't know is, recently I've been having, I don't know, blackouts or hallucinations. I don't know what they are."

"What do you mean hallucinations? Like what?"

Maggie inhaled deeply before continuing. "It's like I can be doing something and then suddenly I'm someone else. My hands don't look like mine, the surroundings don't look familiar. I know it sounds crazy, but it's like for a few moments, I really am someone else and someplace else."

"Well you said you haven't been sleeping."

"That's what I was thinking. I'm hoping that's what it is. But there's more."

"Okay..."

"You know the waitress who works at the Diner?"

"Yes, of course I do. I eat there all the time. You know that."

"What's her name?"

"What?"

"What's her name? - The waitress."

Patty paused for a moment, looking at her friend, trying to figure out where this was heading. "Robin."

Maggie felt tears suddenly well up in her eyes. Patty looked concerned.

"Mag what is it? What's wrong?"

Maggie shook her head and wiped a tear away. "You see, that's the problem - I don't remember her. I don't remember Robin."

"Amnesia?"

"No. It's not that I just don't remember her - I remember someone else. Someone else entirely. Does the name Emily Patterson mean anything to you?"

Patty slowly shook her head.

"Emily Patterson," continued Maggie, "twenty years old, light brown hair - she'd always talk about her boyfriend Steve. Please tell me you remember her."

Again Patty shook her head.

Maggie wiped away another tear. "Well - I remember an Emily Patterson working at the diner. I remember conversations I had with her. I remember her smile. In my mind I saw her a few days ago. I swear Patty, I have never before today, ever seen Robin at that diner. At least that's what my mind is telling me.

I swear to you, I'm not making this up. But you see, it seems as though I'm the only person who thinks she remembers a girl named Emily. Even Jordan said that Robin has been at the restaurant forever. She doesn't know an Emily Patterson. Honestly I don't know what's happening to me."

Maggie stopped talking. She stared at Patty, who was staring back at her, saying nothing. After a few seconds, she saw Patty lean forward, snatch her glass of wine and down about half of it. She looked back at Maggie.

"Okay - this sounds like a lot more than what you told me about before ... Does Sam know all of this?"

Maggie shook her head. "No."

"Good. Keep it that way for now."

"But —"

"Look, I'm not saying never tell him. But first, go to your appointment tomorrow. Talk with the doctor, let him run some tests. You don't know what's really going on. It could be stress. My God look at what you went through just today! That kind of thing will mess a person up! Then toss in lack of sleep on top of it - hell it could even be hormonal. As much as we hate it when guys say that, there is some truth to it. Or — it could be something really serious. But here's just no point in freaking Sam out until you have a complete picture of what's up."

Maggie nodded. "You're probably right. I was planning on talking to him tonight, but it makes sense to wait."

"Good."

Maggie held Patty's gaze for a second.

"Is there anything else?" Patty asked slowly.

"I'm seeing someone."

"What do you mean? Like dating someone?"

"No. God no. I mean every now and then, I'll look around and I see this guy - the same guy all the time - staring at me. I saw him when we were at the gym working out, before that at Pop's Diner... But every time I'm about to point him out to someone, he just isn't there anymore."

"What does he look like?"

Maggie thought for a moment. "In his 30s or 40s maybe. Longer brown hair - shaggy I guess you'd say. Glasses. Average looking really. He doesn't smile. He doesn't do anything. He just stands there and stares at me. I'm thinking maybe he's some sort of hallucination too."

Patty considered what her friend was saying. "Well," she started slowly, "I guess he could be some sort of hallucination ... you know, your imagination going a little wild."

"That's what I'm thinking." said Maggie feeling a little relieved.

"Or ..." Patty continued.

"Or what?"

Patty took a deep breath and stared intently at her friend. "Or he could be the guy Sam's looking for."

Maggie stared at her. She too had considered that possibility but didn't want to believe it. Even though the thought of losing her mind wasn't appealing, it was still marginally better than thinking a crazed killer had her in his sights. It was now her turn to take a sizable swallow of wine.

Maggie shook her head. "Why me? Why would he even notice me? ... IF it is him."

"Well think about it," began Patty, "your husband is the Sheriff. He's investigating the murders. I don't want to scare you, but the guy is probably watching Sam. And if he's been watching Sam, then he knows who his wife is ... and who his daughter is."

The wine was not sitting well in Maggie's stomach. "Great. Just great." she mumbled. "So my choices are, something's wrong with me and this guy is some sort of weird hallucination, or something's just a little bit wrong with me and this guy is actually the killer who's now watching me and my family." Maggie thought for a second. "There is a third possibility."

"What's that?"

"That the man I'm seeing IS an hallucination, but there really is a killer watching us. What you're saying makes sense. Unfortunately. He would be keeping an eye on Sam, wouldn't he? Earlier, outside the Church when I was on my way to the diner - I had a feeling. A feeling I was being watched. It was like the hair just stood up on the back of my neck. Oh God Patty what is going on?"

Patty took ahold of Maggie's hand and looked into her eyes. "You're going to be okay. Everything is going to be okay. Go to your appointment tomorrow and have Dr. Simpson check you out and give you his opinion. And in the meantime, just be careful. And don't mention any of this to Sam until you have a better idea of what's really happening."

Maggie squeezed Patty's hand and got up from the sofa. "That wine isn't sitting well with me at the moment. I think I'm going to make some coffee after all. Would you like some?"

"Actually I think that's a good idea." replied Patty as she followed Maggie into the kitchen.

Maggie started filling the coffee carafe with water as Patty made herself comfortable at the round kitchen table. The bay window next to the table made the spot particularly inviting.

"I'm not saying don't tell Sam at all. I just think you should have all the facts before you drop this on him. He doesn't have any idea?"

Maggie shook her head. "Other than knowing about a couple panic attacks - that sort of thing. I've never really gotten into the details with him. Figured he has enough on his plate without worrying about me."

She finished filling the pot with water and started pouring it into the coffee maker.

"I didn't mean to scare you about that guy you've been noticing." continued Patty. "But think about something ... maybe there IS some guy you've been noticing every now and then. But maybe that's all it is - just some guy who you think is looking at you and then going off and doing whatever. Rosedale isn't that big for starters. And between no sleep and dealing with these horrible murders - well it wouldn't be a stretch to assume that your imagination might be running a little wild and he's just some guy looking for his wife and the whole thing is a coincidence."

Maggie laughed. "Wouldn't that be a hoot. I actually hadn't considered that. Too many possibilities. I guess I could be a little hyper sensitive about things right now."

"You think?" Patty laughed as well. "There are a million different possibilities. I'm pretty sure things will check out just fine with Dr. Simpson tomorrow and there's a very logical explanation for everything. And as far as being careful goes - well quite frankly we all need to be careful these days. That part isn't your imagination. There really is some crazy guy running around. I just hope Sam figures out who it is before anyone else ... ends up like Father McNeal."

Patty reached for one of the bright red apples that was in the bowl in the center of the table and bit into it.

When Maggie heard the crunch of the apple, she turned quickly to look at Patty, who was now happily eating. She felt a little taken aback because for some reason, she couldn't remember putting a bowl of apples there in the first place. But she must have. How else would they be there.

This was just one more thing that didn't make any sense to her. On top of everything, she was obviously becoming forgetful as well. Then again, with everything going on, perhaps she shouldn't be that surprised she was having some issues.

Maggie smiled at her friend. Patty always knew the right thing to say. Suddenly she felt much more positive about her doctor's appointment. She turned her gaze away from Patty to the cupboard where she kept the ground coffee.

As she did so, her eyes swept across the view out the window above the kitchen sink. The view of the street. And there, on the sidewalk about twenty yards away, he stood. Staring at her. Her breath caught in her throat as she stared back at him. She couldn't seem to break his gaze. It felt as though he was pulling her into him.

"Maggie? MAGGIE?" repeated Patty.

But to Maggie, Patty's voice seemed to be a million miles away. So far away. Muffled.

Suddenly she felt a touch on her back that startled her and instantly broke the bond she felt with the stranger. She turned her head to see Patty standing next to her looking concerned.

"Are you okay?" Patty asked with obvious worry in her voice.

Maggie stared at her for a moment and then returned her gaze to the view out of the window. He was gone. Just like the times before. She swallowed hard and looked at her friend. "I'm fine." she said, forcing herself to smile. "Everything's fine."

11

"But the cowardly, the unbelieving, the vile, the murderers, the sexually immoral, those who practice magic arts, the idolaters and all liars - they will be consigned to the fiery lake of burning sulfur. This is the second death." screamed his mother. Her eyes flashing with rage.

Robert sat there - just staring straight ahead. Motionless. His mother was on a rampage. What else was new. She was making him sit in one of the living room chairs while she assaulted him with Bible verses. Waving the Book in her hand like it was some sort of weapon, she recited the verses from memory, screaming them until he could feel her spittle wet his face. He stayed calm.

He didn't look at her. That was the best way of handling these events. He would just sit quietly and focus on how much he hated her. At fourteen he shouldn't have to put up with this. He was almost a grown man. She had no right.

"I know what you do at night - when I'm at Church praising the Lord. You think I don't know?" She brought her face up within inches of his and smiled. "You're going to burn in Hell." She backed away but continued to stare at him - sizing him up. "Why was I cursed with a son like you? You're the Devil himself. You're a disgrace. You'll have to answer to God - may he have mercy on your soul."

And with that, she walked purposefully towards the kitchen, holding her Bible tight to her chest. Robert continued sitting in the chair, motionless. He could hear her talking to herself. He wished she would die. He could feel her spittle slowly sliding down his face. He continued sitting, basking in the silence.

Slowly he drifted into his thoughts. The voices were back. He was grateful for that. They would drown out the distant sounds of his mother's voice still coming from the kitchen. His focus though was broken by the familiar creak of the third step of the staircase. His brother Stephen was coming downstairs.

Stephen was two years his senior. Stephen was different than him. His mother loved Stephen. Everybody loved Stephen. Stephen was perfect. He strolled into the living room.

Stephen was everything Robert wasn't. He was also everything Robert didn't want to be. The girls drooled over him and he loved it. Tall and good looking. He did well in school, played football and was the all American teenager any parent would be proud to call their son. Robert hated him. Hated everything about him. But what he hated the most about Stephen was how good he was at fooling everyone - especially their mother. But he couldn't fool Robert.

Stephen stared at his brother for a moment before a wide grin crept across his face. "Somebody saw you peaking into windows again, huh?" laughed Stephen. "You've got to stop doing that shit. I mean, it's going to start interfering with my social life. When they find out my little brother is the perv who likes to peak into windows, they get a little freaked out. But what the hell, I just tell them you're adopted. You know - that your real mother beat you and messed you up in the head or something." Stephen grinned at his younger brother.

Robert continued staring at the wall. Imagining a knife sticking out of Stephen's neck helped him control his anger.

"Is that you Stephen?" their mother called from the kitchen.

"Yeah Mom! Be right there!" responded Stephen. He looked back at Robert, who continued to stare off into the distance. The smile slowly disappeared from his face.

"Seriously - why do you do that shit? It's messed up."

Robert ignored his question. He was too busy imagining Stephen begging for his life. Stephen continued to stare at him for a few moments longer before letting out a sigh, shaking his head and making his way to the kitchen.

Robert smiled.

He sat there for a few more minutes, listening to his brother and mother talk in the kitchen. He decided he wanted to walk outside for a while. They would probably be relieved that he was out of the house anyway. He stood up, used his sleeve to wipe the side of his face and walked out the front door. The screen door made a loud bang as it slammed shut behind him.   Already it was easier to breathe. He hated being in the house - with them. His house was the last one on a dead end road and stood next to the woods. It was rare to see anyone in front of the house - unless they were coming to visit. But that sort of thing hardly ever happened.   He had no friends so no one would be visiting him. Stephen opted to meet his friends elsewhere and his mother drove herself to her Church and Church functions - which she seemed to enjoy.

He walked out onto the street and looked towards the neighboring houses. He saw kids on their bicycles and one person walking their dog. The noise the kids were making annoyed him. He turned left to go into the woods instead.

People seemed to like his mother.   He had no idea why. He surmised she was probably good at fooling those people as well. They didn't know who she really was.   They didn't know she had driven his father away.

He was sure she probably had some story she liked to tell, where she was the victim, as usual.

He knew his father wouldn't have left him if he had had a choice. Obviously he left because he couldn't stand her anymore. It was her fault. Everything was her fault. She wasn't doing right by the family. That much he knew. The voices in his head didn't like her either. They wanted her dead.

He was pretty sure that one of the voices was his father. He would come and check on him from time to time. He told Robert that his mother was a whore - that all this time she had been cheating on him. That didn't surprise Robert. He had suspected as much. All women were whores anyway. In fact, he was pretty sure Stephen was a product of one of her affairs. That would explain why he and Stephen were so different. It would also explain why he felt nothing when he looked at his brother. Nothing, except hatred.

He entered the woods and made his way to his favorite spot. It was a small clearing that was hidden from view behind a large boulder. He could sit there in peace without fear of anyone bothering him. He looked around to make sure he was alone. It was quiet. The only sound was the rustling of the leaves in the breeze. He was prepared any-way. If someone bothered him, he already knew what he would do.

He sat down on the dirt with his back against the boulder. Shutting his eyes, he let the voices take over. They made him feel good. They made him feel strong. He came out here often. He was tired of being ridiculed and made fun of at school. He was taller than most of the other kids and his voice was much deeper.

Sometimes he would wonder what it would have been like to be more like Stephen. To be popular and have friends. But the times that he wondered, were far and few between. His mother and Stephen were worthless.

His mother wasn't taking care of her family the way she should be - and his brother was born out of sin and therefore probably never should have been born at all. Stephen was a mistake - a punishment for his mother's sins. The voices agreed. They always agreed with him.

He opened his eyes and stared at his hands. They were large and strong. He was strong. That's probably why some of the kids at school were afraid of him. He liked that. He smiled at the thought. They had every reason to be afraid of him.

He looked down at the dirt and watched some ants building a mound. Fire ants. He put his hand on the mound and watched as they attacked, biting relentlessly. He lifted his hand, brought it close to his face and examined it. Already the bites were turning red and swelling up. But it felt good. He liked the way pain felt. It made him stronger. Again he tilted his head back on the rock and shut his eyes. He let the voices run wild.

12

Patty stayed for a couple more hours before giving her friend a warm hug and heading back to her own home. Maggie felt better having had the opportunity to really open up to someone. It didn't solve anything, but it made her more determined to get to the bottom of what was happening. It also made her realize how careful she and Jordan needed to be - until things returned to normal in Rosedale. Her heart ached when she imagined anything happening to her daughter or husband. She knew she wouldn't be able to carry on without them. She just prayed Sam would get to the bottom of it soon and that whatever she was going through, wouldn't interfere with his ability to do so. She certainly didn't want her issues to distract him.

She looked around the kitchen. Sam would be home soon with Jordan and then they could all sit down together for dinner. Safe and sound, tucked away in their home. She had prepared Jordan's favorite - spaghetti. As she set the table she considered how to handle the inevitable question from Sam ... 'What happened at the diner?'.

She thought about it but decided she would simply handle it when it came up. Hopefully she could come up with something that Sam would accept - at least for now.

"Mom! We're home!" called Jordan from the front door, as she and Sam walked into the house.

"In the kitchen!" she responded.

"Hmmm that smells good." said Jordan as she inhaled deeply.   Maggie had to laugh.

It seemed her daughter was always ravenous but never put on a pound. 'The joys of being a teenager.' thought Maggie, smiling.

Sam walked in behind Jordan. Maggie could see concern in his eyes. He walked up to her and kissed her warmly.

"How are you doing?" he questioned, softly.

Maggie looked at him. The gentleness in his eyes always made her heart skip. "I'm good. Really. Trying day. I'm guessing it got to me. But I'm good. How about you?"

Sam sighed as he reached for a glass out of the cupboard. He looked around to make sure Jordan had left the kitchen to drop her things off in her bedroom. "Babe, this is ..." His voice trailed off as he turned on the kitchen faucet and filled his glass with water.

"Yeah I know. It's just so hard to believe."

Sam took a long drink of water. "I really wish you hadn't seen him like that. You know if there was any way I could take that image out of your mind ..."

Maggie walked up to him and hugged him. They stayed like that for what felt like an eternity. Finally they broke apart just enough to look into each other's eyes. Maggie kissed him.

"I'll be okay. It was a shock, but I'll be okay. I promise. You just do your best to find him."

They kissed again.

Jordan walked back into the kitchen. "Can I have some iced tea with my dinner?" she asked.

Maggie nodded as she turned her attention to the loaf of french bread she was cutting.

"Anything I can do?" asked Sam

Maggie smiled at him. "No you just sit down. You must be exhausted."

Jordan poured herself an iced tea and took it to her spot at the table as Maggie placed the food in the center.

The three settled down to a quiet dinner. Even though they were physically together, they were preoccupied and distant from one another.

"How's Susan and her mother?" asked Maggie, trying to get some kind of conversation started.

Jordan shrugged as she sprinkled more cheese on her spaghetti. "They're okay I guess. A little freaked."

And that was the end of the conversation. They sat quietly in the kitchen having their dinner. Each lost in their own thoughts.

A few hours later, with dinner completed and the kitchen cleaned, Sam and Maggie walked together into the master bedroom, shutting the door behind them. Sam rubbed the back of his neck.

"Exhausted?" asked Maggie as she started changing into the t-shirt she liked to wear to bed.

"Totally." Sam took off his shirt and put it on the back of the chair. He looked over at

Maggie, walked over to her and led her to the bed by her arm. They sat down next to each other. Sam still staring into her eyes.

"You're going to your appointment with Dr. Simpson tomorrow, right?"

"Yes, Sir..." said Maggie with a weak smile.

"And you're going to tell him about everything - including what happened today at the diner, right?"

"Yes I am. Sam, I want to find out what's wrong too! I don't understand any of it. But I have to ask you something and if you could just humor me for a second, I'd really appreciate it."

"Ask away."

Maggie took a deep breath. "Does the name Emily Patterson mean anything to you? Anything at all?"

Sam started to shake his head.

"Think ... not just at the diner - but anywhere, anytime. Can you ever remember someone by the name of Emily Patterson?

Shoulder length brown hair - about 20 years old?"

Sam sighed. "Babe, you have no idea how badly I want to say yes. But I can't. I don't ever remember anyone by that name. Ever."

Maggie looked dejected. "Well that's that then. I had to ask."

Sam put his arm around her and drew her to him. They sat like that for a while as Maggie listened to the reassuring sound of his heart beat. After a while her eyes drifted down to his arm and then to his forearm - to the small scar just below his elbow. She traced it with her finger.

"You know you never told me how you got this."

Sam looked down at the scar she was examining.

"I didn't?" he asked.

Maggie shook her head. "Nope."

"Well," began Sam, "I probably didn't tell you because I can't remember."

Maggie pulled away to look him in the face. "What do you mean you can't remember?"

"Just that." said Sam matter-of-factly. "I must have done it when I was a kid, maybe, I guess. It's always been there, as far back as I can remember. But I have no idea what it's from."

"Maybe you chased some bad guy when you were a kid." said Maggie, smiling.

"Ya know ..." started Sam, making it look like he was considering her statement, "you might just be right. After all, I've always been a bit of a hero."

Maggie smiled broadly. "Oh you have, have you?"

"Are you questioning me, woman?" laughed Sam as he started tickling her.

Maggie broke out laughing as well. It felt good.

"Stop!" Maggie implored, still laughing.

Sam grinned broadly and pulled her to him. There they sat for a moment, eyes locked on each other. Both smiling. Both for-getting about everything else around them. In that moment, they were the only two people in the world.

Maggie stared at him - taking in every perfect feature of his face. He leaned in closer and kissed her. What began gently quickly es-calated into more forceful kisses while his hands claimed every curve of her body. Mag-gie shut her eyes and lost herself in his arms. Suddenly nothing else mattered. There was nothing to be afraid of. Everything would be fine.

13

When Maggie opened her eyes the next morning, the sun was streaming through the windows. She laid there for a few minutes, her arms above her head, stretching - enjoying the cozy feeling of being buried under the blankets. She could hear the shower running in the master bathroom. Sam was getting ready for work.

At the start of this new day, it was hard to believe anything terrible had happened the day before. In fact, she had slept better than she had in ages. With a deep sigh and a yawn, she pushed the covers away and sat up on the side of the bed. She would have to get ready as well since she had her appointment with Dr. Simpson. She glanced at the clock, surprised at the time. She walked over to the chair to retrieve her bathrobe.

"Good morning sleepy head." smiled Sam as he came out from the bathroom with a towel wrapped around him.

"Good morning!" replied Maggie. "I'm sorry I didn't get up to make you breakfast! You should have woken me up."

"Nope." said Sam as he started getting dressed. "I looked over at you and you were sleeping so peacefully I didn't have the heart to wake you. Besides, I can pick something up for Jordan and myself on my way in. I'm driving her to school today by the way. I don't want to take any chances."

"Well," smiled Maggie as she gave him a kiss on the cheek, "if you're okay with it, so am I. But ... I'm definitely going to make myself some coffee before I start getting ready. Honestly - I haven't slept that well in forever."

Buttoning his shirt, Sam smiled as he walked over to her.

"Promise me something," started Sam as he put his arms around her, "promise you'll call me the second you're out of Dr. Simpson's office? I want to know what he says."

"Yes sir, Sheriff." replied Maggie, smiling.

"Okay ... well..." said Sam as he looked around the room making sure he had everything. "You going to be alright getting to your appointment?"

"Yes, of course. Why wouldn't I be?"

"Just be careful. And make sure you keep your car doors locked and keep the house locked up even when you're in it."

Maggie saw the trace of worry in his eyes. She nodded.

A few minutes later, Maggie, with coffee cup in hand, was at the front door waving goodbye to her husband and daughter. She stood there for a few seconds after the car disappeared down the road. Shutting the door, she turned to go back to the kitchen, but then remembered her promise to Sam. She went back to the door and locked it.

After putting a few dishes into the dishwasher, Maggie showered, put on some makeup, her comfortable jeans and a shirt and was out the door heading to her appointment in no time at all.

Her drive into town was uneventful. Everything still looked the same. No sign of the fear that now held the town in its grip. Still, she found her gaze lingering on the men she drove by. Could one of them be the man Sam was trying to find?

Dr. Simpson worked out of his home. The house was a lot larger on the inside than it appeared to be from the outside. A comfortable two-story colonial with impressive columns guarding the front door. The landscaping spoke of a man who was meticulous about his environment and about himself.

From what Maggie knew, Dr. Simpson was a bachelor. If he had been married, she didn't know. In fact, as she thought about it, she really didn't know very much about his background at all. He lived only a few blocks from the Sheriff's Office, so before she knew it, she was already pulling into the driveway. She checked her watch. She was on time.

As she got out of her car, she made sure to lock it behind her. Normally she wouldn't worry about doing such a thing, but with the uncertainty in the town lately, better to be safe than sorry. At least she wouldn't have the fear that someone had gotten into her car while she was inside with Dr. Simpson.

She sighed at the unsettling thought that this was becoming the new normal and walked to the front door. She rang the doorbell and shortly after, heard movement inside before the door swung open.

"Maggie!" said Dr. Simpson warmly - a smile spreading across his face. "So good to see you! Come on in!"

He backed away from the door, allowing Maggie to enter and once she had, he shut and locked the door behind her. Maggie glanced around before turning her attention back to Dr. Simpson. She loved his house. Furnishings were clean and light and he obviously had a green thumb, judging from the plants dotted around the living room and foyer. His home was immaculate, decorated in warm earth tones.

"May I get you something to drink? Perhaps coffee or a glass of water or juice?"

Maggie smiled and shook her head. "No thank you. I'm fine."

"Well in that case, why don't we go into my office where we can chat and see what the problem is."

Maggie followed him as he led the way into his office that also had an examination room attached. He sat at his desk while she made herself comfortable on the chair facing him. Even though the morning sun poured through the large picture window to her left, the room still felt darker than the rest of the house - mainly because of the wood panelling that lined the walls. The furniture too seemed older and darker, but in perfect condition. His office was comfortable and meticulously kept and seemed to suit him.

"So ...," started Dr. Simpson, his hands folded on the desk, "what seems to be the problem? On the phone Sam said you passed out?"

Maggie studied him for a moment. Would he think she was simply crazy? She decided that was the chance she'd have to take. She took in a long breath and turned her eyes to the picture window and the view of his perfect yard.

"Well ... there are a number of things..."

"Such as?"

Maggie looked away from the window and this time, looked him directly in his eyes - waiting to see what reaction if any, she might garner. "Such as, I'm not sleeping well - I seem to be having all sorts of strange dreams

... I'm having blackouts or hallucinations - I'm not even sure what they are. That's what happened to me when Sam thought I passed out. It's actually happened a few times, but Sam doesn't know about those other times - I didn't want to worry him ... and I'm having some sort of issue with my memory."

"In what regard?"

"Remembering things that aren't real ... and not remembering things that are."

There was a pause as he started taking notes. After what felt like an eternity, he looked back up at her. "Hmmmm. How long has all this been going on?"

Maggie thought. "I'd say for a few weeks now."

"About the time of Ms. Haskins' murder?"

Maggie hesitated. "Yes, I guess it did start around then, I suppose. Do you think this could all just be because of stress?"

"It's possible. So tell me about your blackouts or hallucinations, as you call them."

"Well, they've been happening more and more I guess - now that I think about it. Maybe it's just a cumulative effect of not sleeping. At least that's what I'm hoping."

"So what happens during these episodes?" inquired Dr. Simpson, still busy taking notes.

Maggie waited until he looked up. "This is going to sound weird I know. But I guess it IS weird."

Dr. Simpson got up from his desk and retrieved a blood pressure cuff from the cabinet behind him and walked over to Maggie. She extended her arm as he wrapped the cuff around it.

"Don't worry about anything sounding weird. If I'm going to help you, I need to know everything. Just tell me as best you can."

"I know ... it's just that it's so hard to explain."

Maggie could feel the cuff tightening on her arm - and then the release as it quickly deflated.   She looked back at Dr. Simpson. "How's my blood pressure?"

"Just fine. Just fine." smiled Dr. Simpson.   "Now, tell me about those hallucinations."

"It's like out of no where I get this weird feeling - like I'm suddenly moving in slow motion and everything around me starts to fade. And then, when I look around, everything's different. It's like I'm not in the same place any more.   I'm somewhere else.   And my hands - my hands aren't mine anymore - they're someone else's too - a man's hands. I can smell things and hear things."

Maggie smiled weakly.   "It's almost as though for a few moments, I'm in someone else's body."

She looked up at Dr. Simpson. He was watching her with no expression on his face.

"I told you it was weird."

"Have you changed anything in your diet recently?"

"Nope."

She watched Dr. Simpson as he flipped through her file. As she did so, she started to take notice of the way he was dressed - sweater vest, bow tie, white shirt. For some reason she hadn't noticed when she first saw him. She had to smile. It reminded her so much of the way her grandfather used to dress when she was a child. The way men usually dressed back then. There was no doubt about it - Dr. Simpson would definitely have been considered dapper back in the day.

"Any changes in your appetite?"

"No."

"Any aches or pains - any headaches?"

"No. Well yes - headaches ... but not more than usual."

She watched as Dr. Simpson wrote her responses in her file.

"Oh - there is one more thing. I guess it's another hallucination."

"What's that?" asked Dr. Simpson, looking up from his desk.

"A man. A number of times I've seen a man who seems to be watching me ... but then he just disappears before I can point him out to anyone. But it's like he disappears so quick-ly he has to be some sort of hallucination."

Dr. Simpson leaned back in his chair, studying Maggie for a moment. "Well that's troubling. Not necessarily from a medical perspective, but because of what's been going on in this town lately. You be careful young lady - just in case."

"I am."

"Would you stand on the scale for me?" asked Dr. Simpson, motioning towards the old scale that sat in the corner of his office.

Maggie walked over to it, kicked off her shoes and got on as he adjusted the weight bar.

"Okay you can get down."

Maggie returned to the chair.

Dr. Simpson came over to her with a small pencil light which he directed at her eyes. He took his fingers and pressed them along the sides of her neck under her ears.

He stepped back.

"I'd like to draw some blood if that's alright with you. Run some tests, see how it looks."

He walked over to one of the cabinets that lined the wall and took a small paper cup out and handed it to Maggie.

"And if you could give me a sample? You can use the restroom attached to the examination room." he said, pointing towards the adjoining room.

Maggie took the cup and looked at him. "Any ideas of what might be wrong?" she asked.

Dr. Simpson smiled. "Truthfully, I'm doing the tests only because they should be done out of an abundance of caution. But you seem to be perfectly healthy and remarkably sane under the circumstances."

He chuckled. "I'm going to stick my neck out and say I'd be surprised if it was anything more than maybe an iron deficiency, lack of sleep or stress. Or possibly all combined. These are unusual times for our town. What you unfortunately witnessed the other day with Father McNeal... terrible, just terrible. Something like that could most definitely have negative effects on your physical and mental health. Could even trigger Post Traumatic Stress in some. But there is something I'd like you to do for me."

"What's that?"

"I want you to start recording every incident you experience that seems out of the norm for you. And I want you to record how much you're sleeping, what you're eating - how much coffee you're drinking, that sort of thing. I'm sure we'll figure this out."

It wasn't much later that Maggie found herself sitting in her car, which was still parked in Dr. Simpson's driveway. Something felt off but she wasn't sure what it was.

She pushed the sleeve of her shirt up and removed the bandage from where he had taken the blood sample. Why did it feel as though Dr. Simpson had merely gone through the motions of an examination? "Iron deficiency! Really?" she mumbled to herself. "At least he didn't tell me to take two aspirin and call him in the morning."

She liked Arlen Simpson and felt badly that she was questioning his care. But she couldn't shake the thought that everything felt - strange somehow. But then, he was the doctor, not her. And perhaps he was waiting to get the test results back on her bloodwork before saying anything more. That was probably it. More than likely he was trying to put her at ease. Suddenly she felt a little guilty about questioning him.

She retrieved her phone from her purse and dialed Sam. He answered on the second ring. Obviously he was anxious to hear all about her appointment.

"How did it go?"

"What? You don't say hello anymore?"

"Hello. How did it go?" responded Sam.

Maggie couldn't help but smile. "Well he doesn't seem all that concerned about anything I told him. He's running some blood-work, that sort of thing, but - he's thinking maybe an iron deficiency or something coupled with stress. Bottom line is - I'm going to live - apparently."

She could hear Sam let out a sigh on the other end. "Thank God. I've been worried."

"Well no need to be. I'm going to be fine."

"Are you heading home now?" asked Sam.

"Actually I was thinking about the grocery store and maybe seeing if Patty wanted to grab some lunch."

"Okay well you be careful and call me when you're home safe and sound. I love you."

"I love you too. Talk to you later."

Maggie smiled as she ended the call. It was good to hear the relief in his voice. She knew he had been more worried than he had let on, which was why she didn't tell him about the man she kept seeing - the one who was either following her, or was her very own hallucination. He had enough on his plate as it was. She would get to the bottom of it on her own. As off putting as her appointment had felt to her, the one thing for sure was that Dr. Simpson didn't appear to be overly concerned. For now, that would do.

She fastened her seatbelt and started the car. As she exited Dr. Simpson's driveway, she told herself everything would be just fine.

He watched as she pulled away. He liked Maggie. She reminded him of someone he once knew - but he couldn't remember who. As her car disappeared down the street, he turned to go into the kitchen. It looked like it was going to be a beautiful day. Perhaps he would do some gardening.

The rest of the day was rather uneventful. After picking up groceries at Hugh's, she had called Patty to see if she was available for a quick lunch, but as it turned out, she wasn't. So Maggie headed home instead.

The evening was quiet. Sam had gotten home at his usual time and had picked up Jordan at Susan's house. After sitting down to a dinner of roast chicken, mashed potatoes and salad, Jordan retired to her room to work on a project for school and Maggie and Sam decided to call it a night earlier than usual.

Maggie was exhausted and Sam was just tired of thinking about murders. If he could fall asleep, it would be his only escape from all of it - even if only for just a few hours.

They fell asleep quickly with Maggie's head resting on Sam's chest - his arm wrapped protectively around her. Her sleep was filled with disturbing dreams. Flashes of scenes, flashes of people's faces, a feeling of despair - of supreme sadness. Fear welling up inside of her. Dr. Simpson smiling at her, Father McNeal hanging on the cross, walking in a forest, the face of the man who was stalking her. It all flashed in her head.

Waking to the realization that Maggie was having a nightmare, Sam held her to him and gently stroked her back until she quieted down. Finally they both fell into a deep, restful sleep.

14

The Saturday morning sun shone brightly. There wasn't a cloud in the sky. The temperature had warmed nicely - although it seemed Rosedale never had terrible weather. But on this morning, the sun, the temperature and the slight breeze all felt comforting and perfect - more so than usual.

Rebecca Sanchez locked the door behind her and started walking towards the town square. It was her day off. A quick shower, her favorite jeans and her hair in a pony tail, she was looking forward to what the day would bring. She only lived a few blocks from the center of Rosedale, in a charming two bedroom bungalow. It was all she could afford on her salary but she felt lucky to have it. In all honesty, she was surprised that she could have afforded a house at all. Rosedale was her home and she liked it that way.

The weekly farmers' market was something the residents of Rosedale enjoyed. The chance to buy some wonderful treats and at the same time, be able to socialize, was something everyone looked forward to - including Rebecca. As she walked she found herself hoping that the woman who made the wonderful apple strudel would be there. As much as she tried to watch what she ate, that strudel had been on her mind for the past two days.

The air had a sweet smell to it this morning. All the flowers were in full bloom and all looked beautiful. As she walked though, she couldn't help but let her mind wander to dark places. The images of the bodies still played in her head over and over. As much as she tried, she couldn't seem to stop that from happening. But, she was hopeful those memories might move further and further back in her mind as time went by.

She turned the corner and saw the farmers' market stretched out in front of her. White tents dotted the town square. Residents were milling about picking out fresh fruits and vegetables, children running and playing, people laughing and a small three-piece band playing in front of City Hall. She searched the crowd for any familiar faces. That's when she spied Maggie who was paying for a bag of tomatoes. She made her way over to her before she could vanish into the crowd.

"Hi!"

Maggie looked up and was happy to see Rebecca standing next to her, smiling. "Hi!" she exclaimed. "Is it my imagination or does this seem busier than usual?"

Rebecca glanced around and nodded. Suddenly she felt uneasy. Maggie saw the change in her demeanor.

"I've been thinking the same thing."

Rebecca looked at her. "That he could be here somewhere?"

Maggie nodded. "I'm trying not to think about that too much - but it crossed my mind. But then again, he may not be." Maggie took a second and then changed the topic. "So what are you here to get? These tomatoes look wonderful!"

Rebecca smiled. "They do. But first I want to see if my apple strudel lady is here!"

"She is." laughed Maggie. "Just on the other side of the square. I saw her earlier. Come on - I'll walk with you."

The two women starting walking slowly towards the other side of the square, stopping periodically to look at what was being sold in the various tents. A wide variety of items were available - from vegetables to knitted hats and everything in between.

"So how are you holding up?" asked Maggie as she held up a pair of hand made earrings.

Rebecca shrugged. "I'm okay I guess. Just wish we could catch the son-of-a-bitch. I don't know - I just feel so ... helpless. Those are nice."

"They are." responded Maggie as she put them down. "And Sam would kill me if I bought more earrings."

Rebecca laughed. "No he wouldn't! That man loves you to death! I couldn't see him ever getting mad at you! And of course, he IS my boss so I probably shouldn't be talking about him like that!"

It was Maggie's turn to laugh. "I promise I won't tell him. Besides - you must know by now that you're like family to him. He has a great deal of respect for you as a deputy too."

Rebecca's grin broadened. "Good to know!"

"Oh fresh bread!" she exclaimed as they walked up to another tent. "Oh my God I have to get some - the smell is killing me."

Maggie smiled and looked around as well, thinking perhaps she too should pick up a nice fresh loaf instead of grabbing one from Hugh's Grocery. Rebecca was already paying for her purchase as Maggie picked up one of the loaves and a small bag of rolls and started to walk back towards the cashier. That's when she saw him. It was the man who was stalking her. Shaggy brown hair, glasses - it was him. She stared at him as she made her way quickly back to Rebecca. This time she wasn't going to take her eyes off him even for a second.

"Rebecca." Maggie said with a sense of urgency - still staring at the man who was just standing there, expressionless, staring back at her.

Rebecca turned to look at her.

"Over there - in front of the tent where they're selling children's books. A man, shaggy hair, glasses. Do you see him?"

Rebecca turned to look in the direction of Maggie's gaze but a group of people had crowded in front of the tent, making it impossible to get a clear view. Frustrated, Maggie tossed her purchases onto the table and started pushing her way through the crowd, trying to get to where she had seen him. Rebecca followed as well, unsure what exactly was going on but clearly aware that something was very wrong. Maggie reached the spot where she had seen him, but as usual, he wasn't there. She looked around frantically. He couldn't have gotten far - not in this crowd. He had to still be around. Rebecca watched Maggie but was clearly confused by what was happening.

"What is it? Who did you see?"

Maggie stopped and sighed. She shook her head in disbelief. "There's a man. I think he's been following me."

"What? Who is he?"

"I don't know. I don't have any idea who he is. I've seen him a few times now - just watching me. But I can't seem to get anyone else to see him! He just vanishes into thin air." Maggie was clearly irritated. "Which makes absolutely no sense."

"Does Sam know about this?" asked Rebecca looking concerned.

Maggie looked her squarely in the eyes. "No - and please don't tell him."

Rebecca started to argue with her but Maggie cut her off. "Please. I don't really know what's going on at this point and it may end up being nothing. And if it's nothing, I don't want to take Sam's attention away from anything important - like trying to find the killer."

Rebecca stared at her, clearly thinking about what Maggie just said. "How tall is he?"

Maggie thought carefully before responding. "I'd say around 6' probably."

"Shaggy hair you said - color?"

"Brown"

"And you said glasses - like prescription glasses?"

Maggie nodded.

"How old would you say he is?"

"I'm guessing, obviously, but I'd say maybe around 30ish, maybe a bit older. It's hard to tell."

Rebecca thought for a moment and then sighed. "I won't say anything to Sam."

"Thank you." said Maggie gratefully.

"I won't say anything to Sam YET." clarified Rebecca. "But if you see this guy again, you have to promise me you'll tell Sam. If anything happened to you and I knew some strange dude was following you I'd never forgive myself - but it wouldn't matter because Sam would kill me first."

"I promise I'll tell him."

"Good. I mean, geez Maggie ... we've got this freak running around killing people...," Rebecca glanced around at the crowd and lowered her voice, "... and you're telling me some weirdo is following you. It could be him!"

Maggie sighed. "I know. I know believe me. The thought has already crossed my mind. If I see him again, I'll definitely tell Sam - I promise. You have my word."

Rebecca nodded. "Good. And in the meantime, I'll keep my eyes open for anyone matching that description. I'll see if I can figure out who this creep is."

"Thanks." replied Maggie gratefully. "Let's go back and get our stuff."

The two weaved their way through the crowd, back to where they had been. After paying for their purchases, they resumed their walk towards the apple strudel Rebecca had been craving. Periodically Maggie looked around, searching the crowd for the mystery man, but to no avail. She wasn't surprised. He had a way of disappearing. She wondered though if he wanted her to see him. But if so, why? Maybe to make her afraid? She was thinking more and more that the possibility of him being some sort of hallucination was slight at best. He seemed too real.

Passing tent after tent they finally made it to their destination. Cakes and pastries of all sorts were stacked on temporary shelves all around them. The smell of freshly baked pastries was intoxicating. Rebecca moved over to the apple strudel while Maggie walked to the opposite side to look at the selection of pies.

"They do look tasty don't they?"

Maggie spun around, relieved to see Wyndham Hart standing behind her. "Wyndham! Good to see you! It's busy today isn't it?"

"My it is, Mrs. Cooper. I suppose everyone has gotten tired of hiding behind closed doors. Time to breathe some fresh air and eat some fattening pies!" He laughed.

Maggie grinned. "I could have done without the mention of 'fattening'... And just when I was eyeing that blueberry pie over there."

"Oh a piece or two won't hurt you, Mrs. Cooper! Besides, at least you have others to share it with. I, unfortunately, would be forced into eating the entire thing all by myself and that just wouldn't do."

"Well ..." started Maggie, smiling, "in that case, I'll buy the blueberry pie on the condition you come by the house and have some with me."

Wyndham beamed. "How could I possibly turn down such a delightful invitation?"

"Perfect! How about tomorrow around noon?"

"I wouldn't miss it for the world." replied Wyndham warmly as he followed Maggie to the cash register. Finally both Maggie and Rebecca, with purchases in hand, walked slowly out of the tent with Wyndham in tow.

"So Deputy Sanchez, any luck on your investigation?" asked Wyndham as the three of them walked slowly through the crowd.

Maggie glanced at Rebecca, knowing she couldn't divulge vey much of what they were doing in the case. She smiled as she watched the two of them engaged in their conversation. Everyone liked Wyndham, it would have been impossible NOT to like him. As they walked, she spotted orchids being sold in one of the tents and decided to look at them more closely. She stopped for only a few moments but when she looked up, she realized Rebecca and Wyndham had continued on, completely unaware that she had stopped.

No matter, she thought to herself, she'd be able to catch up to them quickly enough. She looked at a couple of the white orchids, but then decided against buying them after all. They just weren't quite right - and certainly not for the price. She put back the one she had in her hand and started walking in the direction she had last seen Wyndham and Rebecca.

The crowds were relentless and she felt like a salmon pushing her way upstream. But then, all of a sudden, it hit her. Her hair stood up on the back of her neck and she twirled around - expecting to see the strange man standing directly behind her. But he wasn't. There wasn't anyone looking at her. There wasn't anyone she took notice of. So what was this feeling?

Her breath became shallow and beads of sweat started to form on her brow. She felt the presence of someone. She knew she did. Her eyes darted through the crowd. The feeling of being watched - of someone being right there with her, was overpowering. People in the crowd were knocking into her as they tried to get by, but she continued standing in one spot, looking around wildly.

For a moment she felt like she was going to faint when suddenly the feeling passed as quickly as it started. Her breathing returned to normal and she no longer had the sensation of someone being right there with her. She used the back of her hand to wipe away the beads of sweat. She had to get to Rebecca and Wyndham. She was grateful they hadn't witnessed her going through whatever she had just experienced. They would have thought she had lost her mind and she was starting to get tired of people thinking that.

The more time went by, the more she was becoming sure that she wasn't losing her mind after all - that something strange was in fact going on. Something she would have to figure out. This wasn't her imagination. But if it wasn't her imagination - what was it? She pushed through the crowd a little more forcefully now - eager to find her friends. She didn't want to be alone.

Finally she spied them. They were sitting at one of the small tables next to a tent that was selling cold drinks and snacks. As she approached, she noticed that unfortunately they weren't alone. Alice Topper stood next to their table, towering over Rebecca and Wyndham while a small, frail, brow-beaten man, whom Maggie could only guess was her husband, stood next to her, looking uncomfortable and apologetic.

Based on the expression on Alice Topper's face, combined with her finger wagging, Maggie felt she knew what the conversation was probably about and opted to waste a little time before showing up to the table herself. She understood the frustration and fear that

Alice Topper was feeling. Everyone was feeling it. But, yelling and threatening wasn't going to make things any safer in Rosedale.

Maggie watched from a distance as Alice Topper's face seemed to get redder and redder until Maggie was certain the woman was just going to explode in the middle of the farmers' market. She saw Rebecca smile and appear to respond back in a calm and friendly manner.

Maggie was impressed. She didn't know if she could have handled that woman as well. In fact, she knew for a fact she wouldn't have been able to. It was hard to believe that Rebecca was so young but had such an amazing way of dealing with people. Maggie made a promise to herself that as the wife of the Sheriff, she'd have to work on that. Maybe even find out Rebecca's secret to staying so calm.

A couple of minutes passed before Maggie saw Alice Topper's husband finally take his wife's hand in his and give a slight nod to Wyndham and Rebecca. Surprisingly, he gave his wife what could only be described as a stern look and she suddenly stopped talking. Maggie watched as he extended his hand to both Rebecca and Wyndham and then lead his wife away from the table. From the look on Alice Topper's face, Maggie could tell she was far from pleased, but surprisingly willing to follow her husband's lead. Maggie gave them a couple more seconds to be out of view before finally approaching the table.

"You missed the excitement." smiled Rebecca as she saw Maggie approach. Wyndham was sipping on a small lemonade, obviously enjoying watching the crowds stroll by.

"No I didn't miss anything." confessed Maggie as she sat down at the table. "I saw her. I just wasn't prepared to deal with her. You know - that was the first time I think I've ever seen her husband!"

"I guess she doesn't let him out very often." chuckled Rebecca. "I understand why she's upset. Hell, I'm upset too. But we're doing everything we can do. We just need for the residents to start being more aware and more cautious in the meantime."

"Oh my..." uttered Wyndham as he looked off to his left.

Maggie and Rebecca followed his gaze. But it wasn't hard to figure out what he was looking at. A young man, tall and lanky, maybe in his late 20's and a stocky, conservatively dressed, middle aged woman had started arguing and it had quickly gotten out of control. Voices became loud and suddenly the woman started hitting him. Rebecca jumped up from the table and ran to them.

"Hey hey hey! What's wrong with you?" she yelled as she pulled the woman off.

"She's nuts!" yelled the man, straightening his shirt. "She's fucking nuts!"

"You've been following me! I saw you!" She turned her gaze to Rebecca who still had her by the arm. "He's the killer I know it. I've never seen him around here before and all of a sudden, everywhere I go, he's there! He's the killer I tell you! He tried to grab me!"

Rebecca took a deep breath. She looked around at the crowd that had formed around them. "Okay everybody, get on with your business. This is under control ... just go on and enjoy your day."

She turned her attention to the young man.

"Did you try to grab this woman?"

"Oh hell no. I was trying to get by her and I touched her arm so she wouldn't move in front of me - that's all. I haven't been following her. Nothin'. She's just nuts."

"Do you have some I.D?" she asked him.

He nodded.

"Let me see it." She turned her attention to the woman while the young man was reaching into his jean pocket for his wallet. "I'm going to let go of your arm. Are you going to behave yourself? Cause if you don't, it's you I'll be taking to jail - got it?"

The woman nodded, looking a little embarrassed. Rebecca reached out and took the drivers license the young man was handing her. She looked at it.

"Joe Deluca ... I see you live right around the corner from here."

"Yeah that's right. Lived here a long time."

"Okay." said Rebecca as she handed him back his identification. "Sorry this happened to you. I guess everyone's on edge these days. Do you want to press charges against her for assault?"

The woman looked at Rebecca, plainly in shock at what she was hearing, but wisely she decided not to speak. She looked at the man she now knew as Joe, afraid of what he was going to say. He looked at her for a few seconds and then over at Rebecca.

"Oh hell ... forget it. Just forget it." He then moved his gaze towards the woman who had just assaulted him. "Just don't ever ever talk to me again. Got that? You see me and you just keep walkin'. Understood?"

The woman looked ashamed and nodded her head. "I'm sorry. I'm so sorry. I guess I'm just afraid. I'm not like this, really." Her voice drifted away.

After a few moments Joe sighed and his shoulders softened. "Hey, it's okay. You've got a pretty mean left hook there, but no harm done." he replied. He looked at Rebecca who smiled at him and mouthed the words 'thank you' before he wandered off into the crowd.

Rebecca turned her attention back to the woman who was now standing quietly next to her, looking somewhat embarrassed. Rebecca obviously knew her. "Joyce? You alright now? You want someone to take you home?

"No Deputy Sanchez. I'm fine now. I can get home by myself. I'm so sorry - I don't know what got into me. You KNOW that's not me!"

"Yeah I know it's not. You go home. Get some rest. We're all a little wound up around here."

With that Joyce gave a slight smile to Rebecca and then disappeared into the crowd. Rebecca turned and started to walk back to her table.

"Don't know why everybody's so upset around here!" a man's voice rang out.

Rebecca turned and saw a man about 50, thin and tall - smiling.

"Listen sir - why don't you just move along huh? It's a beautiful day. Go buy yourself something."

"But it doesn't make sense!" the man continued. "If we're supposed to die we die and if we're supposed to live, we live! No point in being scared. Nothin we can do about it anyway! Control is an illusion. We can't escape destiny! It's God's will! God determines who lives and who dies. Who will be in everlasting paradise with him and who will burn in Hell!"

He took the Bible he was holding in his hand and raised it above his head. His voice was getting louder and louder. Again people were beginning to gather. Now he was shouting at the top of his lungs - preaching to the crowd.

"All of you are sinners! You are not worthy. Repent your sins now before you die! The priest may have appeared to be a man of God but he was sacrificed because of his sins. No one will escape the final judgement."

Rebecca took a deep breath and moved towards him. She got into his face and glared at him. "Listen to me and listen carefully," she said in a low, measured voice. "God may decide who goes to Heaven ... but here in Rosedale, I get to decide who goes to jail - and right now I'm starting to think that it might just be you."

"Whatever for, Deputy?"

"As far as I'm concerned, you're disturbing the peace. I asked you to move on and you refused. I'm thinking that might be a good reason, until I can think of something else."

He looked at her intently. He smiled. "You never asked me to move on."

Rebecca smiled back at him. "Oh, but I did - and I'm sure you heard me. At least that's what I'm going to tell the Judge, along with a few other things. So do you really want to argue with me about that?"

The man started to speak and then stopped. He saw a look in Rebecca's eyes that told him this would probably not end well for him if he continued. He cleared his throat, turned and quietly walked away into the crowd.

Rebecca watched him go. She turned back to the table. Wyndham's eyes were as big as saucers.

"Man!" exclaimed Rebecca as she took her seat. "They're just coming out of the woodwork..."

"Yes but you handled that exceedingly well." commented Wyndham. "I certainly couldn't have done what you just did. You are an excellent deputy I must say, simply excellent."

Rebecca smiled back politely. "Thank you Wyndham. But an excellent deputy should be able to do more than just crowd control. Just didn't need him talking about Father McNeal right now."

*   *   *

He sat on a bench eating popcorn. It was a quiet little spot, tucked away from most of the activity. He had the perfect view. The bench sat behind one of the tents just enough that no one would take notice of him. It was like watching a movie, his own private movie. He liked that. He liked watching. So far it had been an interesting morning. People were scared. He could smell the fear. Scared of him. He tried to stop himself from laughing. The band was beginning to annoy him. He never liked music - especially this kind of happy, stupid music. If he listened to anything it was loud and throbbing, with a singer screaming out the lyrics. Add some self mutilation and it was perfect. That's the music he liked. Music that could make him transport into another place. Music that could make him feel alive.

He liked watching the residents of Rosedale going about their day. Perhaps making plans for the future. It was a bit like shooting fish in a barrel. But then, that's what life was like - either you get killed, or you do the killing. He much preferred doing the killing. Besides, it was fun. It was the great equalizer.

Even though he'd never met them, he was becoming familiar with some of them - like that Sheriff's wife. She was pretty - but probably a whore like all the others. As he watched her today though, he noticed something had happened to her - twice. He couldn't figure out what was going on. She seemed panicked, but he couldn't tell why. One time she almost looked right at him. It sent chills down his spine. That was close. Even though she'd have no idea who he really was, he didn't want to take any chances.

There was something about her though. He didn't know what it was exactly, but he felt strangely drawn to her. The voices had started telling him that he needed to kill her. But something was making him feel like he should wait. The time needed to be right. She was special. She was different somehow. But of course the bitch probably knew she was special. The pretty ones were like that. They were the ones who would have liked Stephen. He thought about the ways he could go about punishing her before he killed her. He considered that for a while as he slowly ate more popcorn, scanning the crowd as he did so.

So who would it be? It had been a while and he was starting to get the itch ... starting to feel a little anxious. Maybe it should be someone the Sheriff's wife knew. That would freak her out.

He shut his eyes, took a deep breath and then, ever so quietly, said the words, "Eeny, meeny, miny, moe." Upon the whispering the last word, he opened his eyes and found himself looking directly at someone. He smiled. He knew what he'd be doing later. He got up, threw the bag of popcorn down on the grass and slowly made his way into the flow of the farmers' market - losing himself in the crowd. There was someone he needed to follow.

15

The next day started like any other for Maggie. Although it was Sunday and usually they would have been on their way to Church, that had all changed with the death of Father McNeal. She looked forward to when the Church would send Rosedale another priest to take over St. Boniface. At least then perhaps people could start to heal, instead of being constantly reminded of what they had lost.

However, she did wonder if she'd ever be able to be in that Church again without picturing Father McNeal hanging on the cross. She told herself she would, in time, but that was just what she wanted to believe. She'd have to wait to find out if it turned out to be the case.

But at least she still had plans for the day. She was expecting Wyndham to drop by at noon for some of the blueberry pie she had purchased the day before. That and some strong perked coffee would be a nice treat. Jordan, as usual, had gone to Susan's house. Sam was working so he had driven her there. She had been given strict orders that they weren't to go anywhere and that either Sam or Maggie would pick her up when it was time to come home. As an extra precaution Sam spoke directly to Susan's mother who clearly understood the potential danger of letting the girls out of her sight.

Maggie and Sam had discussed the issue at great length and had decided that forcing Jordan to stay home without any interaction with her friends would only heighten the anxiety level everyone was feeling. So, Jordan could go to Susan's house but next time, Susan would come to Jordan's. That arrangement seemed to make everyone happy.

Maggie glanced at the over-sized clock on the kitchen wall. It was only 9am. She had three hours before Wyndham was expected to come by. She smiled as she thought of him. He was such a charming man. It was always a pleasure to see him and he never failed to make her smile... although she did wonder if she'd ever be able to convince him to just call her Maggie. 'Probably not.' she laughed to herself.

He had kept inviting her over to his house so that she could see his artwork. For some reason, she had never taken him up on the invitation. She made a mental note that she would have to do that at some point in the very near future. In truth, she was curious to see what his paintings were like.

She decided to set the table and make everything a little more special than normal. She knew Wyndham would appreciate the effort. Good toilet training was something he valued. So she brought out the navy blue placemats, her good china and her silver flatware. She took extra time to make sure the flatware was buffed and shiny. She added some pretty white flowers that she had gotten from her garden and before she knew it, the table looked beautiful.

She stood back admiring it for a moment. The way the sunlight poured through the bay windows, made everything on the table sparkle. She walked to the cupboard and took out her electric coffee percolator. Somehow Wyndham didn't seem like the drip coffee kind of person. Again, she couldn't help but chuckle as she poured the cold water into the percolator and then added the ground coffee to the basket. It was ready to go.

Maggie sighed as she looked around. Everything looked perfect. She still had time to tidy up the rest of the house, which primarily meant picking up after Jordan and then taking a nice relaxing shower and getting herself ready.

As she walked to the master bathroom, she thought about the dreams she had had the night before. Even though she tried to write them down, as Dr. Simpson had suggested, it was hard to remember what they were about in any detail that made sense. She could re-member bits and pieces ... but primarily it was the emotion of her dreams that stayed with her.

She found herself waking up a few times the night before - always with that same feel-ing of terror. The feeling of needing to be somewhere, but not knowing where. It was a feeling of being lost. At one point the feeling of emptiness was so strong, she reached over to Sam and found that being able to touch him helped calm her.

But then, after everything that had hap-pened at the farmers' market, it wasn't sur-prising that her mind was in overdrive. Ten-sion was growing in the small community and you could feel it wherever you went. It seemed everyone was suspicious of everyone else. She wondered how long this would continue. How she missed the Rosedale she knew before this insanity started. She could only hope that it would return one day soon.

She turned the water on as hot as she could take it and stood under the shower with her eyes shut just letting the spray wash away the tension she was feeling. She was still exhausted from yet another night of questionable sleep - but she was almost getting used to the feeling. The shower though was helping and soon she felt rejuvenated.

After drying her hair and putting on her makeup, she decided to dress up a little for this special Sunday event and reached for her favorite white cotton sun dress. It was perfect. A few finishing touches and she walked back into the kitchen.

Surprisingly it was almost noon. She decided to get the coffee perking and get the plates ready for the blueberry pie. Wyndham was punctual to a fault and would probably arrive just as the clock read 12:00.

So as the coffee started to perk, she sat down at the kitchen table to wait for the sound of her doorbell. It was already 11:55 so she knew she wouldn't have long to wait. The flowers on the table looked so pretty. She looked out at her backyard. She was quite happy with the work she had done out there. All of the flowers looked as though they were thriving. She loved how they looked and even better, how they smelled. For a moment she got lost in her thoughts.

She felt her eyes getting heavy. She leaned back in the chair. Her eyes shut... and for what felt like a few moments, she was adrift. But then, with a quick intake of breath, she caught herself and her eyes quickly opened. She mustn't fall asleep. Wyndham would be arriving any minute.

She glanced back up at the clock and stopped breathing. It was almost 12:30. She had fallen asleep after all. Where was Wyndham? Perhaps the door bell had jolted her awake. She hurried to the front door and swung it open, expecting to see Wyndham standing there. But there was no one. Obviously it wasn't the sound of a door bell that woke her up. Where was he? She shut the door. She started to worry. Wyndham would never be late. Panic started to grow inside of her.

She ran back to the kitchen and grabbed her phone. Checking her contact list, she found Wyndham's number. He wasn't a believer in cell phones unfortunately, but at least she had his hard line. She dialed the number hoping he would answer, but nothing. She ended the call.

Standing there in the kitchen with her phone in her hand, her thoughts started to run wild. Was she over-reacting? Where was her friend? Looking back at her phone, she dialed Sam. But again, the phone rang the usual number of times before going to voicemail. She ended the call without leaving a message.

She turned off the percolator and grabbed her car keys and purse when suddenly she heard the familiar chime of the doorbell. Without thinking and without checking first, she hurried to the front door and swung it open. Relief washed over her. It was Wyndham.

"Well hello Mrs. Cooper! You look stunning today!" smiled Wyndham.

"Oh Wyndham - thank God." sighed Maggie with relief. "Come on in."

"Mrs. Cooper - what's wrong?" asked Wyndham "Has something happened?"

He walked into the house as Maggie shut and locked the door behind him. She took a deep breath and smiled at him. "Well to be honest - it's not like you to be late for anything and when you weren't here on time, well, I thought something had happened and I got worried. That's all. But it doesn't matter now - because you're here safe and sound! Just me over-reacting I guess."

Wyndham followed her into the kitchen looking a little perplexed.

"Let me make us some fresh coffee. Please, have a seat and make yourself comfortable." said Maggie as she filled the percolator again with fresh water.

"Mrs. Cooper," started Wyndham a little hesitantly. "it's 12:30, on the dot, in fact."

Maggie stopped what she was doing and looked at him. "Yes, it's 12:30." she agreed, unsure of the point he was making.

"Well, isn't that the time we agreed for me to arrive? Please correct me if I'm wrong, of course, but I could have sworn we first said noon but then I mentioned having to run a couple of errands first, so we settled on 12:30."

Maggie stopped what she was doing and thought about what he had just said. "Oh my God. I'm so sorry. You're right! I completely forgot. I guess I'm really not getting enough sleep. For some reason it was noon that stuck in my head. Please accept my apologies for overreacting."

Wyndham smiled. "Absolutely no reason for you to apologize Mrs. Cooper. In fact, I find it rather flattering you would be that worried about me."

"Well of course I'd be worried about you! You're my friend. And I guess with what's been going on around here lately, I'm just a little nervous."

"As you are my friend as well, Mrs. Cooper, I would be feeling the same." said Wyndham flashing is smile. "And I must say this table looks absolutely beautiful! And I certainly am looking forward to that blueberry pie. May I help you with something?"

Maggie glanced around the kitchen. "Well - the coffee will be ready in just a few ... I'll get the creamer and sugar, but if you'd like, perhaps you could cut us a couple of slices of that pie we're both dying to get to." laughed Maggie.

"It would truly be my pleasure." responded Wyndham as he carried the pie to the table and started cutting.

Before long, they were enjoying their coffee and pie and were deep in conversation - not only about the current state of Rosedale, but Wyndham's love of art. She couldn't wait to see some of his work.

"I've always done landscapes because, well, you know, everyone does landscapes - but my real passion is portraits. Perhaps one day you'd allow me to do yours?" he asked.

"I would love that." replied Maggie

"I've always found it fascinating how just one simple stroke can change a face completely. It's in the eyes you know. As they say - the eyes are the window to the soul. All you have to do is look into someone's eyes and you can see who they really are."

"Well in that case, I'm scared to ask what you see in my eyes." laughed Maggie.

"Oh no Mrs. Cooper! No need to be. In your eyes I see a kind, warm, loving woman ... who is also very intuitive."

"Intuitive? Me?"

"Absolutely. I call it sweetness of spirit."

"Well you are very kind Wyndham. But unfortunately from this side, all my eyes are saying is that I'm not sleeping nearly enough."

"Still?"

"Still. I don't like the idea of taking any medication - but I'm thinking maybe I should get some sleeping pills. Even if I just take them for a little while, just so that I can feel a little rested. Maybe with any luck they'll also stop me from dreaming."

"Well to be honest, since all of this started happening, I've been having some rather strange dreams myself. I don't think we realize how this is effecting us - all of us. Best to get through it however we can and hope that soon he'll be caught or ..."

"Die?"

"Well Mrs. Cooper. I didn't want to say that, but yes, 'die'."

Maggie started to respond when her cell phone started to ring.

She look at Wyndham apologetically. "I'm sorry Wyndham, but that's Sam's ring. I should take the call. I'll just be a moment."

"No problem at all. Take your time. And I think I shall have another piece of this sinfully delicious pie!"

Maggie smiled as she picked up her phone. "Hey Babe!" laughed Maggie. "I'm just sitting here with Wyndham completely pigging out on pie."

Wyndham watched as slowly Maggie's smile began to fade and was replaced by a look of shock.

"Oh my God. Where? ... No no no. Does her husband know?... Yeah I'll get Jordan, don't worry about that. You do what you have to do. We'll be fine... I'll ask him. Just let me know what's going on... I love you too."

Maggie ended the call but said nothing for a few moments.

"Mrs. Cooper?" started Wyndham quietly. "Mrs. Cooper?"

Maggie looked up at him. "Sam wanted me to ask if you'd stay with me until he got home this evening. And if you'd come with me while I pick Jordan up at her friend's house."

"But of course I will. What's happened?"

Maggie took a moment to answer. "There's been another murder."

"Oh my no. Who? Who is it this time? Anyone we know?"

Again Maggie took a few moments before responding. "Alice Topper."

16

Sam put the phone back into his pocket. He was standing in the alleyway behind City Hall with his deputies and of course, Doc Simpson. This was starting to feel normal and that scared him.

They were loading the body of Alice Topper into the van, ready to remove it from the scene. Rebecca had contacted Mr. Topper and he was on his way. Sam prayed he wouldn't get there until after they had removed the body. He wanted Doc Simpson to have the time to clean her up a bit before her husband had to identify her.

She had been stuffed into the dumpster after what appeared to be obvious signs of torture and abuse of the body. A restaurant employee from nearby needed to throw some things into their dumpster, but it was full - so he decided to walk half a block further and use this one.

Thank God he did. Had he not lifted the lid to throw something in, Alice Topper may not have been found. The garbage truck was scheduled to pick up first thing Monday morning. They would have dumped the contents into the compactor without ever looking inside and she may never have been found.

Unfortunately the restaurant employee was still shaken up. He threw up a couple of times before Rebecca could calm him down and take a statement. Sam felt sorry for the kid. Hard enough to see something like that when it was part of your job - the kid was just bussing tables for a bit of extra spending money. Sam knew he might never be able to get the sight of Alice Topper, dead and dismembered, lying in a dumpster, out of his mind.

"Well, we're ready to head out." said Doc Simpson as he approached Sam. "I'll see what I can do about preparing the body for identification. I don't want the poor bastard seeing her the way she is."

Sam nodded. "Okay. You go. I'll be here for a while. I'll talk to you back at the Sheriff's office later or maybe tomorrow when you're done."

Doc Simpson nodded and started to turn away when Sam spoke up once more.

"Oh and by the way, just wanted to thank you for taking a look at Maggie. I was really worried about her - but she said you didn't find anything to be concerned about."

Doc Simpson smiled. "No. Nothing. She seems to be a very healthy young woman. But the things that are going on in our town lately... and you being on the front lines so-to-speak, well I'd be surprised if it DIDN'T effect her in some way. You have to know she's probably worried to death about you. And then toss in the fear that someone's following her and it really becomes an overwhelming situation for her."

Sam stared blankly at the doctor. "I'm sorry, what did you say?"

"About what?"

"Someone is following Maggie?"

Doc Simpson looked embarrassed. "Oh I probably shouldn't have said anything but I did make her promise she'd tell you."

"Well she didn't - so why don't you?"

Doc Simpson hesitated.

"Listen," continued Sam, "if someone is stalking my wife, that's a matter for the Sher-iff's office - that isn't a medical issue. So what did she say?"

Doc Simpson took in a deep breath. "Why don't you ask her about it when you get home? Unless of course you want Mrs. Topper here as she is, when her husband shows up."

Sam shook his head. "No - damn it. I want you to take her out of here before he shows up - you're right. And you can rest assured I'll ask Maggie about it when I get home."

"Yes well ...," Doc Simpson replied as he started to walk towards the van, "just make sure to tell her I'm sorry that I mentioned it to you before she had a chance to."

And with that, he got into the van and disappeared down the alley.

Sam looked around but his mind was somewhere else. Suddenly the only thing on his mind was Maggie. Why hadn't she told him that someone might be following her? Well at least he knew she was safe at home and she had someone with her until he got home. That was good. But he'd be talking to her the second he walked through the door. There was no way anything would happen to her - not if he could help it.

"Sheriff? ... Sheriff?"

Sam suddenly realized Rebecca was standing next to him. "I'm sorry. What?"

"As usual, I spoke to the other businesses around here." responded Rebecca. "No one saw anything out of the ordinary and no one saw anyone at this dumpster - either in a vehicle or on foot. I saw her yesterday at the farmers' market. There were so many people around here at that time, there's no way someone could have killed her and placed her here without being seen. Besides, her husband was with her."

"When did you get the call from her husband?"

"Bernice called me at around 7am and told me he had just called. That's when I called him back and found out he thought she was missing. He wanted to file a missing persons report, but I told him it was too soon - that maybe she had just gone for a long walk or something. Christ - I actually said that to him. And then, as you know, the kid finds her at 2:05 this afternoon. This is the first time a victim was dismembered. Why the change?"

"Well I can probably explain that."

Rebecca turned to see Deputy Moyer walking towards them.

"Given the ... ah ... girth, shall we say, of Mrs. Topper - well that kind of weight isn't easy to move around. And especially not easy to hoist up and into a dumpster - at least not for one person. I'd bet he did it just so he could dispose of her in a timely fashion. I say that with no disrespect to the victim of course."

"Oh shit." said Rebecca quietly.

Sam and Deputy Moyer turned to look in the direction of Rebecca's gaze and saw Mr. Topper hurrying towards them. He was obviously distraught.

"Boss, I'm going to go talk to more businesses around here." Deputy Moyer said as he quickly moved away from the Sheriff.

"I'm going to help him." added Rebecca as she hurried away as well.

Before Sam could say anything, Mr. Topper stood in front of him. His distress was palatable. Sam was going to hate this conversation.

"Where is she?" asked Mr. Topper, looking around the scene. "Where's my wife?"

Sam took a deep breath and placed his hand on the man's shoulder. Mr. Topper was a frail man and Sam was concerned he might not be able to handle all of this. He spoke softly, knowing how difficult this was going to be.

"Dr. Simpson has taken her to prepare her for an autopsy. Once we're done here, I'll take you to her because - well - you're going to have to identify the ... her."

Mr. Topper nodded in agreement and that's when Sam saw the tears in his eyes.

"Tell you what, let's go sit in my car and talk for a bit. And then I'll take you to her."

Sam walked to his car with Alice's husband following behind. Sam could tell he was trying hard to hold himself together. Sam respected that. He didn't know if he could, if anything were to happen to Maggie. Holding the passenger door open, Mr. Topper settled into the seat.

As Sam walked around the car to the driver's side, he couldn't help but scan the area. He wondered if the killer was nearby, watching. The thought gave him chills. He got into the driver's side and shut the door. The inside of the car was quiet. Almost too quiet. He could hear Mr. Topper's labored breathing. He turned to look at him.

"Tell me what happened starting with once you left the farmers' market yesterday."

Mr. Topper looked out the windshield and wiped a tear from his eye. "Well actually, something happened while we were at the market."

"What? Did you see someone?"

"No, it wasn't that. My wife and I were walking around, enjoying the day, that sort of thing. But then she saw Deputy Sanchez sitting at a table. I tried to stop her from going over. I mean it was such a lovely day I didn't want anything to ruin it."

Mr. Topper cleared his throat as he tried to push back his emotions. Sam waited. "But ... well you know - you knew ... Alice. There was no talking that woman out of anything once she put her mind to it. She insisted on going up to Deputy Sanchez right then and there in the middle of the farmers' market.

Before I knew it Alice was yelling at Deputy Sanchez, demanding to know what was going on with the investigation. Carrying on something fierce. I felt sorry for the Deputy with Alice yelling at her like that. It wasn't right - I knew that. So I stopped her."

Mr. Topper gave a sad laugh as he remembered. "For the first time in our entire marriage I stood up to her. Told her that was enough, thanked Deputy Sanchez and apologized of course and escorted my wife away. I don't know which one of us was more surprised - her or me."

"Then what happened?"

Mr. Topper wiped another tear from his eye. "Not much for a while. We walked around the market a bit longer. But she was quiet. I think she was just getting madder and madder. I suppose it took her a bit to wrap her head around what had just happened. Anyway, before I knew it, she was demanding we leave. She was angry. But I thought it would pass in a bit. So I thought humoring her might be the best thing, so I agreed to leave."

"You drove?"

"No actually. It was such a beautiful day we decided to walk to the market. So we walked home. Got to say I was never around Alice when she wasn't talking. But she didn't say a word to me the entire time."

"Did you notice anyone watching you or following you? Anything strike you as suspicious?"

"No. Nothing. But to tell you the truth, I was more focused on Alice than anything else. She wasn't herself."

"Then what happened?"

"Well we got home. Put away the things we bought at the market and then she told me she had a headache and was going to lie down for a bit and wanted to be left alone. I obliged of course. When she finally came down, it was time for dinner. I don't think she said three words the entire time. I was beginning to wonder if she would ever snap out of it. I tried talking to her, but she just waved me off. So I just gave up. Figured it would pass in time.

Anyway - after that, she informed me that she would be sleeping downstairs in the guest room. There was no point in arguing with her. As far back as I can remember, that woman never slept anywhere but next to me. Not once."

Mr. Topper sighed as he remembered. "So that's how our evening went. I was upstairs in our room and she was downstairs. I did check on her once though and saw that she was sitting out on the back porch - drinking something - lemonade I think. So I didn't bother her. Just turned and went back up to bed. Figured everything would be fine by morning. Thought by then she would have ..."

Again his eyes teared up. "Why didn't I just tell her to come to bed and stop the foolishness? Why didn't I sit with her on the porch and try to talk to her? Why didn't I know I'd never see her again?"

His voice drifted off.

"Then what happened? You called the Sheriff's office at around 7:00 am."

Mr. Topper nodded. "That's when I got up. I went downstairs expecting to see her in the kitchen. I had prepared myself for a conversation, but she wasn't there. So I looked in the guest room but it was empty. Didn't look like she slept in it at all... That's when I went out onto the porch and saw the glass she'd been using the night before. It was just lying there, broken. That's when I knew something was wrong. That's when I called."

"Do you remember what time you checked on her that night?"

Mr. Topper thought for a moment. "I guess it was somewhere around 11:00 or 11:30."

"And you didn't hear anything when you were upstairs?"

Mr. Topper shook his head. "Our bedroom is at the front of the house. I couldn't have heard her on the back porch. Oh God Sheriff ... what if she called for me and I didn't hear her? How can I live with that?"

There was nothing Sam could say. He waited for a while before speaking again.

"What was she wearing the last time you saw her?"

Mr. Topper gazed out the window. "A pale blue summer dress. It was what she wore to the farmers' market. She was still wearing it when I saw her out on the porch." He paused for a moment and gently shook his head. "I wonder if she ever knew how much I loved that dress on her. I never thought it important enough to tell her..."

Sam started the car. "I'll take you to her. I'm sorry but I need you to identify her. Will you be alright?"

Mr. Topper nodded but continued to gaze out the window.

Sam pulled up to the medical building a few minutes later. He had phoned Doc Simpson from his car to let him know they were on their way. They entered using the private side door and were met by Doc Simpson who extended his condolences to Mr. Topper. He led the man to a private viewing room. Sam stayed outside and waited. Shortly thereafter, Sam heard a heart wrenching cry. Alice Topper had been identified.

17

It had been a long day. Maggie sat at the end of the window seat with her legs stretched out, looking out over her front yard. The street lights were on and everything looked so enchanting, it was hard to believe that suddenly so much ugliness existed in a place that always made her feel safe. She heard Sam in the kitchen. She knew what he must be going through. She only wished that there was something she could do to make things easier on him.

Jordan was up in her bedroom, pouting. She was not happy about having to come home early from Susan's. So, in order to display her unhappiness for everyone's benefit, she refused to say so much as one word over dinner and immediately retired to her bedroom. Maggie didn't like seeing her upset - but she did like seeing her daughter safe and alive. What was it about that age that made it impossible to recognize danger, Maggie wondered.

Wyndham had stayed until Sam got home, as he had promised. As much as Maggie didn't like imposing upon him, she was grateful for his company. They shared stories about Alice Topper over more coffee and then eventually over a couple glasses of wine. They laughed a bit and then felt guilty about doing so. Maggie wished that perhaps she had taken some time to try to get to know the woman better, but it was what it was and could never be any different.

And in the meantime, there was that little thought in the back of her mind that made her feel guilty - the thought that expressed relief that she, her family and close friends were still okay.

She shut her eyes for a moment and rubbed her forehead.

"Headache?"

She opened her eyes and watched as Sam came into the living room, holding two cups of coffee. The lights were off in this part of the house, so the room was softly lit by moonlight and whatever light entered from the streetlights outside. But even though the room was dim, she could still see the tenderness in Sam's face as he handed her a cup and bent down to kiss her on the top of her head as he did so.

"Thank you." said Maggie as she took the cup of steaming coffee. "Just a little headache - nothing serious."

Sam made himself comfortable on the other end of the window seat, so he could face

Maggie. After a quick sip of his coffee, he put it on the small occasional table that stood close-by and reached for Maggie's foot. He smiled. "Nothing a foot massage can't cure." he said as he started to massage her foot.

Maggie smiled and shut her eyes, enjoying the relaxing sensation. It did feel good. In fact, it felt amazing. After a minute or so, she opened her eyes and looked at him.

"How did things go with Alice Topper's husband?"

"About as well as you'd expect. It was hard. I didn't realize it until I was on my way home, but this was the first time I had to inform next of kin. Ms. Haskins and Father McNeal didn't have any family to notify."

"I'm sorry. I can't imagine how difficult that was. How's the investigation going?"

Sam sighed. "We've got nothing. It's amazing but he seems to be able to just vanish. No one sees or hears anything. And he's smart enough not to leave behind fingerprints or anything that could be used as evidence.

Rosedale isn't that big. You'd think someone would see something."

He took her other foot.

"This feels so good ..." said Maggie, grinning.

"That's the idea Mrs. Cooper."

"Oh please, I just spent the entire day being called Mrs. Cooper. It was nice of Wyndham to stay with me, but I really wish I could convince him to just call me Maggie."

"You'll never convince him to do that and you know it." smiled Sam

Maggie laughed. "Yeah I think you're right. He's a sweet man though."

"I saw Doc Simpson at the crime scene - obviously." started Sam carefully. "I thanked him for taking good care of you."

Maggie just smiled as she shut her eyes and tilted her head back against the wall once again.

"But while we were talking, he sort of inadvertently mentioned you think you're being followed by some guy?"

Maggie opened her eyes and looked at Sam. He stopped rubbing her feet and she pulled her legs to her chest. She rested her forehead on her knees for a second before speaking.

"I'm sorry. I know I should have told you. But the thing is, I'm not SURE. With everything that's been going on with me, I can't be sure it isn't just my imagination playing tricks. I didn't want you to worry when there's a chance there's nothing to worry about. Does that make sense? Maggie sighed. "I'm sorry ... I thought I was doing the best thing under the circumstances."

"Not telling me about something going on with you is never the best thing. Understood?"

Maggie nodded.

"I want you to give me a complete description of this guy and I want to know every place you think you've seen him. I know you think it might be nothing - and I hope you're right - but he could be our killer. I'm not taking any chances with you or Jordan."

Maggie didn't want to tell him that she had already discussed this with Rebecca. She didn't want to get the deputy in trouble. So she just quietly agreed. She knew Sam was right. This wasn't the time for her to be keeping information from him.

"Actually ... I have an idea." said Maggie slowly as she thought it through.

"What?"

"Wyndham paints portraits. I don't know how good he is, but maybe I could get him to draw the guy's face. That would be better than me just describing him to you wouldn't it?"

"That would be perfect." agreed Sam. "Good. Call him tomorrow. Okay?"

Maggie nodded.

"Now - as Sheriff of this fine community, there isn't anything else I should know, is there?"

Maggie smiled. "I promise, nothing else."

Sam looked relieved.

"Good. In that case - give me your foot."

Maggie laughed and extended her foot. And that was how they spent their evening. Sitting on the window seat in the dark. It was an evening Maggie would always remember. How she loved him.

18

It was about 1:00 in the afternoon and Wyndham was making sure everything was in order for his guest. Maggie had phoned him first thing in the morning, asking if she could come over to look at some of his paintings. Although rather flattered that she was interested, he also sensed there was another reason for the visit - one she didn't seem comfortable discussing over the phone.

His home was small and charming. Filled with the things he valued the most - books and artwork. Some would say his home was cluttered, but to him, it was perfect. Oriental rugs in rich reds complimented the dark, polished furniture and sparkling crystal vases. His house always made him feel safe. Especially now.

He couldn't stop thinking about Alice Topper. How ironic. He couldn't stand the woman while she was alive, but now dead, he missed her terribly. But then, regardless of how he felt about her, what had happened was dreadful and certainly she didn't deserve such an end. The terror she must have felt during her last minutes on earth must have been unbearable. Wyndham couldn't help but feel sorry for her. Sorry that he didn't take the time to really talk to her. Perhaps they would have gotten along better. He shook his head at the thought of it all and made his way into the kitchen.

Maggie would be by shortly and he was quite excited to show her his work. He hoped she would like it. Perhaps he could give her one of his paintings. Of all the people he knew and cared for, Maggie was his favorite and the thought of her having one of his paintings pleased him.

He was making tea that he thought perhaps they could drink in his art studio. And of course, he had some lovely cookies ready to serve his guest as well. Good toilet training was always important. He feared people were forgetting their manners, much less the importance of being good hosts. He sighed. So much was changing and not for the better, it seemed. Why, most people couldn't even set a proper table any longer.

He started to think that perhaps he should arrange a party at his house - something formal and elegant. As he pictured how it might look, he heard his doorbell ring. Maggie had arrived. He hurried towards the front door, making a quick stop at the mirror to make sure his bow tie was straight and his hair was in order. All seemed fine. He was ready for his guest.

*   *   *

Rebecca was happy to get out of the office. It was making her feel claustrophobic. She wasn't feeling well. She didn't know what was wrong - if anything - but she felt a little 'off'. She had been feeling like that for a couple of days. She hoped she wasn't coming down with something - but she checked and had no fever. Still, she didn't feel herself. Even her concentration seemed off.

Maybe Sam sensed it as well, because he suggested she patrol downtown on foot for a while and get a feel for what was going on in the town. She was more than happy to do so. Perhaps some fresh air and exercise would help. Of course, walking comfortably with the radio strapped to her belt was virtually impossible. She hated having to use it, but since she wasn't in her car, she was stuck with the extra weight on her belt. She only wished she could figure out a way to stop it from digging into her side.

Sam had been talking about having a Town Hall Meeting where he could address concerns and misinformation once and for all. As she overheard conversations between shop keepers and customers, mostly concerning the murders, she thought maybe the time was right for such a meeting.

She wasn't sure how it happened exactly, but news spread quickly concerning the state of Alice Topper's body and it seemed people couldn't stop talking about it. She felt badly for Mr. Topper. Not the kind of thing he should be forced to overhear, although she also didn't think it was the type of thing the poor man would ever be able to get out of his mind. She made a mental note to stop by his house later in the day and check up on him.

For the most part, the residents seemed happy to see a deputy in their midst. Periodically a resident would approach her, asking how the investigation was coming along and if an arrest would be forthcoming. How she wished she could give them good news - but the truth was, they were no closer to finding this lunatic now than they were on Day 1. But still, she reassured them that the Sheriff's Office was doing everything in its power to bring the person to justice and restore Rosedale to its former self. There just wasn't anything more she could say.

She stopped at the street corner, debating which direction she wanted to walk. She wished she felt better. She decided to go into Pop's Diner, which was right on the corner anyway - just to see how they were doing and maybe grab a quick bite. Maybe eating would help her feel better.

Looking both ways to make sure all was clear, she crossed the street and made her way to the front door of the diner. They didn't seem to be losing any business. In fact, they almost seemed busier than normal. Maybe people found it comforting being together rather than being alone and possibly ending up in a dumpster. Looking around, she walked to the counter and sat at one of the empty stools. Having high visibility at a time like this was helpful to the community. It wasn't long before Robin stood in front of her - smiling.

"Hello there Deputy, what can I get you?" asked Robin.

Rebecca smiled back. Robin was always careful to refer to her friend as "Deputy" when Rebecca was on duty. "Do you have a special today?"

"Sure do." replied Robin. "A Rueben on sourdough with a side of our famous home-made fries. It's really good."

Rebecca considered it for a moment. Even though it didn't quite sound like what she wanted, it would do. "Okay. I'll do that and a large coke please."

"Coming right up!" replied Robin as she turned to head into the kitchen to deliver the order.

Rebecca could hear the muffled sound of Robin calling out her order from the other side of the swinging kitchen door. The diner was bustling. Obviously three horrific mur- ders hadn't ruined anyone's appetite. That unsettled feeling washed over her again. She tried to shake it off. She did not want to get sick. Not now. Especially not now. She hoped food in her stomach would help.

As she glanced around, waiting for her order to arrive, she saw a familiar face, who unfortunately, saw her at the same time. She took a deep breath when she realized he was walking towards her. It was that guy from the farmers' market, the one who was preaching Hell and damnation, that she had threatened to arrest. She really didn't need this right now. But she prepared herself for what was probably going to be a miserable conversa- tion.

She straightened her back as he ap- proached. He was smiling, although some- thing about it told her it wasn't genuine. He walked directly to her, pushing past a few cus- tomers who were on their way to a table.

"Deputy," he gushed, "so very nice to see you again."

Rebecca nodded and smiled.

"I'm assuming you won't threaten to arrest me because I said hello to you?"

"For the moment I'd say you're safe. But - maybe you should move along because you never can tell."

He laughed. "I commend you for having a sense of humor in the face of all of this adversity."

"Well tell you what - I'm going to have my lunch here in a little bit and I'm just not in the mood for chit chat. So, unless you have business with the Sheriff's Office - I would strongly suggest you move along."

"And I would be happy to do so. I completely understand why you wouldn't want to talk to me. After all, you stopped me from warning the residents of this fine town yesterday and look what happened - another sinner was taken - and rather brutally from what I understand."

Now Rebecca was getting annoyed. "Listen. I'm going to tell you once more to get out of my face or we're going to have a problem here. Do you understand? In fact, I want to see some I.D. - now."

He stared at her with a smile frozen on his face, reached into his back pocket and produced a wallet. He took out his drivers license and showed it to her. She took it from him.

"You stay here." she instructed him as she moved just outside of the front door of the restaurant, where she could still keep an eye on him. She took the radio from her belt and identified herself. It wasn't long before she heard Bernice on the other end.

"Hey Bernice, I need you to check someone out for me. He's a real pain in the ass. Name is Daryl Burns. The address I have is 3354 Longfellow Drive, here in Rosedale."

"Back to you in a minute." responded Bernice through the radio.

Rebecca waited. She watched him through the glass door. He just stood there smiling at her. So much for a relaxing lunch. After a couple more minutes, Bernice reappeared on the radio.

"Nope. We've got nothing outstanding. There have been complaints about him in the past from his neighbors, that sort of thing, but nothing current."

"Okay. Thanks Bernice."

Rebecca returned the radio to her belt and walked back into the restaurant. She returned the drivers license to him.

"Alright Mr. Burns. It appears that as of right now, you're in the clear. But, I would suggest in order to keep it that way, you stop trying to cause problems. We both know that's what you're trying to do. No need for you to go around trying to stir things up. They can get good and stirred without any help from you. But I do promise you one thing ... I'll be watching. So I'd say it would be in your best interest to help me forget about you. Do we have an understanding?"

He smiled at her and nodded. "Yes Deputy, I think we have an understanding. You have a good day - and I'll be praying for you."

"Why thank you Mr. Burns - putting in a good word for me is certainly something I appreciate."

With that, he exited the restaurant. Rebecca was happy to see him go. He just rubbed her the wrong way. The last thing this town needed was someone getting people more worked up than they already were. She sat back down on the stool. She watched as Robin came through the swinging door, carrying her lunch.

"Here you go, Deputy - fresh off the grill." said Robin, placing the plate in front of Rebecca. Rebecca looked down and was surprised that actually the sandwich looked much better than it had sounded.

She flinched - the radio was digging into her side again. She looked away from her plate for a second to adjust it and when she looked back, her plate was no longer there. Confused, she looked up just in time to see Robin coming through the swinging door, carrying her lunch.

"Here you go, Deputy - fresh off the grill." she said, placing the plate in front of Rebecca.

Rebecca froze. What had just happened? How was that possible? How could she see Robin walk over to her holding a plate of food and then see the exact same thing play out for a second time? Suddenly Rebecca felt a hot flash run through her body. She forced herself to slow her breathing. There had to be a logical explanation for what had just happened - or at least what SEEMED to have just happened.

"Did you ... did you take my plate back into the kitchen?" She asked in a measured tone.

Robin looked confused - unsure of what Rebecca was asking - or why. "What do you mean? I just brought it out to you. Is something wrong with it? Do you want me to take it back?"

Rebecca shook her head. "No - no it's fine, really. I don't know what I'm trying to say. It was just a crazy thought - that's all. Or the best case of déjà vu I've ever had." Rebecca tried to force herself to laugh it off. "Don't worry about it. I'm just over-tired and not feeling quite myself."

"Are you sure? If you don't like the Reuben, I can get you something else."

"No - it's perfect. It's not the food at all - looks wonderful ... I'm just ... You know maybe I'm coming down with something. Could I get this to go?"

Robin looked a little confused but brushed it off. "Sure." she responded, taking the plate from Rebecca. "I'll put it in a box for you. Do you want the Coke in a to-go cup?"

"Yes, please.   That would be great. Thank you."

Rebecca tried to smile but inside she was worried. What had just happened? That was the strangest thing she had ever experienced and couldn't even begin to think of an explanation for it.   In no time at all, Robin came back holding a plastic bag and a to-go cup of Coke and put it in front of Rebecca. As Rebecca went to pull out her wallet to pay for her lunch, Robin stopped her.

"On the house." smiled Robin. But her smile faded quickly as she looked at her friend. "Why don't you get some rest? Eat your lunch and see if the Sheriff will let you go home. I don't like seeing you like this. You just don't seem like yourself."

Rebecca nodded as she picked up the plastic bag.

"Thanks. That sounds like a good idea."

With that, Rebecca exited the restaurant. The breeze felt good. Getting out of the diner felt even better. All she could think was that something was terribly wrong.   But she couldn't begin to guess at what that might be. She turned left and headed back to the Sheriff's office.   If she wasn't feeling better after eating her lunch, she was going to talk to Sam. She needed to go home.

He watched as she crossed the street, carrying her take-out bag. He wondered why she had decided to leave and not eat at the diner. It was too bad. He liked watching her and would have enjoyed watching her eat her lunch ... so close to him. She had no idea how close she was.   Luckily for her he was quite happy thinking back and remembering Alice Topper and didn't feel the need to find another victim quite yet. But that could change.

He had no way of knowing when the voices would start talking to him. Or when they would start making demands of him. He wasn't sure of the fat woman's name until later, when he overheard everyone talking about the murder. He tried not to laugh. If they only knew.

Of course he believed her husband's display of emotion was strictly for show. Deep down he was probably grateful the bitch was gone. He saw how she treated him. Sometimes women just got too full of themselves for their own good. They needed to be brought down a peg or two. Or sometimes they just needed to die. Talking to them was usually a waste of time.

He bit down into the burger. Juices mixed with ketchup and mustard collected at the corners of his mouth. He used the back of his hand to wipe his chin. He always had a healthy appetite after killing someone.

He glanced back out the window again, but this time couldn't see Deputy Sanchez. No matter. He'd find her. He could find anyone. He would watch for a while until that feeling rose up inside and the voices starting talking. His father was proud of what he had done. His father understood. But until then, he had something to look forward to and the memory of Alice Topper to occupy his thoughts.

He starting thinking about the Sheriff's wife. And from there, he found himself thinking about the daughter. He had learned her name was Jordan. He smiled. That might be fun. But still, there was something about the Sheriff's wife. Too many times now it felt like she knew he was watching. But that was impossible. Or at least he thought it was impossible.

She was the type who probably thought she was smarter than everyone else. He had seen that before. Those women needed to be taught a lesson. He started to mull over possible scenarios as he took another bite of his hamburger. He wondered if killing her daughter and her husband might prove to her that she didn't know shit after all. He smiled. He might just have to find out.

He stuffed a handful of fries into his mouth. He liked this town.

*   *   *

"Why Mrs. Cooper! Please, please come in!" exclaimed Wyndham, as he backed away from the door, allowing Maggie to enter. She smiled.

"I really appreciate you agreeing to see me on such short notice. I hope I'm not imposing."

"Oh certainly not. I was thrilled that you wanted to see my paintings. And even more thrilled that we could spend more time together. I do so enjoy your company. But this time, let's see if we can end the visit on a much more positive note."

"I couldn't agree more." replied Maggie.

Wyndham motioned towards the kitchen, allowing Maggie to pass in front of him. She had never been to his house before. It seemed they always saw each other when they were out and about and never got around to an actual visit. She was happy that regardless of the reason, they were finally able to get to know each other as friends.

They entered Wyndham's kitchen. The cabinets were dark like all the furniture in his home and there was a beautiful oriental rug positioned perfectly in center of the floor. A small kitchen table with two chairs sat next to a wall of paintings in elaborate frames - making the room feel more like an art gallery than a kitchen. On the counter was a silver tray that held a couple tea cups and a small plate of cookies. In the center was a beautiful silver tea pot. Wyndham poured the hot water into the pot and then picked up the tray.

"I thought we could sit in my art studio. It's beautiful in there this time of day and that way, you can take a look at my artistic attempts, as I like to call them."

"That sounds lovely." replied Maggie as she let Wyndham lead the way. He took her to a room which obviously had been a sizable back porch in years gone by, but since then, had been enclosed with floor to ceiling windows, giving it the feel of a greenhouse. He was right. The room was beautiful. Off to the

corner was another small table with two deli-
cate looking chairs. As Wyndham set the tray
on the table, Maggie looked around. It was
breathtaking. There were paintings everywhere - beautiful paintings - some on easels,
some in frames hanging on the wall that sepa-
rated the studio from the rest of the house and
yet others simply stacked on end sitting on the
floor. She was speechless. It was far more
than she had imagined.

"Oh my God Wyndham. These are beautiful. Really beautiful. I had no idea you had
such talent." Maggies's eyes travelled the
room. She could hardly believe what she was
seeing. "I don't know why you never took
your paintings to a gallery! I'm sure people
would pay a great deal to have one of these."

"You're too kind Mrs. Cooper. But in
truth, I've never painted with money in mind.
I paint because I enjoy it and the feeling I get
when I look at one of these creations - well
let's just say that feeling couldn't be matched
by any amount of money. Please have a seat."

He pulled out one of the chairs for Maggie.

"You mentioned you also do portraits?" Maggie asked as she settled into the chair.

Wyndham grinned as he poured the tea. "Yes indeed. Would you like to see them?"

"Yes I would."

"Well then, you shall." Wyndham put down the tea pot and made his way to the far end of his studio, behind an easel that held a partially completed painting. When he turned around, she could see he was holding a few canvases which he propped up so she could view them. He also reached for a large portfolio that he brought back to the table and presented to Maggie. She was in awe. They were absolutely beautiful. The attention to detail was amazing. They all looked so real she had to remind herself these weren't photos but actually paintings, or in some cases, pencil drawings. It was almost unsettling.

"I don't know what to say. I never could have imagined this."

Wyndham beamed. "You are too kind Mrs. Cooper. And in fact, before you leave here today, I would be honored if you picked out your favorite painting and considered it a gift from me to you."

"I couldn't possibly..."

"No - I insist. I would find great pleasure in knowing that one of my paintings was bringing you joy. And perhaps that way I could also be sure you would never forget me. Now, Mrs. Cooper," he said, sitting down on his chair, "I got the feeling that looking at my artwork was only part of the reason you wanted to come here today. So, I'm all ears."

"I'm sorry, did I make it that obvious?" She looked at him intently. "You're right - I need your help."

"I would be honored to help you in any way that I can. Please continue."

Maggie took a deep breath. "Ever since the killings started here in Rosedale, or at least shortly after the first one, I've noticed a man who seems to be watching me - or stalking me - I'm not sure. But every time I try to point him out to someone, he seems to vanish before they've been able to look."

"Oh my, I assume you've told your husband?"

"That's why I'm here actually. We talked about it and felt that maybe, if I could describe what he looks like to you ..."

"That I could draw him for you and that way Sam could see what he looks like!"

"Exactly!"

"Oh this is terribly exciting actually. I could be like one of those sketch artists you see on the police shows."

Maggie smiled. "Do you think you could do that?"

"Oh absolutely. Let me get my pad and we'll start straight away."

With that Wyndham walked over to the cabinet that stood against the wall and took out a large pad of sketch paper and a few pencils. He returned to the table, placed the pad on his lap, tilting it against the table. Holding a pencil in his hand, he looked at Maggie.

"I'm ready when you are Mrs. Cooper."

19

As it turned out, Rebecca didn't go home after all. She ate her lunch at her desk and re-played the incident at the diner over and over in her mind. She couldn't believe she had overreacted as she had. Certainly what she thought had happened simply couldn't have, so it couldn't have been anything else other than her imagination. Maybe it truly was just some sort of déjà vu.

Regardless, it wasn't something she was going to be upset over. In fact, the more time that passed, the more she doubted her own memory of the event - if there even was an 'event'. But she didn't rule out the possibility that she might be coming down with something. She was still feeling a little under the weather.

She told Sam about her run in with Daryl Burns and the conversations she overheard while walking the streets. She agreed with him that maybe a Town Hall Meeting would help put people at ease, since so much misinformation and speculation was being shared. She could tell Sam wasn't comfortable with the thought of having to have such a meeting when there was so very little to share with the residents, but at the same time, he knew there really wasn't a choice at this point.

Doc Simpson had stopped by the Sheriff's office to share what the autopsy revealed about Alice Topper's death. Sam had Rebecca and Jason join in on the meeting, keeping Bernice out of ear shot on the other side of a closed door. However it was understood and accepted that she would probably always do her best to eavesdrop. This seemed to hold true yet again, given the look on Bernice's face when they finally exited Sam's office.

It looked as though Alice Topper had still been wearing her blue dress when killed - which further confirmed the killer had managed to take her while she was sitting out on her back porch. There were signs of blunt force trauma to the head and some defensive wounds - although not many. She didn't go willingly and looked like she tried to fight back - although, as Doc Simpson pointed out, due to the nature and extent of the blunt force trauma, her resistance would have been minimal.

The rest of the day progressed without any major issues and before Rebecca knew it, it was finally time to go home. After making sure that Bernice had a friend coming to escort her home, Rebecca got into her patrol car and headed home.

She still wasn't feeling quite herself, but whatever it was, it hadn't progressed to anything beyond that. Soon she was relaxing in a hot bath. It felt amazing. She leaned her head back on a towel and shut her eyes. Visions of Alice Topper threatened to invade her thoughts, but she did her best to push them aside. She wondered if she'd ever be able to rid herself of those images. She took a washcloth, submerged it into the water and then placed it over her face and continued to stay in the bath until the water started to cool.

Finally she got out, put on a t-shirt and sweat pants and started to think about dinner. Apparently feeling a little off didn't do anything to diminish her appetite. She was starving. After standing in front of the refrigerator, staring blankly at the half empty shelves, she decided that ordering a pizza would be the best option. After checking her purse to make sure she had the right amount of cash on hand, she called Vic's and placed the order for her favorite garlic and pepperoni pizza.

Before she knew it, she was sitting on the sofa, enjoying her pizza, drinking a Coke and watching a romantic comedy on television. She liked to tell everyone that romantic comedies were lame - she had a reputation to maintain after all - but secretly she loved them. By the end of the evening, the pizza box was empty except for a couple pieces of crust and the guy and girl worked things out and had finally found true love. All in all, it was a satisfying evening.

She took the empty box to the kitchen and left it on the counter, telling herself she'd put it in the large trashcan outside on her way to work in the morning. She moved around her tiny house, checking the doors and windows, making sure everything was secure, before shutting off the lights. Even with the lights off, she could still see in the darkness. The streetlights always provided enough light for that.

She made her way into her tiny bathroom and brushed her teeth. She stared at herself in the mirror for a few minutes. She didn't look sick. But why was she feeling like this? Maybe it was stress. Who would have thought a tiny town like Rosedale would be the target of some lunatic serial killer. They needed to catch him soon. The town couldn't handle another murder.

With that thought, she flipped the light switch off and made her way to her bedroom. She took off her sweatpants and crawled into bed, pulling the comforter up around her. She found herself staring out the window at the stars. It looked so peaceful outside. Slowly, her eyes shut and before she knew it, she had drifted off to sleep.

But as quickly as she fell asleep, the dreams started. Dreams of being chased, of people with unfamiliar faces staring at her, feelings of overwhelming fear and panic. Her breathing quickened as she tossed and turned. But then, a feeling of calm started to take over. In her dream, someone was talking to her - someone was holding her hand. Her breathing returned to normal. She was letting herself relax.

"Rebecca..." a voice called softly. "Rebecca..."

Rebecca stirred. She was slowly waking.

"Rebecca..."

Without even thinking and still half asleep, she started to respond to the voice as she stirred. She was somewhere between being awake and being asleep. She was on that threshold where dreams have the ability to invade reality if only for a few brief moments.

As she started to respond again to the voice, she suddenly woke with a start. She bolted up and sat with her back up against the headboard. She looked at her right hand. Someone had been holding it. She knew it wasn't a dream - she could still feel the pressure of someone's hand on her skin. Someone was in her house.

She looked around the room wildly. She couldn't see anything. Quickly she slid out of bed and quietly opened the drawer in her nightstand and took out her gun. She switched off the safety and held it in both hands. She wasn't alone - she was sure of that. Then she heard it. It was a muffled voice. It seemed to be coming from one of the other rooms - maybe her living room. She wasn't sure. It wasn't clear enough. She couldn't make out what they were saying, but someone was definitely saying something.

She blinked her eyes a few times, trying to sharpen her vision and shake off any remnants of sleep. She held the gun out in front of her and slowly made her way out of her bedroom. Was there more than one of them? She couldn't make herself think clearly enough to figure it out. What was wrong with her? Why couldn't she focus?

Suddenly she felt a touch on her back. She spun around but saw no one. What was happening? Her breathing quickened. Luckily the house was small and she could check easily. With her gun still at the ready, she checked her doors and windows. Everything was intact and locked. This made no sense. None of it made sense, except for the fact that she could somehow feel that someone was there. She could feel that she was being watched.

Quietly she made her way back to her bedroom and retrieved her phone from the nightstand. She positioned herself in the corner of her bedroom with her back pressed up against the wall. This gave her the best view of her bedroom door. If anyone were to walk in, she had a clear shot. She took her phone in her left hand and dialed Sam. She held the phone to her ear, all the while staring at the door with her gun ready. She was relieved when she finally heard it ring.

*   *   *

Across town Sam and Maggie were sound asleep. He had been anxious to see the sketch Wyndham had made of the man Maggie thought might be following her. He stared at it over dinner, hoping that the face looking back at him would be familiar in some way. But it wasn't. He would find him though. He'd find him and get to the bottom of why he was following Maggie.

He tried to make Maggie feel better by telling her, as convincingly as he could, that when he found the guy, they would probably discover it was nothing at all. At least that's what he told her. But deep down, he prayed he wasn't looking at the face of the killer. He didn't want to think a killer was stalking his wife.

In the meantime, he showed the sketch to Jordan as well, with instructions that if she should ever see the guy, she was to have someone call Sam immediately - and for her to stay with adults until he arrived. She understood. Luckily she was beginning to understand and accept the seriousness of what was happening in Rosedale. She had stopped complaining about not being allowed out with her friends. He was grateful for that. He didn't want to scare her - but he needed her to understand the danger she could put herself in if she wasn't careful.

After dinner and an in-depth conversation about personal safety, Jordan retired to her room to watch television while Maggie and Sam retired to theirs. He was exhausted. They were all exhausted. At this point, it was almost hard to remember what Rosedale was like before. How it was to live their lives without fear. He hoped it could be that way once again soon. In the meantime, he had a sketch of someone he wanted to find.

They didn't talk much, but rather just held each other as they drifted off to sleep.

At about 2am though, Maggie thought she heard Sam's phone chime. At least that's what she thought had woken her up. She laid there for a minute, listening to Sam's heavy breathing, waiting to hear if it rang again - but it didn't. She decided it must have been her imagination after all and fell back into a deep sleep.

20

Maggie sat at the kitchen table nursing her second cup of coffee. Sam had already left for work and had taken Jordan with him. Neither he nor Maggie felt comfortable letting Jordan walk to school by herself. As Maggie sat there, thinking about what she wanted to do, it dawned on her that it had been a while since she had gone to the gym. Maybe that might help her feel better. She thought about calling Patty and seeing if she wanted to meet there. She needed to do something to take her mind off things. Sam had inadvertently left Wyndham's sketch on the kitchen counter. She'd take it to him later, perhaps after she was done at the gym. She certainly didn't need it. She could see that face in her mind as clearly as if he were standing directly in front of her.

In a few days there would be another funeral to attend - Alice Topper's. Apparently the Church had sent a replacement for Father McNeal. She hadn't met the new priest yet, but whoever it was, she was hopeful he'd be able to help the community heal. He was certainly coming at a difficult time.

She dumped out the remaining coffee and tidied the kitchen. A quick call to Patty and before long, she was ready and in the car heading to the gym.

She was looking forward to seeing Patty. They hadn't really had a chance to talk since her appointment with Dr. Simpson and she knew her friend wanted to know the outcome. Of course, as she thought about it - she wasn't sure of the outcome herself. Basically, Dr. Simpson couldn't find anything wrong and believed it was all stress related. Maggie didn't completely agree, but at least it sounded good and would put everyone at ease. Her dreams however, were becoming increasingly strange. She made a mental note to pick up some sleeping pills while she was out. Maybe that would help. As far as that feeling of being watched, or the panic attacks she was still having from time to time, she decided to chalk that up to lack of sleep. It seemed to be the answer that made everyone else happy, so she decided not to argue the fact. There was no point. Unless someone could experience what she was experiencing, there was no way to explain how bad it was.

She pulled into the gym parking lot. It wasn't nearly as busy as it usually was. She guessed that people were simply more cautious now than they once were and only ventured out for the more important things.

As she got out of her car, she saw Patty walking towards her.

"Well that was perfect timing!" smiled Patty.

"Hi!" responded Maggie, collecting her bag from the back seat. "How have you been?"

"Busy - but the question is ... how have you been? I haven't talked to you since you saw Dr. Simpson."

The two friends started to walk slowly towards the front door.

"I've been good ... well as good as you can be with another murder in Rosedale."

"Oh my God I know! Wasn't that awful? I mean truth be told, I never liked the woman. I thought she was mean, bossy, nasty and just a dreadful human being - but still... "

"I know - she wasn't my favorite person in the world either, but I feel just awful that she went through what she did - I feel even worse for her husband. He really did love her, you know. I'm thinking maybe we should take some food or something over to him - just check up on him, make sure he's doing okay."

"That's not a bad idea." agreed Patty. "I don't think he has family around here so he probably is alone. And something tells me she didn't have a lot of friends who would check up on him. Why don't we plan on doing that, say tomorrow?"

"Okay. Oh - and before you ask, I told Sam about that guy I've seen watching me - or looks like he's watching me."

"Good - I was just about to ask actually. What did he say?"

"Going to keep an eye out for him - see if he can figure out who the guy is. But he did say there's a very good chance it's nothing. And when you think about it - it can't possibly be the killer. Why would the killer want me to be able to identify him? That doesn't even make sense."

Patty thought for a moment. "You might be right. I never thought of it that way. Well at least I feel better now knowing you told Sam."

With that, they reached the doors. As they entered, they looked around. The place was deserted except for the few trainers who sat at their desks near the front doors, looking a little bored. It was like having their own private workout space.

An hour on the bike followed by weights and Maggie had worked up a sweat and at least for the time being, managed to push all unwanted thoughts out of her mind. It was exhilarating. Everything almost felt normal. A handful of other clients wandered in over the course of an hour, but only one approached her asking about the investigation and wanting to talk about Alice Topper's murder. As soon as Maggie explained she wasn't at liberty to discuss her husband's investigation, they apologized and went back to their workout.

After a quick shower to clean up, the two went to the diner for lunch before Patty had to run off. She was showing a house later that afternoon and still had to get a few things ready. Maggie watched her friend pull away before getting into her car. First she was going to drop the sketch off to Sam, since the Sheriff's Office was so close to the diner and then a run to the grocery store so that she could grab some things to cook up for Mr. Topper. She felt like a new woman. The workout was exactly what she needed.

She pulled out of the parking lot and headed to the Sheriff's Office. She couldn't help but glance down at the sketch staring up at her from the passenger's seat. Wyndham had managed to draw him perfectly. It was exactly the face she saw staring at her. But if it wasn't the killer - who was it, she wondered. And why was he so fascinated with her?

That thought stayed in her mind as she pulled into the parking space behind the Sheriff's Office. She grabbed the sketch and entered through the back door. There was always a strong musty odor in the Sheriff's Office. She noticed that every time she came in. She thought it was a shame they never updated the space. As soon as she entered the main room, Bernice immediately looked up from her desk and smiled.

"Well hey there, Mrs. Cooper! The Sheriff didn't tell me you were coming here today!"

"He didn't know." smiled Maggie. "He forgot something at home and since I was in the neighborhood, I thought I'd drop it off to him. Is he in his office?"

"He sure is! Can I get you a cup of coffee or anything?"

"Oh no, I'm fine. Just came from lunch. He's not in there with anyone is he?"

"Nope. All by his lonesome. Help yourself."

Bernice motioned towards Sam's office. Maggie nodded and started to walk in that direction.

She saw Deputy Moyer busy at his desk. He looked up at her and smiled. "Ma'am."

"Hello Jason. How are you doing?"

"Doing okay Ma'am. Be better once we catch this guy though."

"I hear you." responded Maggie as she continued to walk to the back office. Something seemed off to her. Something had changed. What was it? She looked around. Rebecca was no where to be seen, so obviously she was out on patrol. But that's when she noticed Rebecca's desk no longer faced Jason's like it always had. In fact, it looked like her desk had been pushed up against the wall and had become the dumping ground for extra office supplies.

'That's strange' thought Maggie. But then, perhaps Rebecca was finally getting that new desk Sam had been promising her.

She tapped on Sam's door lightly before opening it. He looked up from his desk as she walked in and grinned.

"Well this is a nice surprise." he said as he approached her.

"It was everything I could do this morning to make you forget this sketch so I'd have an excuse to drop by and see you." she said smiling as she handed it to him. "I don't want to keep you from what you're doing, but I thought you should have this."

"Yeah I realized I left it at home the second I walked into my office. I was going to swing by the house later and pick it up, so this is great. Do you want Bernice to get you a coffee or something cold to drink?"

"Oh no. She asked me when I came in. But as lovely as it is to visit, I should get going. Patty and I are going to cook up some meals and take them over to Alice Topper's husband. We're pretty sure he's all alone and probably isn't eating."

"That's a good idea. And you're probably right."

Slowly they started to walk out of Sam's office.

"I met the new priest today."

Maggie looked surprised. "Oh what's he like?"

"Seems like a nice enough guy. Father Michael Bauer. Older than Father McNeal. Seems like a nice guy. I told him about everything that's been going on around here. Suggested he be super careful."

"I'm surprised that didn't send him packing."

"Nope. Seemed pretty cool about it."

Maggie looked around and chuckled. "So where are you making poor Rebecca sit these days?"

Still smiling, Sam looked at Maggie. "Who?"

She laughed. "Rebecca! Don't be cute."

Sam looked confused. "I'm not. I'm sorry Babe, I don't know who you're talking about. Should I know a Rebecca?"

Maggie's smile faded. She stared at him. He wasn't joking. "Deputy Rebecca Sanchez. She and Deputy Moyer work for you."

Sam stared at her for a moment. "Babe - I've never had two deputies - you know that. Only Jason. That's it. I mean, Rosedale isn't all that big.   I'm sorry, I don't know who you're talking about. Are you pulling my leg?"

Maggie froze. She stared at him for any sign that he might be playing some sort of misguided joke - but she saw nothing. He was being sincere.   Sam had absolutely no idea who Rebecca Sanchez was.

Maggie turned to Deputy Moyer. "Deputy - does the name Rebecca Sanchez mean anything to you? Have you ever heard that name before?

Deputy Moyer looked up from his desk. He took a second to think about it and then shook his head. "Nope. It doesn't mean anything to me. Should it?"

"Bernice?" called Maggie.

"Yes Mrs. Cooper?" she answered from her desk.

"Does the name Rebecca Sanchez mean anything to you?"

"Well, let me think." replied Bernice as she came around the corner.   "There was a Rebecca I knew a long time ago - of course I can't remember when exactly. But from what I remember, her last name was Gibbens, I think. Not Sanchez."

"Ok then," interrupted Sam, "everybody back to work - We were just wondering if either of you remembered her, that's all." He looked at Maggie. "Why don't I walk you to the car? I don't like you moving around outside by yourself these days."

Maggie nodded. She wanted to say something, but she couldn't speak. Her head was spinning. Why didn't anyone remember Rebecca?

Sam took hold of her arm to steady her as they walked out the back door. As soon as it shut behind them, Maggie went into a panic.

"Oh God Sam - you have to believe me. I swear, you had another Deputy by the name Rebecca Sanchez. You did. In fact, she was working here yesterday. I remember what she looks like. She and I hung out together at the farmers' market. I am NOT making this up!

You have to believe me! Why don't you re-member her? Why don't ANY of you remem-ber her? Something is happening and you don't realize it. You have to trust me. Please."

Sam stared at her. He looked deep into her eyes. Finally he took a deep breath. "Babe I love you more than I ever thought possible. But I'm beyond worried about you. I want you to call Doc Simpson as soon as you get home and I want you to tell him about this and see what he says. In fact, ask him if he can prescribe something to help you relax a bit. I don't know but maybe the nightmares you've been having combined with the stress, it's all catching up. I mean, I keep forgetting you were first on the scene with Father Mc-Neal and seeing that kind of thing can really mess with you. Because Babe, look at me ... I never had a deputy named Rebecca Sanchez. Ever."

Maggie threw her arms around him and hung on as tight as she could. She loved him so much. But she knew this wasn't some sort of reaction to seeing Father McNeal. Something else was happening and she needed to figure it out. But in the meantime, she couldn't have Sam thinking she was unstable. She couldn't blame him for not believing her. What she was asking him to accept made no sense - even to her.

She released her grip on him and backed up just enough to be able to look into his eyes. She hated the thought of not being honest with him.

"You're probably right." she began. "I've been having terrible nightmares and, well, I just can't stop thinking about all of these murders. I didn't tell you because I didn't want you to worry, but I've been having those images of Father McNeal play in my head like some sort of movie, over and over. It's been just horrible. I thought I could handle it by myself. Obviously I can't."

Sam sighed. "I knew it. Tell Doc Simpson and tell him about the memory thing. I'm pretty sure he can prescribe something that'll help. And in the meantime, I don't want you to worry. Everything's going to be fine. I promise. Now are you going to be okay driving home, or do you want me to take you?"

Maggie shook her head. "No - I'm fine now. I really am. I feel better now that we talked. And I'll call Dr. Simpson - see what he says."

"Promise?"

"Yeah - I promise."

"Alright then. You be careful driving home. And don't bother stopping at the grocery store. If you want, I'll go by there tonight and get what you need. I just want you to get some rest."

He opened the car door for her. She sat down in the driver's seat and he carefully shut the door and leaned through the window.
He kissed her.

"I love you Mrs. Cooper."

"I love you too."

He tapped the hood of the car as he slowly made his way back inside. He watched as she exited the parking lot.

She started driving home. Her head was spinning. She was a couple blocks away from Sam when she changed her mind and made a U-turn. There was something she needed to check out before she went home. Plus, she needed to talk to Wyndham again. As she drove she checked the street signs. She's was pretty sure she knew where she was headed, but not positive. She had only been to Rebecca's house a couple times before. Suddenly she saw a street name that sounded familiar. She turned left and then recognized a small park on her right. Two blocks later, she turned onto the street where Rebecca lived. She drove slowly, looking carefully at the houses until she finally recognized the one she was looking for. 1311 Miller Street was the house. This was Rebecca's house.

She parked her car on the street and started to walk towards the front door. The house looked different. The flowers Rebecca had planted in the flower bed were no longer there. All that remained were dead flowers and weeds. The cute house that Rebecca had lived in and cared for looked totally different. How was that possible? As she got closer, she saw peeling paint and the dirty windows. In fact, one of the front windows had a crack running through it. She carefully walked up the steps and made her way to the door. She knocked.

A few moments went by until she heard sounds coming from inside and then the turn of a lock. The door opened.

"Yeah what do you want?"

Maggie was at a loss for words. There in front of her was a man, possibly in his 40s. He was wearing a dirty t-shirt and jeans and holding a can of beer in his hand. He looked like he hadn't bathed in days. Finally she found her voice.

"I'm sorry to bother you, but I'm looking for a friend of mine. She used to live here - in this house.   Her name is Rebecca Sanchez. Does that name sound familiar to you?"

He stared at her, confused and annoyed at being disturbed. "No - it doesn't sound familiar. I don't know any Rebecca okay?"

"She used to live here - before you."

He smirked. "Listen lady. I've lived here for as long as I can remember. Got that? No Rebecca or Becky or Jane or Mary. Nothin'. Just me. Anything else I can do for you?"

Maggie shook her head. "No, but I —"

He slammed the door in her face before she could finish. She stood there for a while, staring at the closed door. Finally she made her way back to her car. She got in, shut and locked the door and sat there, silently staring out the windshield.

She tried to fight the tears that were welling up in her eyes. What was happening? What was wrong with her? Was it her, or was it everyone else? She started to cry. She had never felt so alone before. The tears came and she couldn't stop them. In anger, she hit the steering wheel until her hands hurt. She missed her friend. God she missed Rebecca. The realization that she would never see her again overwhelmed her. What was wrong with everyone?

It took a while to calm herself down - but she finally did. She knew that if there was any chance of being able to figure out what was happening, she needed to be able to think clearly. She wiped the tears from her eyes, picked up her phone and called Wyndham. Although surprised to hear from her so soon, he was happy to have her come by. He could tell it was important. It wasn't long before she found herself pulling into his driveway. As she was getting out of her car, Wyndham had already come out of his house and was standing on his front porch waiting for her. After the initial hello's, they were soon sitting at the cozy table in his kitchen. He had already made some tea. He stared at Maggie, waiting for her to speak.

She looked at him. "I need you to trust me, believe me, don't ask any questions and most importantly, do not tell anyone about me being here or talking to you. Not even Sam. Can you do that?"

Wyndham stared at his friend. He could sense how serious this was. "Mrs. Cooper ... Maggie ... you have my word of honor. You're my friend. You never have to question my loyalty."

Maggie smiled weakly. "Thank you. First, I need another sketch from you. But I can't tell you why - or who it's a sketch of. Can you do that?"

"Of course."

"And then - well when I was here yesterday - you told me to pick out a painting to take home with me - so that no matter what - I'd never forget you..." Maggie smiled. "Well it seems I left here without a painting yesterday. But I'd very much like to do that now, if the offer still stands."

"Absolutely!   But in return," smiled Wyndham, "remember, you must never forget me!"

Maggie got up from her chair, walked over to Wyndham and hugged him. After a moment she pulled back and looked at him. "I promise." She took a deep breath before continuing. "But first, let's get that portrait done."

Immediately Wyndham got up from the table, walked out of the kitchen, only to return a few moments later with his sketch pad and a pencil. He sat down and waited for Maggie's instructions.

21

He sat on the edge of his bed, staring out the window. He was angry at his mother for making them move. They had been in New Orleans for only a couple of weeks and he had already grown to hate it. Of course, his mother blamed him for the move. She blamed him for everything. She claimed everyone had started talking about the family - about him - and she felt the only thing to do was leave. The last straw seemed to be when her Church friends started talking about her behind her back. Funny - she never asked him if he had done those things people were talking about.

Not once. He smiled to himself. Maybe she didn't want to hear it. He would have been happy to tell her, if only she had asked. But maybe she liked lying to herself.

She had a friend who lived in New Orleans. Betty Shelton. Betty had gone to high school with his mother all those years ago, before Betty's father got a new job and the family relocated to New Orleans. Betty not only helped them find the house they now called home, but also got his mother a job working with her at a burger and wing joint a few blocks down on Mazant Street. It would take him a little while to figure things out - but he would, eventually. Stephen, seemed happy with the move. It would be only a matter of time before the girls were lining up. As far as Robert could tell, moving didn't really seem to change things very much. They would all continue being who they were - but now in different surroundings.

He got up from the bed and walked to the front door. He needed some air. The house was hot and stuffy inside even with all the ceiling fans going at top speed. The screen door squeaked as he pushed it open and slammed shut behind him. Under the small bay window, sat two white plastic chairs. He made himself comfortable. The house was tiny. It was painted bright green with white trim, complete with a white railing that framed the porch. Some overgrown bushes took up the flower bed below. Grey cement steps led down to the very tiny front yard that butted up to a chain link fence surrounding the property. It looked as though everyone had a chain link fence around their property. The neighbors were close. Very close. Too close for his liking. It felt claustrophobic. Row after row of little shotgun houses - street after street as far as he could see. He had heard about something called the Lower 9th Ward. It sounded interesting. Maybe, once he got his bearings, he would check it out. Old habits would be impossible to break.

He heard his mother moving around in the house, getting ready to go to work. Once she was gone, he'd go explore.

"Okay." said his mother as she stepped out the door. "I'm going to go to work. Stephen won't be home till late. You're going to have to feed yourself. There's food in the fridge so you won't starve. Just make sure you clean up after yourself. I'm not your maid you know?"

Robert continued staring out at the street.

"I'm talking to you! Are you listening to me?"

He slowly turned his head to look at her, but before he could respond, a car pulled up in front of the house. It was Betty, there to pick up his mother.

"I'll be home late. Betty wants me to see the sights after we're done with our shift. Don't do anything stupid - you hear me? There's only so many times we can move."

With that, she walked down the steps and let herself into Betty's car. He heard her laughing as she shut the car door. He saw Betty look at him, but she didn't say anything. He wondered. The look in her eyes. Could she hear the voices too?

He stood up and went back in the house. The door banged as he did so. He liked it better now that he was alone. He stood there looking around. It was a three bedroom shotgun. He hadn't known what a shotgun house was before, but it seemed to be popular in New Orleans. The living room was small but comfortable. The furnishings were sparse. Most of it came from Goodwill. There was a sofa, chair and an old television set. A couple small tables had old table lamps sitting on them. His mother had put up a framed painting of angels above the sofa that she had also gotten from Goodwill. His bedroom was opposite the living room at the front of the house. It was small, but had a single bed, a nightstand and a small chest of drawers. He didn't need anything more. He liked the fact that he could see out to the street. Next to his room was a small bathroom he shared with Stephen and then there was Stephen's room. It was about the same size with the same minimal furniture, but Stephen had taken the time to tape posters and photos to his walls. To Robert, it just looked stupid and cluttered. As he walked further back into the house, the tiny kitchen was on the right, behind the living room. It was just big enough for one small table. That was more than adequate. His mother never cooked anyway and he couldn't remember the last time all three of them ate together. Usually he would eat in his room, or in front of the television and typically Stephen would be out somewhere.

Opposite the kitchen, at the back of the house, was his mother's room with its adjoining bathroom. He walked to the door and stood there, staring at it. It was pink, frilly and repulsive. It looked like the room of a twelve year old girl - not a grown woman. She had draped scarves over her lamps in order to create softer lighting. She didn't think Robert knew, but he was fully aware that she was sneaking men into her room by way of the back door, when she thought her sons were asleep. Whore. He wondered how long it would take her new friends at the Church down the street to figure out she wasn't who she pretended to be.

He leaned up against the wall and crossed his arms. He stood like that for a while, staring at her bed - staring at her bed imagining her lying there, dead. The thought pleased him. It made the voices happy as well.

22

Maggie got into her car. Wyndham's painting of a forest in spring, rested in the back seat - his name scrawled across the bottom right corner. Wyndham Hart. She already knew the perfect spot for it in her living room. As she put on her seatbelt, she glanced over to the passenger seat and took a moment to gaze at the sketch Wyndham had made. Rebecca's face smiled up at her. Wyndham hadn't recognized the face. But then, Maggie didn't expect he would. She was determined however, that regardless of what was happening, she would never allow herself to forget her friends.

Just as she started to back out of the driveway, her phone chimed. She looked at the screen and was relieved to see that it was Patty, not Sam, who was calling her.

"Hello?"

"Where are you?"

"I'm in the car going home. Why?"

"Sam called me. Said he sent you home and he wanted me to check up on you and make sure you were okay. So I'm here, but you're not!"

Maggie felt a rush of panic. "Did you tell him I wasn't home?"

There was a pause.

"No I didn't. I thought I'd call you first. See if you answered. Now what is going on?"

Maggie let out a sigh of relief. "Good. Listen. Are you inside?"

"Yeah - I let myself in. You gave me a key ages ago, remember?"

"Good.   I'll be there in a few minutes. Just don't say anything to Sam and if he calls before I get home, just tell him you let yourself in and I'm sound asleep and you don't want to wake me."

There was another pause.

"Okay.   But when you get here you have to tell me what the Hell is going on."

"Deal.   I'm be home soon."

And with that, Maggie disconnected the call.   She needed to get home.   Her mind was racing.   She was remembering Ruth, the cashier at Hugh's Grocery - who just wasn't there one day and no one seemed to remember and Emily, the waitress at the diner who simply vanished one day and again, no one remembered.   How many others had there been?   A horrible thought crossed her mind - if it happened to them, could the same thing happen to Jordan or Sam - or to her?   Beads of sweat started to form on the back of her neck.   The serial killer and now this.   Were they somehow related?   She didn't know.

None of it made any sense. The only thought she had, was keeping her family safe. They had to be safe. She looked at the clock in her car. It was only 2:15. She still had time before Sam and Jordan got home. When Sam asked about the painting, which she knew he would, she would just tell him Wyndham had dropped it off. She didn't want him to know she didn't go straight home like she promised she would. She hated lying to him. But there was no other choice.

After a fairly stressful drive home, she pulled into her own driveway, turned off the car and was reaching into the back seat to take out Wyndham's painting when Patty walked out to meet her. She was relieved to see that Sam's car wasn't there. She had worried that he may have come by the house to check on her. The only car she saw was Patty's which was parked out front on the street. Patty took the painting from her hands, allowing Maggie to grab her purse and the sketch of Rebecca. They entered the house and Patty locked the door behind them. She noticed the sketch in Maggie's hand.

"Who's that?"

Even though Maggie had come to expect that reaction, it still made her feel off balance. "Just someone I used to know. And this is a painting Wyndham did - he gave it to me."

Maggie leaned the painting against the wall and then walked over to the armoire that sat opposite the sofa. She opened one of the large doors and laid the sketch down flat on the shelf.

"So let me get this straight - all this mystery and intrigue is about a painting and a sketch? You had me worried that something was really wrong."

Maggie looked at her friend. She then turned and walked into her kitchen to get herself a bottle of water from the fridge. She unscrewed the cap and took a healthy swallow before turning back to Patty. "No. It's not about the artwork. And something is wrong. But - you have to promise me you won't tell

Sam that I wasn't home. And actually, if you could, maybe you could go one step further and say Wyndham dropped the stuff off while I was sleeping - but only if he asks."

"Okay I don't like this. Why are we lying to Sam?"

Maggie sat down at the kitchen table and put her head in her hands. Patty sat next to her and watched her friend, waiting for her to speak.

"Something IS wrong. But I can't tell you what it is because I'm not sure."

"This doesn't make any sense - you know that, right? What do you mean something is wrong - with what?"

Maggie took a deep breath. "As my friend, I need you to trust me and believe in me no matter what. Just blind faith. And for the time being at least - no questions. Can you do that?"

Patty thought for a moment. "You're probably the most normal friend I've got - and

I mean that in a good way. So ... I guess I can go with the flow."

"Good - but know I'm not doing anything wrong. Not doing anything to hurt anyone. I need you to have my back though, no matter what. And you absolutely can't let on to Sam that anything is weird. You have to make him believe everything is completely normal and I am perfectly fine."

Patty stared at her friend. "You're going to be a difficult friend, aren't you?"

Maggie smiled. "Absolutely. You don't know the half of it."

"Well ... since you are up from your nap and feeling 'perfectly fine' - I guess I'll head home. Oh - and while you were sleeping, Wyndham dropped off a couple things."

Maggie smiled at her friend. "I'm gonna owe you."

"Damn right you are." replied Patty, giving her friend a long hug. "But just promise, whatever is going on - that you stay safe - okay?"

"That's a promise. I'll walk you to your car."

The friends walked slowly out to Patty's car. In the back of Maggie's mind, she couldn't help but wonder if she would ever see Patty again.

Patty started her car, put on her seat belt and blew Maggie a kiss as she pulled out of the driveway. Maggie watched as she disappeared around the corner. Sam would be home soon. She had to think carefully about how she was going to handle things with him. She couldn't let him keep thinking something was wrong with her. The look on his face when she insisted some woman named Rebecca had worked for him, was a look she never wanted to see again.

She turned to go back into the house, when out of the corner of her eye, she thought she saw the figure of a man. She quickly turned her head to look and at that moment, stopped breathing. It was him. The face Wyndham had sketched. The man who was following her. She looked around wildly hoping to see someone on the sidewalk, but there was no one. It was just the two of them. Not taking her eyes off of him, she started to walk back to her house - prepared to start screaming if he were to move closer. Finally she broke into a run and managed to get inside and lock the door.

She slid onto the floor and made her way to the window. Ever so slowly she raised her head up to try to look without being seen. She just prayed he wasn't on the other side of the window. Her heart seemed to be beating so loudly she couldn't hear anything else. Finally she could see over the window sill. Nothing. She couldn't see him. She tried to think. Panic was making that difficult. Could he have moved closer to the house? Staying low to the ground she moved out of the living room and then moved quickly through all the rooms, making sure windows and doors were locked and drapes were drawn. She ran up the stairs thinking she could get a better look from the second floor.   Jordan's bedroom faced the front of the house. She looked out onto the street but saw nothing. He wasn't there. She ran into the master bedroom and looked out onto the backyard. No sign of him.

She sat on the floor trying to get her breathing to return to normal - her back up against the wall.   Whoever it was, she was safe. He couldn't get inside. She kept telling herself this wasn't the killer. But if he wasn't the killer - who was he? She shut her eyes, trying to calm herself. She couldn't let Sam see her this way. She felt exhausted. Slowly her breathing returned to normal.   And that's when she heard it.

"Maggie ... Maggie?"

Her eyes sprung open and then widened in fear as she realized - she was staring at him. He was in the room with her.

23

As much as he had gotten used to living in New Orleans, he still missed his home up in North Carolina. That would always be where he belonged. There he had space to breathe ... to roam without people crowding into him, playing their stupid music, touching him. His father had lived up in North Carolina. That's where he should be. But again, his mother found yet another way to erase him from their lives - as though he never existed. Robert decided he wasn't going to let her do that anymore. Not to say New Orleans didn't have its perks. He had come to learn a lot about the Lower 9th Ward. He smiled when he remembered. Yes he had learned a lot over the course of four years. Stephen had gotten a job as a salesman. He liked it. He still lived at home though and helped out with expenses from time to time. His mother liked that. She never wanted Stephen to leave. He was the love of her life. Besides, there would never be a girl she thought was good enough for him. Robert, on the other hand, was a different story. No one could believe he was only 19. He looked like a man in his 30s and he was strong. Very strong. Stronger than Stephen. His hands were twice the size of Stephen's. There were times he would look down at his hands and imagine them wrapped around his brother's neck. Squeezing. What would his mother say then?

He wasn't in school any more. That was a relief. He had hated school. Hated everyone there. He still had no friends, but if he was being honest with himself, he liked it better that way. To him, the voices in his head were all he needed. He got odd jobs around town for spending money. He liked the jobs where he could be by himself. But he could never hang on to a job very long. People tended not to be comfortable around him. Maybe it was the way he looked ... the way he looked at them ... the intensity of his eyes. Maybe it was his voice. It was deep - deeper than most. Some people found that intimidating. He often times wondered if they could see into his head - into his mind. If they were hearing the voices when he heard them. He enjoyed their discomfort. It made him smile. He enjoyed watching people - always did. But he never liked talking to them. He could always feel them trying to pry open his skull - trying to get inside of him. He didn't like that. His thoughts were his own - not for anyone else. They had no rights to them.

He sat on the front porch of the house, in the darkness, lighting matches, watching them burn down to his fingers and then throwing them into the garden. It didn't hurt. He had done it so many times, he could barely feel it. But there was something about fire that fascinated him. When he gazed into the flame, he never knew what he might see gazing back at him. Could be the Devil himself.

Lately his father had been talking to him a lot. He wasn't surprised. Ever since they had moved to New Orleans his father was visiting him more often. His mother had been whoring it up all over town. She had been cheating on his father without any remorse at all. Her and that friend of hers - Betty. He could barely remember the last time he'd seen her sober. She was a disgrace.

He lit another match and held it close to his face.

It was 2 o'clock in the morning. Stephen was asleep and his mother had come home, drunk again and had passed out in her room.

He waited for the flame to go out in his fingers but continued to stare at it. It was time. He threw the match into the bushes and walked down the steps, around the side of the house and to the shed that stood by itself in the corner of the back yard. The door let out a soft creak as he opened it - though he wasn't concerned anyone would hear him out there. He figured his mother wouldn't hear a train passing through the house.

He pulled the small chain that hung from a lightbulb in the ceiling. The light was barely stronger than the moonlight, but it was still good enough for him to find what he was looking for. He looked around until he saw it - leaning up against the corner - the sledge-hammer.

He picked it up. It felt good. The weight was perfect.   He could tell his father was pleased with his choice.

He shut off the light, closed the shed door and slowly walked back along the side of the house to the front porch.   The distant sound of music floated in the air. Seemed like there was always a party somewhere.   There was always noise. He longed for quiet. Maybe later, he'd move back home.

He turned and walked up the front steps, keeping the sledgehammer hanging safely next to his side. He opened the screen door slowly and then, guided the door shut behind him so that it wouldn't slam. He didn't want anyone waking up. He shut his eyes for a moment and took in a deep breath. He felt an excitement building in him. It was time. She wasn't taking care of her family. Talking to her wouldn't make any difference - he was sure of that. His father agreed. This was best. He had dreamed of this moment.

He opened his eyes and walked to his brother's bedroom door. He put his hand on the doorknob and slowly turned it and pushed the door open, just enough to be able to see in. His brother was in bed. His back was facing the door. He could tell Stephen was asleep by the sound of his breathing. He stared at him for a few moments. He always slept hard - even when they were kids. Robert smiled.

Stephen had no idea his stupid life was going to change.

Just as carefully as he opened Stephen's door, he shut it again. Now he walked slowly and quietly towards the back end of the house. The house was dark and other than the distant muffled sounds of a jazz band playing somewhere in the city, it was silent. Finally he stood in front of his mother's door. He was almost giddy with excitement. He had waited so long for the right time. It had finally come. He would be free.

Silently he turned the doorknob and opened the door. His mother appeared to be asleep - or perhaps simply passed out. It didn't matter. The lamp on the far side of the bed was still on. But the scarves covering the shade and the low wattage of the bulb itself, meant it produced nothing more than a weak glow. It looked like a dream.

He shut the door behind him and slowly walked to the side of the bed. He stared at her face. It was curious that he didn't feel anything. He knew he probably should, but he didn't. The woman lying there in bed meant nothing to him. He could feel how proud his father was. He smiled and slowly raised the sledgehammer high over his head. The first blow would be the most important. It had to be just right. In his head, he counted to three and then, with all his strength, he brought the sledgehammer down onto her head.

He was surprised how oddly quiet it was - for something so violent. It only made a strange popping noise - like dropping an over-ripe melon. The force of the blow caused her body to bounce up and for a moment, it looked as though her eyes, now open, looked right at him. He smiled. He hoped she knew it was him. Again, he brought the sledge-hammer down on her head. He started laughing.

Again and again - blow after blow. Finally his arms were tired. He looked at her. It was hard to make out what she used to look like. But he could still see one of her eyes. It seemed to be staring at him. He smiled at her. He looked down at his arm and saw a bit of, what appeared to be, brain matter. He sighed. It had been over too soon. He put the sledgehammer down, resting it against the bed and went into her bathroom to wash off the blood.

He stripped off his clothes and put them in her hamper. He left her room, making sure to open and then shut her door quietly and then walked back towards his bedroom. On the way, he looked in on Stephen and saw he was still asleep - completely unaware of what had just happened.

Putting on fresh clothes, Robert suddenly realized how hungry he was. He made his way back to the kitchen and prepared himself a bowl of red beans and rice, which he ate while sitting alone at the kitchen table. It was delicious. He decided he would have to have it again soon.

After finishing his food and drinking a large glass of milk, he put the dirty dishes in the sink, took a medium sized knife from the drawer and walked back towards his bedroom. Shutting the door behind him and being careful to be quiet, he reached up to the top shelf of his closet and retrieved a container he had hidden behind some sweaters. He took it down and unscrewed the cap. The smell of gasoline immediately filled his room. He grabbed a couple of t-shirts from his dresser drawer and walked out of his bedroom, back to his mother's room. There, he liberally poured gasoline on the bed. He took the matches from his pocket, lit one and threw it on her. The flames started almost immediately. The heat was intense. Then, he turned and walked back to his brother's closed bedroom door. He took the two t-shirts and laid them at the base of the door. He poured gasoline on them and then sprinkled what remained on the living room furniture. He left the bottle on the sofa, lit another match and threw it on the t-shirts. He stood there basking in the moment, before turning and walk-

ing out the front door. He gently closed it behind him so it wouldn't slam. He always hated the way that door slammed.

24

Maggie tried to scream, but no sound would come out. She looked around wildly. There was nowhere to go.

"Shhhh. Shhhhh." he said, holding his finger up to his mouth. "Don't be afraid. I'm not here to hurt you. I promise."

Maggie was so scared she could barely understand what he was saying. "Who are you? What do you want?" She felt tears welling up in her eyes as desperation over took her. "Please don't hurt me."

"I'm not going to hurt you. I'm not." As if to prove his point, he held his hands up, palms facing her and slowly backed away.

For some reason - either the fact that he was backing up, or perhaps it was the look in his eyes - she started to feel calm. She didn't really know why. It was almost as though she knew him - but that didn't make any sense. Still cautious though, she stayed where she was. She had reached up to her nightstand and grabbed a crystal vase she was now holding in her hand - just in case. She studied him. Pleasant looking. Kind eyes. Average build. Blue jeans and a t-shirt. His hair was brown and shaggy as she remembered and he was wearing the same glasses she remembered.

"How did you get into my house?"

He slowly lowered his hands. "First thing's first. My name is Paul. Paul Treadway. And as far as how I got into your house - I'll get to that - later. There are other things you need to know first and I don't know how much time I have - I'm getting better at this but still not great."

"Better at what? Breaking into houses?"

"No - that's not what I meant. But I will explain."

"Well why don't you start with explaining who you are, Paul Treadway and what you're doing in my house? Huh? I've seen you before but every time I wanted to find out who you were and why you were stalking me, you'd take off."

Paul took a deep breath and scratched his forehead. He was obviously trying to figure out what to say. "That wasn't my intention, believe me."

He seemed so nervous and worried himself, that Maggie realized she was getting more and more relaxed with this strange encounter. She studied him a few moments longer.

"Okay - you said I needed to know something. Why don't we start with that."

Paul nodded nervously. "Alright then ... First of all - you are rather psychically gifted, did you know that?"

Maggie just stared at him.

"Okay, obviously you didn't know that - how would you?... Let's start with this: Have you noticed anything strange going on here in Rosedale? Things that just don't make a lot of sense?"

Maggie stopped breathing for a moment. She stared at him but didn't want to let her guard down. "Maybe."

"Okay - good." he said nervously. "There's a reason for that."

Maggie watched him cautiously. "And what would that reason be?"

Paul took a deep breath. "You're going to need to trust me, okay? Cause there's a lot I have to tell you, but I have to do it in a certain way. So please - no matter how weird you think it is, at least just for a little while, I need you to keep your mind open to ... possibilities."

Maggie was about to say something dismissive, but then the thought crossed her mind ... she HAD been noticing strange things happening - that was true. So how did this guy know that? But then, perhaps she really was losing her mind and this Paul Treadway didn't actually exist. But if that were the case, she really wouldn't lose anything by going along with it for a few minutes. She looked at him again.

"Alright. I'm all ears. But let me tell you - you come near me and I swear I'll find the most painful way imaginable to use this vase."

He smiled at her. "Deal."

He took a deep breath and looked at her for a moment before speaking. "Rosedale. It all has to do with Rosedale and how Rosedale works. This place isn't what you think."

He stopped talking and waited for Maggie to respond.

"You need to leave. Now."

"I will - I promise - but please just give me a few more minutes. Truthfully I may only have a few minutes anyway. What have you got to lose?"

Maggie considered what he was saying and against what she thought was her better judgement, she motioned for him to continue.

"Let me ask you - have you ever tried to leave Rosedale? I mean, have you ever gotten in your car and just driven out of town to see what was out there?"

Maggie started to feel uncomfortable. She couldn't explain why. She slowly shook her head.

"Why not? Don't you find that a little odd? Think about it. And apparently you're married, right?"

Maggie slowly nodded.

"So where did the two of you meet? When? How long did you date? Where did you get married?"

Maggie started to feel dizzy. Why couldn't she answer these questions? They weren't difficult questions. So why was her mind drawing blanks?

"We'll talk again. But for right now, I need you to think about what I've said. Think about it. Please, ask yourself those same questions."

Maggie shut her eyes and rubbed her temples. She was starting to get a headache.

"What you're saying doesn't ..." She opened her eyes but he was gone. She looked around, she couldn't see him. It was as though he had vanished. She got up and looked around the second floor and then down on the main floor. It didn't make sense. She hadn't looked away for that long. He couldn't have left without her seeing him go. She ran to the front door and then the back. Both were still locked. She stood there for a moment leaning against the back door, looking at her kitchen. What had just happened? That couldn't have been real ... but ...

A couple of hours later and Maggie was still feeling shell-shocked. Was it her imagination or did it really happen? Whatever the case, she certainly couldn't risk telling Sam.

She was going to have to figure this out her-self. She sat at the table nursing a now cold cup of coffee - just staring off in the distance, trying to figure out what was going on.

She glanced at the clock. Sam and Jor-dan would be home soon. She probably need-ed to get dinner started. She didn't want Sam to think anything was wrong. She had to con-vince him that after her nap, she felt so much better.

With that thought in mind, she pulled a few things from the refrigerator and started putting dinner together. While doing that, she remembered her conversation with Patty and she realized she wasn't going to have any-thing to take to Mr. Topper the next day. As things were boiling away on the stove, she made a quick call to Patty who completely un-derstood and assured Maggie that she would take care of it herself - not to worry.

She disconnected the call, feeling better at least about that, when her thoughts re-turned to Rebecca. She thought back to their day at the farmers' market. She knew she didn't simply imagine Rebecca. She was a real person and she lived in Rosedale, she worked for Sam. But ... what had happened to her and why didn't anyone remember her? Of course those questions made her think about the things Paul had said - or whoever he was. All of those questions about Sam. Why couldn't she remember? Surely she should remember when they met or how they met. The more she thought, the more questions she had. And then there was Jordan. At which hospital was Jordan born? Did Jordan have a favorite doll? Why couldn't she remember? What was wrong with her? Surely these are things a mother would remember. Suddenly she ran to the armoire that stood in the living room and threw open the doors. There were photo albums stacked along one side. She grabbed one of them. Maybe there were photos of Jordan as a little girl in one of these - or maybe a photo of her wedding - something that might help her remember. But as she started paging through the album, her heart sank. Each page she turned was empty. She grabbed another and it was the same. And then another. There were no photos in any of the albums. They were all empty. How could that be?

Her head started spinning. Suddenly the world felt up-side-down and she couldn't make sense of anything. She stopped and took a deep breath. She was shaking. She had to put the albums away and get back to cooking dinner. Sam would be home any minute and she couldn't take the chance of him thinking something might be wrong.

Her heart was beating through her chest as she set the table. What did all of this mean?

Just as she put the last napkin on the table, she heard the familiar sound of the front door opening.

"We're home!" called Jordan from the front door.

Maggie swallowed and with all her might, forced a smile on her face. "I'm in here! Dinner's ready!"

Moments later Jordan and Sam walked into the kitchen. Jordan was all smiles as usual and Sam looked concerned - which seemed to be pretty normal for him recently.

"I'm just going to clean up first. I'll be right back." announced Jordan as she gave Maggie a quick kiss on the cheek on her way out of the kitchen.

Sam walked up to Maggie and put his arms around her. "How are you feeling now?"

Maggie smiled. It was strained, but she was pretty sure it looked convincing. "I'm actually pretty good! You wouldn't believe how I slept this afternoon! I was shocked! I was surprised to see Patty sitting here when I woke up. You didn't have to call her to check on me. I told you I'd be fine."

Sam smiled and kissed her.

"I didn't want to take any chances. You had me pretty worried. Are you sure you're feeling okay?"

"Absolutely."

"Oh what's with the painting in the living room?"

Maggie looked surprised. She had actually forgotten about it. "Oh that! Apparently Wyndham dropped it by when I was sleeping. He told Patty he wanted me to have it to remember him by."

"Well that was nice."

"It was wasn't it?" replied Maggie as she made a mental note to call Wyndham the next day to tell him what she had just told Sam. She felt heartbroken. She had never lied to Sam and yet here she was - lying like a pro. She tried to shake off the feeling, telling herself she didn't have a choice - that as soon as she had something reasonable to tell him, she would.

"I also picked up some sleeping pills for you on my way home. I thought it wouldn't hurt. Maybe if you had a good sleep for a few nights in a row, it might make a difference."

"I'll give it a shot." replied Maggie, smiling. "You're probably right. How's the investigation going?"

Sam shook his head. "Nope. We aren't going to talk about that tonight. I don't want you thinking about any of that stuff and then dreaming about it later."

Maggie smiled at him. She loved him so much.

Before long, they were finishing up dinner. Jordan had retreated to her room, as usual - leaving Sam and Maggie sitting at the table, finishing their coffee.

Maggie found herself staring at him when he wasn't looking and at the same time, thinking about those questions she had started to ask herself. She wondered if Sam would remember, or would he think it strange that she was asking. She tried to think of a way to ask him some questions in the least suspicious way possible.

She forced herself to laugh. Sam looked up at her.

"What's so funny?"

"Well, I was talking to Patty this afternoon - after I woke up. We were talking about relationships and that sort of thing. And the really stupid thing is, for some reason, I couldn't remember where exactly we met each other. Isn't that weird?"

"Oh."

Maggie pressed on. "Yeah I felt really silly. I mean, who forgets something like that, you know? I'm thinking again it's probably due to lack of sleep and all of that - maybe another symptom or something. So - as stupid as it is, I have to ask, I mean, it might help jog my memory - where did we meet?"

Sam stared blankly at her for a moment and then got up with his coffee cup in his hand. "Do you want another cup of coffee?" he asked as he walked to the coffee pot.

"Ah, no, I'm fine. So... do you remember how we met?"

Silence.

"Or what Church we got married in?"

Silence

"Do you remember what my dress looked like?"

The silence was deafening. With each question, Maggie felt the panic in her growing.

Finally Sam looked at her and smiled.

"I'm going to go hang that painting in the living room."

And with that, he took the hammer out of the drawer and exited the kitchen, leaving Maggie sitting at the table.

She couldn't move. She felt nauseous. What had just happened?

Before long she heard Sam hammering. She got up and carried the rest of the dishes to the sink. She stood there for a moment, leaning against the counter, trying to think.

"Well what do you think?" He called to her from the other room.

She turned and walked into the living room. Wyndham's painting hung above a small bombay chest. It was perfect. As she looked at it, the only thought she had was that she must always remember her friend. No matter what happened, she must always re-member.

"That looks great." she said, trying to sound normal.

It wasn't long before Sam was making sure all the doors were locked and they were heading up to bed. As they shut the door be-hind them, he reached inside a small paper bag that he had brought upstairs with him. It was a bottle of sleeping pills. He handed them to Maggie.

"Here. Read the directions for the dosage - I'm not sure what it is, but hopefully this will help you sleep."

Maggie forced herself to smile. "Thank you. It certainly can't hurt and hopefully I'll wake up tomorrow morning feeling like a brand new woman."

She forced a laugh, took the box and went into the master bathroom, shutting the door behind her.

Her smile faded quickly.

She stared at herself in the mirror. She felt numb. She tried to replay that moment with Sam - when she was asking him the questions. Why did he act so strangely? It was almost as though he wasn't hearing her. She felt panic rising in her once more. Why didn't either one of them remember those things? Suddenly it felt as though her world was starting to spin out of control. Nothing made sense. She then looked down at the box of sleeping pills. She shrugged and decided it wouldn't hurt to take a couple. It certainly had been a confusing day and her head was throbbing. But most importantly, she just didn't want to think anymore. Maybe the sleeping pills would prevent that. She needed - she wanted, to sleep.

She opened the box and took out the bottle. She shook a couple of the small white pills into the palm of her hand. But as she stared at the pills, she decided against taking them. It was as if there was something in her telling her not to take them. After a moment, she put the pills back in the bottle and put the bottle up in the medicine cabinet. She would take a couple the next night if she needed them. In the meantime, Sam was right - she was exhausted. She couldn't think about things if she wanted to and felt that she would sleep even without the pills. She would tell Sam she took them. She left the bathroom, shutting off the light as she did.

25

The next day started as any other. Maggie made every effort to appear happy and back to her old self - but in reality, she was anything but.

Over pancakes and coffee she told Sam she was going to spend the day running errands. She told him she felt amazing.

It was a lie.

Finally it was time for Sam to head off to work, with Jordan in tow.

She kissed and hugged both of them as they walked out the door. If they had been paying attention, they would have noticed the hugs lasted a little longer than usual. She was afraid of letting them go. Afraid she'd never see them again and no one would remember they had ever existed. Except her.

She stood just outside the front door waving good-bye until they were out of sight. She went back in the house and locked the door behind her. In truth, she had hardly slept at all the night before. She had been checking the clock almost every hour waiting until it was time to get up. She knew what she wanted to do but was nervous at the thought of what she might discover. But then, what was she expecting to discover? Some things were just impossible. At least that's what she told herself.

After a quick shower, she donned her jeans and pull-over, grabbed her purse and was out the door. She was taking a road trip.

Her stomach fluttered as she backed out of the driveway and turned down the street. She'd be going in the opposite direction of the Sheriff's office. Under the circumstances, that made her feel marginally better. The sun was shining as usual. It was a perfect day for a drive. She knew that until she did this, she wouldn't be able to rest. The fact that neither she nor Sam could remember basic things - like where they met each other, kept her awake all night long. She needed to find an explanation and this might give it to her.

She turned left at the end of her street and this time, made a right turn on Woodland Avenue. She looked at the people who were out walking and jogging. She wondered if any of them had been experiencing odd things lately, as she had. Then she had an even stranger thought, as she wondered if they continued to exist after she drove passed them.

She drove past houses and small businesses, old people, young people and children. She stared at them as she passed, not knowing what she was expecting them to do as she drove by. Why was it that nothing looked quite the same to her?

As she drove, she was bothered by the fact she couldn't remember ever leaving Rosedale. She couldn't remember ever driving out of town. How was that possible? She started to feel a little nervous as she realized she was driving through what was referred to as the "out-skirts" of Rosedale. She had never driven this far before - at least not that she could remember. But she would follow her plan - she would drive out of town, staying on Woodland Avenue until it took her to the next stop along the way. There, she would possibly have some lunch, look around and then come home. That would be that and she could get back to living her life. Something felt wrong though and she knew it. Deep down she knew it.

She remembered that she needed to call Wyndham in case Sam were to see him and thank him for dropping off the painting. How she looked forward to the day when she could stop lying to Sam. She hated herself for it.

She picked up her phone and dialed Wyndham. He answered on the second ring, obviously happy to hear from her. Without going into detail, she gave him a quick outline of what she had told Sam and Wyndham seemed to have no problem with supporting her story should the need arise. He didn't even ask any questions - which was something Maggie was grateful for.

Just as she ended the call, she passed a large sign that read "You Are Leaving Rosedale". Why did that make her feel so nervous? It was just a sign.

The road passed by beautiful farmland. The gentle hills made the drive particularly pleasant. She smiled. There was no other traffic on the road. Just then, she noticed a sign off on the horizon at the top of one of the hills. She felt relieved and a little giddy. Everything was fine. As she got closer and closer, the sign became clear. She pulled over to the side of the road and slammed the car into park. She stared up at the sign in disbelief. There, in large, bold letters was a sign that read "Welcome to Rosedale"

Her breathing quickened. She jerked the car back into drive, looked to make sure the way was clear and pulled back out onto the road - but this time going the other direction. She pressed hard on the accelerator. This didn't make sense. She strained trying to see what was ahead of her. Finally another sign. She couldn't explain what had just happened, but it didn't matter. Nothing mattered except leaving Rosedale. But as she got close to the new sign, she began to make out what it said. She didn't need to see it any closer - she already knew what it said. Without slowing, she made a frantic u-turn, almost losing control of the car and drove as fast as she could. Her mind was playing tricks on her. That had to be the answer - that was the only answer. Once again she pressed the accelerator to the floor, hanging on to the steering wheel with both hands as tightly as she could. Suddenly, there, on the horizon - a sign. As she approached, she slowed the car and pulled over onto the side of the road. She put the car in park, got out and walked up to the large sign that once again, welcomed her to Rosedale. She stood there staring at it. She looked around in every direction as though hoping to see something that might explain this - but there was nothing. Just her, farmland and a sign.

She started to feel faint as a wave of heat seemed to race from her feet all the way through the top of her head and then back down again. She wanted to scream. She wanted to scream because she didn't know what else to do.

She got back into her car and locked the doors. For over an hour she sat there, in her car, staring up at the sign, crying one minute and screaming the next. For the first time, she actually felt hopeless. Try as she did, she couldn't come up with any explanation that would help all of this make sense. She needed to talk to Paul again. Paul Treadway seemed to have answers. She needed those answers.

Finally, after calming herself down and wiping her tears away, she started the car back up and got on the road - this time, passing the welcome sign. She was heading home.

She reached over to the passenger seat and picked up her phone. She dialed Patty but then disconnected the call. There was no point in asking her if she had ever left Rosedale. Maggie already knew the answer. No. No one had ever left Rosedale.

Another thought crossed her mind and she called Patty again, but this time she waited for Patty to answer. After a quick conversation, they decided to grab some lunch at the diner. Maggie was grateful for the company. She didn't want to be alone.

It wasn't long before she was pulling into a parking spot on Main Street, just a few doors down from Pop's Diner. She got out of her car, locking the door behind her. She stood there for a few moments looking up and down the busy street. People were walking along the sidewalks, going in and out of the small shops that lined the street. She inhaled the sweet aroma coming from the bakery a block away. She thought back. He said it had to do with the way Rosedale worked. What did he mean by that, she wondered. It didn't make any sense. It was all crazy.

She tried to shake off the feeling of impending doom and hurried to the restaurant. The familiar smell of coffee and bacon greeted her as she walked in - making the bell that hung at the top of the door announce her presence. She looked around for Patty when Robin walked up to her, smiling.

"Hey sugar! Patty is at the back in the second booth on the left. Can I bring you something to drink?"

"A Diet Coke would be good actually." responded Maggie, forcing herself to smile.

She started to walk towards the back of the restaurant, but glanced back at Robin who was busy filling a soda glass with ice. It was almost hard to believe that there was ever someone named Emily Patterson who worked at Pop's Diner - even for Maggie. She realized that now, when she looked at Robin, it felt like Robin had been at the diner for as long as she could remember.

She turned away and resumed her walk towards Patty, when she stopped dead in her tracks. She felt the blood drain from her face.

'For as long as she could remember.'

That's what everyone said, wasn't it?... 'For as long as they could remember.' They worked somewhere for 'as long as they could remember.' They lived somewhere for 'as long as they could remember." They've known someone for 'as long as they could remember'. Robin - the new kid at the grocery store - even Sam. Even Sam. Her mind started racing.

According to Sam, he had the scar on his arm for 'as long as he could remember' - the guy who lived in the house that used to be Rebecca's - same thing ... Why was it that no one spoke in terms of months or years gone by. What was she missing? What did it mean?

She hurried to the booth at the back of the restaurant where Patty was sitting. She threw her purse on the bench and then quickly slid in. "I have to ask you a question."

Patty looked at her for a moment and then smiled. "Oh hi Patty! How are you? - Oh I'm good Maggie and you?"

Maggie shook her head.

"I'm sorry - Hi."

Patty chuckled. "Yeah okay, never mind - you look like you're going to explode."

Maggie nodded and started to speak when Robin showed up at the booth and put Maggie's Diet Coke down on the table.

"Are you ready to order?"

Maggie smiled impatiently at her. "Could you give us a few minutes, please?"

"You got it!" replied Robin and she moved away from the table. "Just wave at me when you're ready!"

Maggie refocused her attention on Patty, who was sipping her coffee, waiting for Maggie to get on with it.

"You're a real estate agent, right?"

Patty stared at her. "Well yeah ... but you know that. Why are you asking?"

"How long have you been a real estate agent?"

Patty thought it over before finally starting to speak. "Well, I've been a real estate agent for as long -"

" - as you can remember?" finished Maggie.

Patty looked at her. She was obviously a little confused by the conversation. And, it appeared, starting to feel a little uncomfortable. "So what's your point?" Patty asked as she took another sip of her coffee.

"Bear with me here because I really need you to think about this."

"Okay." replied Patty. She was no longer smiling. She put her coffee cup down.

"In actual years - think back - how many years have you been a real estate agent? Even in general terms ... five years, ten ...?"

She could see Patty trying to process what she was saying, but still she wasn't answering.

"Or maybe - when did you get your real estate license?   Anyone would know that, right? How many years ago - about how many years ago?"

She stared at Patty waiting for a response. But then something happened. There was a look that came over Patty's eyes. It was like a veil had covered them. Maggie had never seen it before. It looked as though something had disconnected - as if Patty was somewhere else and Maggie was staring at a shell. Something was happening. Something was wrong. The color had drained from Patty's face.   Then Maggie heard a sound that drew her attention down onto the table. Patty's hand was beginning to twitch so badly that her finger nails were hitting the side of the coffee mug, making a frantic clicking noise. It seemed however that Patty wasn't even aware of it.

Maggie grabbed her friend's hand and squeezed. "It's okay. It's okay. Patty? Look at me. It doesn't matter. Nothing matters. How's your coffee Patty? Huh? Does it taste good? Do you think I should get a cup of coffee too? I'm starved, how about you?"

She watched as Patty slowly started to blink her eyes. The color seemed to come back to her face as well. She turned to Maggie. She was obviously confused. "What? I'm sorry - what did you say?"

Maggie took a deep breath. Relief washed over her. She had no idea what she had just witnessed, but she was grateful it had passed. Obviously there would be things she couldn't share even if she wanted to - if that was in fact what caused whatever she had just witnessed.

"I said ... I said maybe we should order now." she responded nervously - not knowing if Patty would know any different.

But instead Patty smiled at her and then waved to Robin. Everything was fine - at least for Patty.

During the following hour, Maggie did her best to keep a pleasant conversation going while her mind was screaming a thousand different questions.

Patty didn't appear to remember anything happening out of the ordinary. And even stranger, she didn't seem to remember the questions Maggie had been asking her. It was as if Maggie had never brought anything up at all.

"Bye guys!" called Robin from behind the counter as Maggie and Patty headed out of the restaurant. "Come back soon!"

"So what are you up to now?" asked Patty

"What do you mean?"

"Well, what are you planning on doing after you leave here? That last conversation I had with you still has me a little worried. Are you okay?"

Maggie looked at her friend and saw the concern in her eyes. In that moment all she could think was how much she hoped Patty would be safe from whatever was happening. She smiled at her friend.

"I'm fine. Really. And ... well I'm still sorting things out. But I don't want you to worry about me. I promise I'll be careful."

Patty studied her for a moment. "Well, I promised I wouldn't ask any questions. But don't forget - if you need anything, I'm here for you. It's going to cost you but I'm here for you."

Maggie laughed.

They walked until they reached Maggie's car. Patty was parked directly behind her.

"I'm just going to go home." said Maggie. "Maybe take a nap for real. Feel a bit of a headache coming on." Maggie opened her car door. "Why don't I give you a call tomorrow?"

"Sounds good!" replied Patty

And with a small wave and a smile, Patty got into her own car. Before Maggie could get herself settled, her friend had already pulled away. Maggie sat there for a minute, trying to sort things out in her mind. She wished it made sense. But it didn't. She started her car and was about to pull out of the parking space when she started feeling a bit queasy. She put the car back into park - hoping the feeling would pass quickly. She rested her forehead on the steering wheel. Her heart started pounding. She shut her eyes because it felt as though everything had started spinning. She tried taking deep and deliberate breaths in and then out. In and out. But then, all of a sudden she felt a breeze on her face, which made no sense because she was in her car. She opened her eyes only to discover she was in fact, no longer in her car. She was outside. She looked down at her hands. A man's hands. Not hers. It was happening again.

She looked at her clothes - old blue jeans and a black, long sleeve pull-over of some sort. She looked around. There were trees, a hedge, houses. She saw people walking by. She heard sounds that she couldn't quite make out. She looked to the left, across the street. It was a school. It was Jordan's school. Her breath quickened. What was happening? She saw Jordan walk out the front door. Then time seemed to skip because suddenly she was no longer on the other side of the street watching, but she was on the sidewalk behind Jordan. She watched as Jordan turns to face her - but it's like slow motion. She's screaming. Jordan is screaming.

Maggie's heart felt like it was about to explode. She shut her eyes once more and focused on her breathing. It felt like it took forever but finally, she felt a change. The sensation of being outside vanished. She opened her eyes and found herself back in her car. It took her a second to get her bearings and collect her thoughts. She was in a panic. She looked at the time. Jordan wasn't supposed to be getting out of school yet - it was too early.

It didn't make sense - but she didn't care. It wasn't the time to try to figure things out. She put the car back into drive and pulled out of her parking spot - almost hitting a car that was driving by. She drove as quickly as she could. She had to get to Jordan's school. Before long, she was pulling up in front of the building. She turned the car engine off, stepped out and looked around. She was about to run into the school to ask for her daughter when she saw the front doors swing open as a group of students walked out. Jordan was one of them. She was deep in conversation with a fellow student and hadn't noticed Maggie at all.

"Jordan!" yelled Maggie. "Jordan!"

It took a second, but finally Jordan looked up and saw Maggie. She smiled, said something to the friend she was talking to and then ran down the steps to Maggie.

"Hey! What are you doing here?" Asked Jordan as she hopped into the car.

Maggie glanced up and down the street, before getting back in the car. She locked the car doors and then turned to Jordan. "What's happening here?   Why are you leaving school?"

"We got out early today that's all!"

"That's ALL?" responded Maggie, feeling frustrated. "Did you let your father know?"

"No."

"And why not?"

Jordan sighed somewhat impatiently. "I totally forgot we were getting out early today. And then, I didn't want to bother him! It's no biggie. I've walked home a million times! It would have been fine."

"You don't know that! How many times do we have to tell you not to take any chances, huh? My God Jordan! Your father and I have told you how important it is for you to be careful and this is what you do?"

Jordan looked down. "I'm sorry. I guess I should have called either you or Dad, but I just figured I could walk home and it was no big deal. It won't happen again. I promise."

Maggie looked at her daughter. She sighed. "Okay. Just never again. We couldn't stand it if anything happened to you - do you understand?"

Jordan nodded.

Maggie looked around. He was there somewhere. She could feel it. Her hand was shaking slightly when she picked up her phone. She called Sam to let him know that Jordan was with her. She didn't tell him anything else, not about her vision, not about feeling she was having. She knew how it would sound - again. With a final look in her rear-view mirror, she pulled out onto the street and headed home.

*   *   *

He watched her drive away. He was angry. He had been watching the Sheriff's daughter for a while now and he had planned everything out. How dare she ruin things for him? He stared off into the distance for a few moments and considered his options. He wondered if it was just coincidence that the mother showed up. Something didn't feel right to him. He pulled down on the sleeves of his black t-shirt. He needed to walk. That would help clear his head. Maybe he'd go out later and look around.

*   *   *

It wasn't long after that Maggie and Jordan had arrived home. She told Jordan that they would tell her father that she had called Maggie to come pick her up. She told her that way her father wouldn't be angry. Jordan was relieved. So was Maggie. Quite frankly she couldn't figure out how she could possibly explain to Sam what made her drive to Jordan's school. A 'vision' just didn't seem like a viable explanation.

They entered the house and as usual, Jordan went upstairs to her room. Maggie went into the kitchen. She made herself a cup of coffee and then sat at the kitchen table and stared out through the bay window.

Everything felt up-side-down. She thought about what had happened today with Jordan. She wondered if in fact it really was a premonition. She had no way of knowing if Jordan would have actually been in danger, but then, she was leaving school early - by herself. Maggie shuttered to think of what might have happened if she hadn't been there to pick Jordan up. How could she rationalize any of this? She thought back to Paul Tread-way ... if what was his name. She needed to speak to him. She remembered him telling her that she had some sort of psychic abilities. Was that what happened? It was some sort of psychic warning that Jordan was in danger? She didn't know.

And then that whole episode with Patty.

She shook her head and took a sip of her coffee. She would figure this out. She had to.

Then something crossed her mind. "Jordan!" she called from the kitchen.

"Yeah?" replied Jordan from upstairs.

She considered what she was going to say. "Why don't you bring your things down here and spend some time with me?"

After a few moments, Jordan finally replied. "Okay - I'll be right down."

Maggie sighed. Suddenly she was afraid of Jordan staying upstairs. What if she just disappeared? What if she called her down for dinner and she wasn't there to respond?

26

The next day arrived without any further surprises - much to Maggie's relief. Sam had praised Jordan for calling her mother to come pick her up at school and Jordan was grateful that her mother had covered for her. Little did she know that Maggie was in fact, covering for herself as well.

After Jordan and Sam left the house, Maggie sat on the living room sofa which faced the bombay chest - and Wyndham's painting. It was still there. She told herself that because it was at least still there and his name was still on the bottom right corner, that it must have meant that Wyndham was still around and hadn't vanished as others had. She reasoned that if he had, then no one would remember him and like Emily's Employee of the Month photo, either the painting would be gone, or it would be signed by someone else.

She got up and moved closer to the painting to study it. Yes, that was still his name in the corner.

She sat back down on the sofa. She needed to talk to Paul Treadway. She had too many questions and it seemed that he, whoever he was, had answers. Was she just supposed to wait and hope she would see him again? What if ... She remembered what Paul had told her and then remembered her experience with Jordan. Maybe she did have some sort of psychic ability. Was it really that far-fetched, especially with everything else that was going on. Something seeming "far-fetched" was no longer a good reason for not believing in it.

She took a deep breath and shut her eyes. She focused on her breathing - deep breath in and slow out ... deep breath in and slow out. In her mind, she kept imagining Paul Treadway. She felt ridiculous, but what did she have to lose at this point? At least no one could see her. Over and over again in her mind, she kept repeating his name, kept imagining him standing in front of her. She started to laugh at herself. She opened her eyes and went in the kitchen. She'd just have to wait until or if he showed up.

She went to put the breakfast dishes into the sink and when she looked up through the window - she saw him. He was standing there on the sidewalk as he had been that time before. She dropped the dishes into the sink and ran to the front door. Throwing it open, she ran out onto her front yard. She didn't want him to disappear. Not now. Luckily he was walking towards her. Relief washed over her.

Before long, they were sitting at the kitchen table. She had so many questions, she hardly knew where to start.

"After what you said to me the other day - I tried to leave Rosedale. I tried. But I can't. It's like I'm in a fishbowl. And I can't remember things I know I should. And what's weird, Sam - he's my husband - he can't remember things either and neither can a friend of mine. But, it's different with them. It's like on one level they aren't hearing the question I'm asking. They seem to tune out what I'm saying. I don't understand what's happening with that. I mean, I was scared with my friend because, I thought she was going to have a heart attack or something. Please tell me. What's all this about? Who are you?"

Paul looked at her. She saw compassion in his eyes. "This is going to be difficult to hear. But I need you to stay calm and trust me. Can you do that?"

Maggie slowly nodded.

"Alright then. Have you ever heard the name Vicki Allyn?"

Maggie thought for a moment. It didn't mean anything to her. She shook her head. "No."

Paul continued, "Vicki Allyn is one of your best friends..."

"But I don't - "

Paul raised his hand. "Please just listen. This is going to be difficult I know - but I need you to listen."

Maggie nodded.

"Your friend, Vicki Allyn, reached out to me. I'm a psychic medium. She reached out to me because she wanted to see if I could connect with you."

Maggie looked completely confused. Paul took a deep breath before continuing, trying to find the right words. "This place you call Rosedale - doesn't really exist. I mean, it exists in your mind - you think it's real - it exists in everyone's mind who lives here - but it isn't actually a physical place."

Again he stopped and watched Maggie for a moment before continuing. "You really aren't here - physically that is. You - your body - your physical body, is actually in a hospital bed, at Piedmont Hospital, in Atlanta. You're in a coma Maggie."

He paused so that Maggie could digest what he was saying. She sat motionless - listening to him but not uttering a word. He continued. "The doctors thought you should have been waking up by now, but for some reason you're not. That's why Vicki talked to me. She wanted to see if I could make contact with you and see if I could bring you back."

Maggie stared at him. Then without any warning, she slapped him hard across the face. She didn't know if she was feeling angry or scared. In truth, she had no idea how she felt about anything he was saying - other than the fact it sounded ridiculous. "Not real huh? Well, that felt pretty real to me and pretty darn physical. So now what do you want to say? Huh? You're crazy, you know that?"

Paul rubbed the side of his face. "I know this is hard to get your mind around. Let me show you. Slap me again."

"What?"

"I said, slap me again, just like you did. Come on. Do it."

Maggie set her jaw with determination. "Okay. Just remember you asked me to do this."

And with that, she went to slap him across the face once more, but this time everything was different. Instead of hitting him, her hand passed through his face as though he was just an image imprinted on the air. She froze. She stared at her hand and then back at Paul. Slowly she reached her hand up to his face and watched as her fingers slid through him. She jerked her hand back. She wanted to say something - anything - but the words wouldn't come out.

"It's kind of a mind thing. If I choose to be solid to you, I am - but if I choose not to be, well then I'm not. Welcome to Rosedale.

Everyone in this town is actually, physically, somewhere else ... probably in a hospital or nursing home somewhere ... in a coma. Some for years, some for days."

"No ... that can't ..." she whispered under her breath, shaking her head ever so slightly. Her thoughts were all over the place. She couldn't believe what he was saying - could she? It all sounded so crazy. So unbelievable. But her hand had passed through him ... people were vanishing ... That wasn't normal. As crazy as it sounded ... could it be true?

"When the essence of who we are," continued Paul, "our souls or that unseen part of our brains - that thing that makes us sentient beings - isn't dead but isn't truly alive either, it's like it has to go somewhere ... so it comes to Rosedale, or to some other place like Rosedale and stays busy and lives. It's the ultimate in mass hallucination."

Finally Maggie found her voice. "We have people here who just vanish and no one remembers they were ever here ..."

"They've either woken up and resumed their lives or they didn't make it."

"Meaning they died."

"Yes."

"But then why doesn't anyone remember them? Once they leave, no one misses them, no one remembers them."

Paul took a deep breath. "If they did remember them, it would open a flood gate of questions and that would be the end of Rosedale. I'm not an expert on this by any means.   Truthfully I've only experienced something like this once before. I didn't know this sort of thing existed before then.   But it seems if people start noticing the cracks in the reality of these places, it causes a sort of short circuiting. It's kind of like parting the curtain on the Wizard in the Wizard of Oz. Once you do, the whole fantasy comes crashing down. In order for Rosedale and places like Rosedale to do what they were intended to do - they must be believed in their entirety. Usually the mind manages that and protects itself. Protects the fantasy."

"But I'm seeing the cracks. Why can I see them?"

"Maybe there are a few people who do. Maybe they have psychic abilities like you. I don't have all the answers. But perhaps they just chalk it up to any number of rational explanations. People have always been able to accept things they really don't understand. The average person may not fully understand electricity but they will flip the switch and expect the light to come on. But - I think you're extremely psychically gifted which I believe is what allows you to part that curtain just a little. And, if I hadn't shown up - who knows, maybe you would have finally just put those questions behind you and continued living here as you have."

"You're expecting me to believe something that.." Her voice trailed off as she tried to wrap her mind around what he was saying.

"If I choose to believe you, which I don't quite yet, how long have I been ... in a coma?"

"For about two weeks. But they say you should have come out of it by now and you haven't. Somehow you're fighting coming back and you shouldn't Maggie. You need to come back."

Maggie thought about what he was saying and finally shook her head. "No. Even if what you're saying is true - I can't. Not yet."

27

He sat on a bench in Jackson Square watching people walk by. It was almost dawn but still he could hear music playing somewhere and the raised voices of drunk patrons as they stumbled out of bars. New Orleans.

He needed to make plans. He hated the city. He wanted to go home. There was nothing holding him here any longer. He was free.

His father was proud of him. He could tell. The whore got what she deserved. And, as far as Stephen was concerned, Robert decided he wasn't going to be missed. Always more concerned about himself. And besides, he was fairly sure Stephen was only his half brother anyway - an insult to his father. He did wonder though if perhaps he should have killed Stephen with the sledgehammer as well. If he had to do it over again, that's what he would do. He had a slight concern that Stephen had survived the fire. But, if he had, Robert felt sure his father would advise him on how to handle the situation.

He thought back to the feeling that washed over him as soon as he felt the sledgehammer make contact. A grin spread across his face. It had felt good. Finally. All those years of being ridiculed and mistreated. He showed them. He finally showed them.

He decided to stretch out for a while and get some rest. Then, in the morning, maybe see about getting a few odd jobs. He only needed to earn enough money to get him back up to North Carolina. Maybe he could hitch a ride with a trucker going that way. It didn't matter though. He'd figure it out. He always did.

He made himself comfortable on the bench and shut his eyes. The voices in his head were lulling him to sleep. They had grown louder than ever since he killed his mother. He took that as a good sign. He wondered how long it took the fire department to get to the house. Maybe he'd go by there and see how everything looked. Or maybe he wouldn't. He hadn't decided yet. Going back though always felt good. He rested his hand on the handle of the knife he had tucked into the waistband of his pants and fell asleep.

He didn't sleep long however. He couldn't. The adrenaline was still coursing through him. He needed to walk. The sun had come up which would have made it impossible to sleep anyway.

He got up, checked to make sure he still had his wallet and knife and then started walking. Maybe it wouldn't be safe to stay around New Orleans any longer. He needed to go back to the house. If it had completely burned down, then he would have time. They would assume that his body was somewhere in the rubble. But if it was still standing, then he needed to find a ride right away.

He stopped by a convenience store and got himself a bottle of Coke and some chips. After drinking almost half the bottle in one swallow, he started walking. He kept his head down and concentrated on his steps. When he did that, he knew he was invisible. It was a trick his father had told him about.

Left foot, right foot, left foot, right foot.

He started walking back in the direction of the house. The closer he got, the more excited he felt. He could still smell the gasoline and feel the heat from the fire. All of it played like a movie in his head. It was exhilarating. He couldn't help but feel giddy at the thought of revisiting the scene.

Finally he turned the corner and was on his street. A little further down he saw the police cars and the fire trucks, all parked out in front of the house. There seemed to be people everywhere. He couldn't help but smile. He felt excited. He had caused this. People were paying attention to him and it was on his terms. There were a lot of residents standing on the sidewalks and road, watching what was happening at the house. He could slip in behind them without being seen.

As he got closer, he realized the house had not been completely destroyed as he had hoped. It still stood. He was a little disappointed with that, but then when he realized he might be able to see them wheel out the body of his mother, he was happy again. He had always enjoyed the feeling of killing someone. But there was just something so special about having killed her. Maybe it was because it was so important to his father.

He scanned the scene and was relieved to see both an ambulance and the coroner's van. He was in luck. He hadn't arrived too late after all.

He continued to mingle in the crowd, keeping his head down and his eyes towards the ground, listening to bits of conversations as people were discussing their shock and sadness. He heard them and their stupid guesses as to what had happened. Some said an electrical fire, he heard one person swear they had heard an explosion ... but a couple were saying they heard it had been a murder. A murder. Not murders but "a" murder. He thought about it. Maybe his brother had survived. Well if he had, he had. No point in worrying about that. Stephen never saw him do it anyway so what difference did it make. With any luck, maybe the fire messed up that perfect face of his. If only he had it to do over again.

Finally he noticed the crowd had grown silent. He looked over to the house. As hard as he tried, he couldn't stop the smile from spreading across his face. A body bag on a gurney being wheeled out into the street and into the coroner's van. His mother. He wished he could have been a fly on the wall when investigators entered her room and saw her.

He realized he must have inadvertently laughed out loud because he saw someone - a woman - turn and look at him. He put his head down again. He had to be more careful than that. The voices were telling him that it was time to go. They were right. He noticed she had started pushing her way through the crowd in the direction of a police officer who was standing next to his police car. He cursed under his breath. Just when things were getting interesting, he would have to leave. But, he told himself, he could come back later.

Keeping his head down, but his eyes up, he started walking quickly in the opposite direction, away from the house, away from the police officer and away from the activity. People were making it more and more difficult for him to walk as they continued towards the scene. He found himself pushing them out of his way. He needed to leave before that woman said anything to the police officer. He wondered who she was. Was she someone who knew his mother? Maybe she recognized him. How stupid could he be? Of course he would have been recognized. He thought he was invisible, but maybe not. Did his father lie to him about that? It didn't matter now. He needed to leave.

He pushed his way through the crowd, shoving anyone who didn't move out of his way fast enough. A few cursed at him but he ignored them. Finally the crowd was thinning out and he started to jog and then run, all the while trying to remain calm. But then he heard it.

"Hey you! Stop! Police!"

He stopped running. His mind was racing and his heart was pounding. He had just turned 19 so he knew he would be charged as an adult - no question. But then, he didn't know who was behind him. Was it just one cop? If it was, he might have a chance.

Slowly he turned around. Three police officers, with guns drawn, were standing there. This wasn't good. His mind raced. The voices were all jumbled up in his head. He couldn't make them out. He needed to hear his father, but he couldn't hear what he was saying because they were all talking at the same time.

"You Robert Kraus?" asked the officer in the middle.

Robert stared at him and then slowly nodded his head in an exaggerated motion. The officers glanced at each other.

"Put your hands up in the air."

Robert continued staring at him.

"I said - put your hands up in the air. I'm not going to ask you again."

Just then Robert heard his father's voice. It was clear.

"Fuck him."

Robert smiled and reached for the knife that was hidden in his waistband. He raised it above his head and started to charge the officer.

Then everything went black.

28

"What do you mean 'not yet'?" asked Paul.

Maggie looked at him. "We have a serial killer here in Rosedale.

"What?"

But Maggie continued as though she hadn't heard him.

"I'm not going to just leave the people I love. What if something happens? I mean, my husband and my daughter ..."

Maggie suddenly stopped talking. A sudden realization hit her. She looked at Paul with disbelief. "My husband ... my daughter - are you telling me they're just some random people in a hospital somewhere?"

Paul took a moment but then nodded. Both sorry and relieved that she was making the connection.

Maggie got up from her chair and walked to the far side of the kitchen, trying to process all of the things Paul was telling her. "That's impossible. I love them. How is any of this possible?" She thought for a moment and then looked back at Paul. "I don't understand how I can be in a coma for only two weeks like you said, when I've lived a lifetime here. I have a family, friends. It doesn't make sense!"

"I guess the best way for me to explain is, it's a lot like a dream. You can be asleep for just a few minutes but in your dream, it isn't just a few minutes - it can feel like years, or feel like nothing. Time is relative. It's measured differently here."

Maggie wiped a tear from her eye. "I haven't asked, but now I need to know. Who am I? Am I Maggie Cooper? Why was, why AM I in a coma?"

"You may want to sit down."

Maggie forced a small laugh. "Oh this isn't sounding good."

She walked back to the table, sat down and looked at him. He looked obviously uncomfortable.

"Your name is Maggie Willis. Willis is your married name."

Maggie looked shocked. "I'm married?"

"Yes - well, yes. David Willis is the man you married."

Maggie waited for him to continue since there seemed to be more he had to say but was searching for a way to say it. "And you had a daughter together. The two of you named her Laura."

Maggie stared at him. "Why are you phrasing things like you are? It's a strange way of saying what you just said."

Paul took a deep breath. "Because they died. You were away that weekend, at a convention. You were - are - an interior decorator. There was a trade show out of town. While you were gone, there was a home invasion. It went badly. They didn't make it."

Paul stopped talking and watched Maggie. Suddenly it felt like she couldn't make her mind work. She couldn't seem to focus on what she was hearing - couldn't seem to get her mind to understand the words. She only knew Sam and Jordan. She loved them with all her heart. Why couldn't she remember David and Laura? Suddenly she felt overwhelming guilt and shame over the fact that she felt nothing towards these people. They were strangers to her. Just names. "But if I was out of town ..."

Paul took her hand and held it. "It was a few months later. I guess you just couldn't take the pain anymore. I mean, it's understandable. You felt alone and, according to Vicki, you felt some sort of misplaced guilt for not having been there when it happened."

Maggie pulled her hand away from Paul's grasp. "What are you saying?"

"You tried to commit suicide. Pills. Vicki found you in time."

For what seemed like hours, Maggie simply stared at him. No one spoke. The only sound that could be heard was coming from the ceiling fan in the other room. They sat like that for what seemed to be an eternity.

Maggie cleared her throat and stared out the window for a few moments. She wiped a tear from her eye with the back of her finger. She needed to pull herself together. Finally she looked at Paul. "Did they ever catch the person who did it?"

"Yeah. A couple of street punks who were just going to rob the house, but then things got out of control. They caught them. They're in prison."

Paul stared at her for a moment before speaking again. "You said there's a serial killer in Rosedale?"

Maggie nodded. "Yeah. Three people so far. It's bad. They can't find him."

Then something crossed her mind.

"Is that why..." Maggie was having a hard time speaking. She started again. "I thought I was going crazy. Maybe I am, but, I've been having - I don't know what they are - premonitions or visions. I think somehow I'm connected to the killer, some sort of psychic connection, if that makes any sense. At times it's like I'm looking through his eyes. It happened yesterday when I thought Jordan was in danger. Is it because I'm still wanting to protect my husband and my daughter?"

Her tears started flowing but she did her best to fight them.

"If I had to guess ... If the desire to protect your family is strong enough, anything is possible. In your mind, maybe because you weren't there to protect David and Laura ..."

"... at least I can try to protect Sam and Jordan? I'll be right back." said Maggie as she hurried to the bathroom and shut the door behind her. She stared into the mirror and let it out. She cried until she couldn't cry any more. All of it was real and yet none of it was real. How would she ever get through this? Was this really happening? If only she could just shut her eyes and make it all go away.

After a while she stopped crying. She turned on the cold water and splashed some on her face before returning to the kitchen. She was grateful Paul was still there.

She returned to the table and sat down. She was calm. She cleared her throat before speaking. "There's something I still don't understand. If none of this is real. If none of this exists on a physical level. How is he killing people? That doesn't make sense - if we're just energy."

"Have you ever heard the saying 'your thoughts create your reality'?"

Maggie nodded.

"He believes he can kill them. They believe he can kill them. So he is able to."

"But what happens to them? They can't die, not in reality."

"They can. Back in the real world - maybe a heart attack, maybe they just stop breathing, maybe the doctor's don't know why. It's sort of like someone dying from fright. No - this serial killer of yours is a very real danger to everyone in Rosedale."

Maggie considered what Paul was saying. "Ironic isn't it? A real danger to a place that isn't real. But people remember his victims..."

She thought through her statement for a moment. "Maybe it's because remembering the victims, doesn't part the curtain on the Wizard. It's explainable within the confines of Rosedale. But, regardless, if this is me wishing I could have protected two people I can't remember, or me wanting to protect Sam and Jordan - the fact is, I'm not leaving until I can do something to make sure they're going to be okay."

"You may not have a choice."

"I may not - but if I have to go back I'll be fighting all the way. I need you to help me, Paul. Please."

Paul stayed for another half hour until Maggie realized she was risking Sam and Jordan coming home. Promising he would return, Paul vanished, as usual. They had discussed everything - including what she could do about the killer. She had a plan. But she also realized she was working against the clock. She could try to fight going back, but ultimately she would have no choice and truthfully, didn't know if it was really possible to fight it at all. She only hoped that she could do what she needed to do before it was too late.

As she started cooking dinner, she couldn't help thinking about the day when she would simply vanish from Rosedale. No one would remember her. No one would remember she ever existed. The thought of losing Sam and Jordan broke her heart - but the knowledge that they wouldn't remember that she had ever existed, seemed to crush it. It was all the more reason she was going to have to find the way to make things safe for them. One thing she had asked Paul though, was for him to think of a way to help her remember Sam and Jordan, when she finally did wake up in his world. The physical world. She could only assume that her memories of them would be wiped away like their memories of her. She didn't want that to happen. She never wanted to forget them - or her friends.

Before she knew it, they were all sitting down to dinner together. She couldn't help but stare at them - wanting to absorb each detail of their faces, the way their voices sounded or how they laughed. She wanted to remember everything.

Later that night, alone with Sam in their bedroom, they made love like they had never made love before. And then later, as they stretched out on the bed, still holding each other, she took the time to make sure she had memorized every detail of his body. From the three tiny moles at the base of his neck to the small scar on his elbow, to his beautiful hair or the way his blue eyes sparkled when he smiled... and of course, how he kissed her. She never wanted to forget how he kissed her.

Finally it was time to go to sleep. He held her in his arms as she wept silently.

29

Detective Boudreaux drove through the intersection on his way to New Orleans East Hospital. The rain had finally stopped but it made the air heavy with humidity. He hated humidity. It fogged up his glasses. He would always threaten to move somewhere cooler, but everyone knew it was just an idle threat. His family had lived in New Orleans for generations and would probably continue to live in New Orleans for generations to come.

He thought about the conversation he had with Officer LeBlanc. Officer LeBlanc had been one of the three officers who confronted the suspect on Mazant Street. Even though the three were on mandatory leave, as was the procedure in an officer involved shooting, he felt sure that once the investigation was complete, they would be returning to work. He hoped so. Officer LeBlanc was a good cop.

He had been to the crime scene. What a mess. He had seen his share of murders over the years, but nothing quite as bad as this. The mother had been beaten beyond recognition. The murder weapon appeared to be a sledgehammer. Her other son had suffered burns to his body trying to escape the house fire. Luckily for him it could have been far worse. He would still need a few skin grafts but he would recover - at least physically.

What had gotten into this kid, he wondered. He hadn't seen him yet, but from what he was told, he was a strange one. Hell, why was he calling him a kid. He was 19 and an adult in the eyes of the law. But then, to Detective Boudreaux, pretty much anyone under the age of 40 was still a kid.

He pulled in front of the hospital, in the special area reserved for police, and parked his car. From what he heard, they had operated on the kid. They removed the bullet but he wasn't waking up.

He walked into the lobby and checked the Directory next to the elevators. He had no idea why he always did that. He knew I.C.U. was on the second floor. He got on the elevator, pressed the button and soon he was in I.C.U. staring down at his suspect.

"Do you really think the handcuffs are necessary?" asked the attending doctor.

Detective Boudreaux shrugged.

"Procedure."

His suspect, Robert Kraus, was unconscious. An I.V. drip was attached to his arm and various monitors were flashing and beeping. They were the only indication he was still alive.

"So what did he do?" questioned the doctor.

"Turned his mother into ground beef with a sledgehammer."

"Oh God."

"Yeah - and then tried to burn his brother up when he torched the house. Luckily his brother got out in time." He took a moment to study his suspect. "Strange lookin' fella, ain't he? You sure he's only 19? Looks older."

The doctor checked his notes. "Nope - 19. They say murderers don't look how you'd expect them to look. This one does."

"Yup" agreed Detective Boudreaux. "So how long before he wakes up and opens them pretty eyes of his?"

"Well, detective, he may never wake up. We don't know. He was without oxygen for quite a while ... so now it's just wait and see. We'll keep him here in I.C.U. for a couple of days until he stabilizes and then send him to a step-down unit. And then if he still isn't showing any signs of waking up from his coma in a couple of weeks - well, hospital beds are worth their weight in gold around here, we'll send him to one of the State run long-term care facilities. That is of course unless his family steps up to pay for something better."

Detective Boudreaux looked at him and smiled. "Well we know that's not going to happen."

The doctor chuckled. "You're probably right."

"So how long can this go on for?"

The doctor sighed. "Could go on for years. Other than being in a coma, he has no health issues to speak of. No reason to assume he'd die any time soon."

"Sweet Jesus. Well if he ever does open those baby blues, he'll have charges waiting for him. But in the meantime, I thank you for the enlightening conversation Doctor. You take care now, ya hear?"

"You have a good evening too, Detective. And if he wakes up, you'll be the first to know."

Detective Boudreaux smiled, gave a one finger salute and walked out of the room. He had another murder case he needed to work on.

30

Maggie spent the next few days trying to digest everything Paul had told her. She believed him, even though doing so scared her. At least she had answers and a plan. She tried to stay focused. If she thought too much about the situation, she was afraid she would just roll up into a ball and cry. She couldn't do that. Besides, she was all cried out. If she had to leave Rosedale, which was apparently inevitable, at least she would do something for the people she had come to love. For Sam. For Jordan. At least she would try.

She knew that Paul didn't have all the answers. But at least he at a general understanding, which was more than she had. What concerned her was when she asked if Sam had been a Sheriff on the other side. As he told her, it wasn't necessarily so, pointing out she had been an interior decorator. Perhaps deep in his subconscious he had always wanted to be in law enforcement - to be a Sheriff. But in reality, he could have had any occupation on the other side. It was anyone's guess.

Ever since the murders started in Rosedale, she had been bothered by the fact that something about the investigation felt a little "off". Now, as she looked back, she realized what it was. A case involving a serial killer was being investigated only by the Rosedale Sheriff's office. Should there not have been a homicide detective? What about a forensics team ... or maybe even the FBI? Why didn't the Sheriff's Office - Sam - ever reach out to another agency for assistance?

Why was there no database search? Why did he never reach out beyond the limits of Rosedale? Now she understood.

The more she thought about that, the more concerned she became. If he wasn't actually a Sheriff, would he know how to go about catching a very real killer. Everyone loved to say that nothing had ever happened in Rosedale. If that had continued to be the case, his lack of experience and resources wouldn't have been a problem. But it might be now. Perhaps that also explained why her appointment with Dr. Simpson seemed so ... superficial. Who knew who these people actually were when they were on the other side.

She had started to think of it as "the other side". It was easier to wrap her head around it that way. There was this side and the other side. But she still had so many questions.

She wondered if Rebecca had woken up on the other side, or if she had died there. She chose to believe that Rebecca had woken up.

That she was surrounded by family and was now living her life without any memory of a place called Rosedale. Maggie thought about the possibilities. Maybe on the other side, she might bump into Rebecca one day. But then, what if she herself couldn't remember Rosedale or the people who had lived there? Paul said he was addressing that problem since he knew how much Maggie wanted - needed - to remember. But she knew he could only do so much. She would just have to wait and see how things unfolded. In the meantime, she needed to focus.

Sam and Jordan had already left for the day. She had started a strange morning routine. She would call both Wyndham and Patty to make sure they were still there. It made her feel more at ease to hear their voices. She knew the alternative might mean they had woken up - but it could also mean they had died and she just wasn't ready to deal with that possibility right now.

She made herself a cup of coffee and took it to the kitchen table where she sat, staring at a small box she had placed there earlier. She opened it. It was her sewing box. She dug around until she found a large needle that had made its way to the bottom. She closed the box and pushed it aside. She sat there, holding the needle in her right hand. She took a few deep breaths and shut her eyes.

Paul had said she was psychically gifted. She wasn't so sure of that, but then, maybe that was something she would rediscover on the other side when the time came. But if he was right, she should be able to do this.

She focused. She tried to make herself feel like air. She focused on Rosedale, on her energy, on the energy of everything around her. She felt ready. She felt calm and relaxed. She felt like she was floating. She opened her eyes and looked down at her hands - at the large needle in her right hand. Slowly and carefully she guided the needle to her index finger on her left hand and pushed it into her skin.

The pain was immediate. As was the blood. She cursed as she hurried to the kitchen sink and ran cold water over her finger until the bleeding stopped.

'Well that isn't the way to do it.' she thought to herself.

She took a dishtowel and held it tight around her finger. Frustrated she looked around the kitchen. She stared at the refrigerator. She smiled. At least that wouldn't hurt.

Again she shut her eyes and focused on her breathing. Deep and controlled. Floating, calm and relaxed. More breaths in and out, in and out. Finally she opened her eyes and reached for the refrigerator handle and opened the door.

She slammed it shut and ran her fingers through her hair. Why couldn't she do it? She knew what she wanted to do. Maybe she should have talked to Paul about this in a bit more detail. She decided to do that the next time she saw him.

She had started to walk out of the kitchen when her phone chimed. It was on the counter next to the sink. As she got closer she saw it was Patty. She reached for it. And then she froze. She reached again and started to giggle. She tried it slowly a third time and watched with fascination as her hand passed through the phone. She was learning to manipulate the energy in Rosedale. Normal rules would no longer apply. But of course, now she wanted to answer the phone and was starting to get a little nervous about the whole thing. Panic was beginning to set in. She backed away from the phone and tried to calm herself. She shut her eyes and focused again, hoping beyond hope she could reverse what she had done. Deep breaths in and out, calming thoughts, focusing on what she wanted to achieve. The phone stopped ringing. She didn't care. After she had reached total relaxation, she reached for the phone. But this time, she could feel it in her hand. She picked it up. She had done it. She wished she could tell someone what had just happened, but knew it was out of the question. She would wait until she saw Paul again. She had to tell Paul. Her plan was beginning to come together. She smiled. It would be hard to kill someone when you couldn't grab them.

She calmed herself down. She was giddy with excitement. She couldn't wait to experiment with her newly discovered talent. She dialed Patty's number.

"Hello!" said Patty when she answered the call.

"Hi! I'm sorry, I was in the other room and by the time I got to my phone, it stopped ringing."

"No sweat. I was just calling to check on you. Making sure everything's alright."

Maggie thought about what she was about to say. She was going to need Patty's help in a while, but she had to be very careful about what and how much, she told her. "Actually, I'm happy you called. There's something I'd like to talk to you about. Maybe we could get together for lunch or something this week?"

"Yeah, sure. I can do day after tomorrow if that works for you?"

"Great. The diner at, say, 12:30?"

"Okay! See ya!" responded Patty, who then disconnected the call. Maggie stood there for a little bit, thinking about what she was going to say to her friend. She would figure it out. That was the least of her worries.

*　　*　　*

He lived in a small apartment over the hardware store. It was all he needed. He lived there for as long as he could remember and didn't see any reason not to continue doing so. Sometimes he tried to remember why he decided to settle in Rosedale. He couldn't remember. Must have been too long ago. Didn't matter anyway. The town was made for someone like him. Obviously it was a good decision. The apartment consisted of one room that doubled as his bedroom and living room, a small kitchen, bathroom and access to a washer and dryer. Luckily it had come furnished. It wasn't much, but it gave him the freedom to do as he wanted - and it was cheap. Really cheap. The owner of the hardware store hired him do odd jobs from time to time. Everyone knew if there were small jobs anyone needed done around their homes, the hardware store had someone who could do them. It was a perfect set up. It even allowed him access to places he would never have been able to get into under normal circumstances.

He had bought some chicken from the place down the street and was now eating it in the quiet of his apartment, as he sat there by the window, watching the people walk by below. It was a perfect vantage point. Using his fingers, he ripped apart the chicken breast and shoved a piece into his mouth. He liked the quiet. He could sit there for hours, just watching.

He saw the Sheriff earlier, talking to a group of people who were standing around on the sidewalk. He watched him carefully, memorizing every little detail about him. There was something about him he hated. He couldn't figure out exactly what that was though. Maybe it was just the air of confidence Robert despised. Perfect little family. He was still angry that the Sheriff's wife had come to get her daughter from school. She had ruined everything. It seemed odd somehow - the way she looked around before getting into her car. It was almost as though she knew she was being watched. But that was impossible.

He took what was left of the chicken and threw it into the trash, wiping his hands on his pants.

He had the urge. It was time. The voices were loud again. Maybe he'd go for a walk later.

*　　　*　　　*

Maggie spent the rest of the day practicing her new skill. It was getting easier and easier. It seemed to be taking less effort every time she did it. That was good. When the time came, she would need to be able to count on this new trick of hers.

Sam called to let her know he was going to be home late, so she picked Jordan up from school and made dinner for the two of them. She had been trying to come to terms with all the things she had learned - trying to figure out a way to cope with it. She had come to the conclusion that even though she knew she wasn't Jordan's mother on the other side, she was still Jordan's mother here, in Rosedale. The only mother Jordan remembered. She could not have loved her more. The two talked about what was going on in Jordan's school, about her friend Susan and about what she wanted to be when she grew up.

Maggie could only hope she would have that chance. Maggie put the leftovers into the fridge for Sam as Jordan headed up to her room.

She looked at the clock. Sam wasn't going to be home for at least a couple more hours and with Jordan safely in her room, it was the perfect time.

Maggie went up to her bedroom and locked the door. She shut off most of the lights and sat down in the chair next to the window. Even though the thought of connecting with a murderer scared and repulsed her, she knew she had to do just that. Instead of fighting it, she would have to encourage the connection and fall deeper into it. She needed to learn about him. She needed to see who he was. It was the only way she was going to stop him.

She and Paul had discussed how she would try to do this. He claimed her ability to connect with him came from her strong desire to protect her family - much like children who suddenly had the ability to lift cars off a parent trapped beneath. They showed super human strength and she was now showing a super human psychic link. Now though, she wished she had attempted this while he was still there with her. It didn't seem as scary then as it did now that she was actually getting ready to do it.

She got comfortable, shut her eyes and focused on her breathing. Slow and steady. She needed to relax and go wherever the experience wanted to take her. She forced herself to think back to those times she had connected with him. The man she could now only assume was the killer stalking Rosedale. There was a sensation she had during those times. It was hard to explain, but it almost made her feel closed in - as though locked in a small, dark, confined space. She tried to remember that feeling and let it wash over her. In her mind, she saw the hands - his hands ... she felt her chest move in and out, not with her breath, but with someone else's. His. After a while she slowly opened her eyes, both afraid it hadn't worked and afraid it had.

But as she opened her eyes, she saw that she was still in her bedroom, sitting in her chair. But something was different. She felt different. Something was happening. And then, suddenly, it was as though the room started to spin. She thought she was going to be sick. It was like being on a roller coaster that threw the rider up-side-down. She shut her eyes in an attempt to settle herself. And then, with her eyes shut, she started to hear things. In the distance at first, but then louder and clearer. The sound of a clarinet ... no, a trumpet ... maybe both... people... a lot of people talking, laughing. She felt herself being shoved off-balance. There were so many people. Crowds. Then the sensation of her arm above her head, coming down in front of her ... Intense heat on her face. What was it? A fire? Did all these people die in a fire? She wasn't sure.

She opened her eyes and looked at her hands. As before, they weren't hers, they were his. She tried to touch her face, his face, but she didn't have control of them. He did. She was just along for the ride.

Now she saw what he was seeing. She felt excited but didn't want to do anything that might break the connection. She had to remain calm and keep her thoughts at bay. A room. Small. Dirty. Then a light. A sink. A bathroom maybe? And then just for a split second, she thought she saw a reflection in something shiny to the right - she wasn't even sure what. Was it his reflection? It happened so quickly she couldn't be sure. But it was only for a moment. Just not long enough. Just not long enough. Then darkness.

She continued to sit there. But slowly, she could feel things returning to normal. She shut her eyes and when she opened them again, she was sitting in the chair in her bedroom. She glanced at the clock and was surprised to see so much time had passed. She felt frustrated. She thought back to the reflection. At best, maybe she could make out dark hair. But that was it and even that was a stretch.

She would try this again. For now though, she felt exhausted. It was as though the experience had drained everything from her. She started to get up and in that moment, a horrible thought crossed her mind. What if he could see through her, the way she could see through him? The possibility sent chills running down her spine. She doubted it. But if he could, hopefully soon it wouldn't matter anyway.

31

It was still early, but Wyndham was already up, dressed and preparing his breakfast. He looked out his kitchen window as the smell of fresh coffee began to fill the air. He loved this time of day. He was definitely a morning person.

He poured his coffee and took it over to his kitchen table where his plate of scrambled eggs and toast was already waiting for him.

As he ate his breakfast, he couldn't help but think of Maggie. He was worried for her. He had promised he wouldn't ask any questions - and he most certainly wouldn't go against his word - but there was something going on that frightened him. He wasn't sure what it was, but he just felt something wasn't right. He could only hope that she would be safe. He thought very highly of her. In fact, she was probably his most favorite person in all of Rosedale. He was extremely proud of the fact that she took one of his paintings. It was nice to know it meant that much to her.

As he sat there eating, he started thinking about the sketch she had him make. That thought led to another which led to another until finally he was thinking of doing a sketch of Maggie. How wonderful it would be to have a sketch of her in his house. His dear friend. Of course, he'd have to do it from memory since he wanted to surprise her. He would hang it in his living room and then, the next time she came over, oh she would be surprised.

He smiled at the idea. That would be his project for the day. He glanced at the clock.

He was expecting a handy man to come over in a couple of hours to do some jobs around the house. His gate out front was in dire need of a coat of paint. He was actually embarrassed he had let it go this long. And, he needed a dimmer switch installed for the foyer light. At some point he knew he also wanted his shed out back organized. But that could be done at a later date. There was no rush. He had all the time in the world to have it done. But for now, he was excited to start working on the sketch.

He took his dishes to the sink to let them soak and walked out to his studio. The morning sun made everything sparkle. He was excited to get started.

*   *   *

Paul watched as Maggie paced back and forth in the kitchen. "... I just couldn't make it out. It was too quick. And I have absolutely no idea what any of the other stuff meant. If it even meant anything at all. It didn't sound or feel like anything around here." She sighed in frustration. "But the reflection ... now that was something. So, if I do it again - WHEN I do it again, I'll be more prepared for what I might see. Maybe I'll be able to see what he looks like."

"And then what?"

Maggie waited for a moment before answering. "I'm going to find him and kill him."

Paul stared at her.

"Look - how can I tell Sam I know what the killer looks like? What am I going to say - that I dreamed it? Hey give me a second to get into my trance darling so I can tell you where he's hiding out? ... Oh that would be special." Maggie sighed. "I won't be in any danger. With my new trick, he wouldn't be able to touch me much less hurt me. But the beauty of it is, he'll believe that I can kill HIM. So I will. I'll just tell Sam he tried to attack me, the killer will be dead and everyone here in Rosedale will be safe."

"And the killer dies in some hospital bed somewhere on the other side."

"Exactly."

"So how do you propose finding out what he looks like and where he is?"

Maggie looked dejected. "I haven't figured that part out yet."

They both sat at the kitchen table in silence. The same expression on their faces.

"How much time do I have?"

Paul shook his head. "No way of knowing. According to the doctors, you're still fighting it - but I don't know."

"I wonder if I'll get a warning that it's about to happen. Any guesses?"

Paul shook his head. "It could be like flipping a switch or it could be like waking up out of a dream where you start being aware of things around you. But honestly - I have no idea."

Maggie sighed. "Well then I guess I need to keep trying to connect with him. It's my only chance. So - I'll do that and I need you to promise me again that you'll do everything in your power to help me remember when I get back to the other side."

"I promise. But just be aware of something."

Maggie looked at him, waiting for him to continue.

"There's some stuff I'm just guessing at. Pure speculation. I could be wrong. So you need to be careful."

*   *   *

Wyndham was surprised at how quickly his sketch was coming along. Maybe it was the subject matter, but he felt it was going to be his favorite piece. "It's all in the eyes," he mumbled to himself as he did a few finishing touches and stepped back to admire his work. It was beautiful. The woman staring back at him from the sketch pad looked like she was about to speak. Luckily he had some extra frames in the attic and he knew one of them would be perfect. He took a bottle from the shelf and gave the portrait a good spraying. Once it dried, he wouldn't have to worry about the sketch smearing. It would look this way forever.

Just as he replaced the bottle, his doorbell rang. For a second he wondered who it might be and then he remembered - the handy man.

He chuckled to himself that he could actually be that forgetful. Perhaps his memory was starting to fail him. He wiped his hands on a small rag he had grabbed from his studio and opened the front door.

The look of the man standing in front of him gave Wyndham a start. It was a knee jerk reaction that he hoped the man hadn't noticed. There, standing in front of him, was a surprisingly large man dressed in jeans and a black t-shirt with dirty brown hair and a slightly protruding forehead. What caught Wyndham off guard though were his eyes. They were dead. They reminded Wyndham of a shark's eyes. It was oddly disturbing.

"Are you Wyndham Hart?" the man inquired.

Again Wyndham felt uneasy. The man's voice took him by surprise. Very low and there was no inflection at all. It sounded strangely flat. Still, in his head Wyndham felt terrible for having these thoughts. Bad toilet training was something he apparently suffered from as well.

"Yes, I'm Wyndham and you must be the gentleman from the hardware store - the one who's going to be helping me out today."

The man in front of him nodded yes, in a very slow and exaggerated manner. Wyndham tried not to stare. He didn't want to appear rude. "And your name is?"

"Robert Kraus".

Wyndham waited for a few moments, expecting Robert Kraus might want to say something more. But he didn't, so Wyndham continued. "Well I'm thinking we might want to start with painting the gate? That way it will be well on its way to drying. And then maybe the dimmer switch? How does that sound?"

"Fine."

Again Wyndham waited for a few moments until he was sure this man wasn't going to speak any further. It was awkward but, as Wyndham told himself, he's a handyman here to do his job, not to socialize. "Well in that case, why don't you go out to the gate and I'll join you in a few moments with the paint and the paint brush."

Without saying a word, Robert turned and walked down the steps to the gate.

Wyndham shut the front door and collected the paint and painting supplies to take out to Robert. He also told himself he needed to be less judgmental of others. He was probably a very nice man - just shy. Wyndham would try to make him feel more at ease.

*   *   *

Paul left, leaving Maggie to continue practicing and trying to connect with the killer. She felt frustrated and exhausted but wasn't going to give up.

Every now and then her mind would wander to her other life. Would she know Vicki, who according to Paul, was her best friend? And would she instantly remember her husband and daughter - the ones on the other side? It broke her heart to think that she would have to forget in order to remember. None of this made sense and the more she tried to navigate through it, the more confused, frustrated and depressed she became. She needed to focus.

She practiced her trick and was now extremely good at it. But she still needed to figure out where this guy was. She had plenty of time, so she decided to go back up to her bedroom and try again. Maybe this time she'd get lucky.

She was halfway up the stairs when it hit her. She was dizzy. Very dizzy. She hung onto the railing to stop from falling and sat down on a step with her head on her knees trying not to pass out. Like the time before, her heart started pounding and the room was spinning around her. She took deep breaths in and out and shut her eyes. She recognized the feeling and she wasn't going to fight it. She would welcome it.

After a few moments she felt different. She opened her eyes and discovered she was no longer sitting on her staircase, but rather she was outside. She could feel the warmth of the sun on her back. She looked down at her hands and this time, she wasn't surprised to see they were a man's hands - this time she was happy. Lawns, trees, a sidewalk. This wasn't Jordan's school. Where was this? A street. A residential street. Is this where he lived? Then a quick glance at a front porch. She recognized the porch. She recognized the house. It was Wyndham's.

She could feel herself panicking. She shut her eyes and took deep breaths. She had to end this. She had to get to Wyndham before the unimaginable happened.

Deep breaths in and out, in and out and although it seemed to take forever, she finally found herself back in her house on the stairs.

She ran back down to the kitchen and grabbed her purse and keys from the counter and raced out the front door, not bothering to lock it behind her. She needed to get to Wyndham's immediately.

She started the car and gunned it. Before she knew it she was racing down the street and talking to herself at the same time. It was going to be okay. She was going to get there in time. She had to. It seemed to take forever, but finally she turned onto his street and then into his driveway. Throwing the car into park and grabbing the key out of the ignition, she ran to the front door and started pounding on it, calling his name at the same time. She tried the door but it was locked. She rang the doorbell over and over again. Her heart felt like it was in her stomach. She was expecting the worse.

But then she heard a sound coming from inside the house and watched as the door handle turned. For a second she felt afraid that maybe she would be staring at the face of the killer. But before she could give that a second thought, the door opened and there in front of her was Wyndham looking very surprised. She couldn't help herself. She threw her arms around him and hugged him.

"Oh my Mrs. Cooper. What on earth is wrong?" asked Wyndham as he ushered her into is house, closing and locking the door behind her.

Maggie forced herself to smile while trying to shake off the panic that was still inside of her.

"Please Mrs. Cooper." continued Wyndham as he motioned to his sofa. "Have a seat and tell me what's happening."

Maggie sat down and took a deep breath. "I'm so sorry. I didn't mean to upset you. Please don't ask why, but I got this overwhelming feeling there was someone here with you. I guess I was just being silly."

Wyndham looked at her. A slightly confused expression crossed his face that Maggie failed to notice. "Well, in fact there was."

Maggie stared at him.

"It was just a handyman doing some things around my house. But he left a little while ago. Painted my gate and look!"

Wyndham got up, walked to the foyer switch and moved the dimmer control up and down. "I can now have wonderful soothing light in this foyer in the evening."

He noticed Maggie wasn't speaking. "Mrs. Cooper?"

Maggie's thoughts were spinning in her head. "What did he look like?"

Wyndham started to speak when she cut him off.

"Actually, even better, could you do a sketch of him for me?"

Wyndham looked a little perplexed but remembered his promise of no questions. "Yes of course. Let's go to my studio."

Maggie followed him there and sat at the small table while he sketched. She looked around. Now she was wishing the room wasn't so exposed. The windows she thought were so beautiful earlier, now made her nervous. She wondered if he was out there watching them.

It felt like hours had passed before Wyndham put down his pencil, although she knew it had only been maybe 20 minutes.

"Well it certainly isn't my best work, but here he is." said Wyndham as he turned the pad around for Maggie to see.

She stared at it without saying a word. Finally. She knew what he looked like. This was the person she had been connecting with. This was the killer.

"I really do hate to be uncharitable," started Wyndham, sounding apologetic, "but I must say God wasn't very kind to this poor fellow."

Maggie had to agree. It was his eyes. Something about his eyes that sent chills down her spine. She found it almost impossible to look away.

"But," continued Wyndham, "Robert did a fine job even though he isn't much of a looker and definitely not much of a talker either."

Maggie looked up from the photo. Her eyes were wide. "Robert? That's his name?"

Wyndham smiled. "Yes of course. Robert. Robert ... oh heavens what did he say his last name was? I'm so forgetful lately ... " Wyndham's brow furrowed as he thought back. "Kraus! Yes that's it! Robert Kraus. I can certainly give him good references as far as his quality of work goes."

Maggie couldn't believe what she was hearing. Was this possible? "Robert Kraus?" she repeated, trying to appear calm. "I wonder where he lives."

"Oh that's easy," replied Wyndham with a smile on his face. "He lives in the apartment right above Smith's Hardware, on the far end of Main Street. He does odd jobs for the hardware store, so if you'd like to hire him, just call the store and they'll set up an appointment for you."

Maggie could barely breathe. "May I take the sketch with me?"

Again Wyndham looked confused over the request, but a promise was a promise. "Yes of course you can."

They stood and started to walk towards the front door. Maggie held onto the sketch.

"Are you sure you don't want to stay?" asked Wyndham.

Maggie smiled at him. "No, I have to go really, but ..." She glanced up and noticed the sketch he had made of her hanging on his wall. It was beautiful. She looked back at Wyndham. He was smiling so much it looked as though he was simply beaming.

"Do you like it?"

"Oh Wyndham it's beautiful."

"I'm happy you approve. It shall stay on that wall and every time I walk past, I will think of my good friend."

Maggie stared at him, trying to figure out how to word what she was about to say. "Wyndham, I can't tell you why I think so, but I need you to believe me, trust me and not doubt anything I'm about to say."

The smile on Wyndham's face slowly disappeared and was now replaced by a look of solemn concern. "Yes, of course."

Maggie took a deep breath. "I have reason to believe you're in danger. Possibly from the serial killer. In fact, this Robert guy probably IS the serial killer. I can't tell Sam yet because he'll want to know how I know and ... well, I can't tell him - the same way I can't tell you. But you need to believe me. I know this sounds awfully mysterious, but - do you have someone in town you could go visit for a few days? That might be a good idea. And I want you to promise me you're going to be extremely careful. If anything - and I mean anything - doesn't feel right, or if you see this man again, you'll do what you have to do to be safe."

Wyndham stared intently at his friend. "Oh my. Well, this is a bit of a surprise now, isn't it?"

He could see just from looking at her that what she was saying was the truth. He didn't need to ask how she knew. That didn't matter. He would believe her.

He stepped up and hugged her as tightly as he could. They stood like that for a few moments until he finally stepped back and looked into her eyes. "I promise. I promise I'll be safe. I haven't been around this long to have someone else decide when my time is up. I'll be safe and you be safe too, Mrs. Cooper. You and I are destined to be friends for a long, long time."

32

The next morning Maggie could barely focus on making breakfast for her family. She tried as hard as she could to make herself appear perfectly normal when inside she was absolutely panicking. Today was the day. She was still formulating the plan in her head, but she knew she couldn't keep putting it off. It had to be today. She was having lunch with Patty and still needed to figure out what she wanted to say to her. Part of her felt she should keep Patty out of it - but if things went wrong, she felt she needed to have her around. Frustrated that she couldn't make up her mind, she decided to think about it later. She seemed to be having issues making any decisions. Maybe it was because she didn't sleep well, but she wasn't feeling herself. She was feeling off somehow. She chalked it up to her nervousness or maybe because she had spent almost every waking moment looking at the sketch Wyndham drew of the killer. She would have no problem identifying him.

Finally she was walking Sam and Jordan to the door. Jordan gave her a quick kiss on the cheek and headed out to Sam's patrol car. Maggie however couldn't seem to say goodbye to Sam. They stood there together looking at each other. Sam could tell something was different, but he didn't know what.

"What are you thinking Mrs. Cooper?" asked Sam as he put his arms around her and looked into her eyes.

"I'm thinking how much I love you and how I never want to lose you."

Sam smiled. "That's not ever going to happen ... and I love you too."

"Guess I'm feeling kind of sad this morning for some reason. Could I get you to hold me for a little bit before you leave?"

Sam pulled her to him. She buried her face into the base of his neck.

"You never have to ask me twice to do that."

There, in Sam's arms, Maggie took deep breaths in and out, in and out, until she relaxed. In her mind, she repeated his name over and over. She thought of how he looked at her, how he smiled at her. She thought of how much she loved him. A few moments later, she slowly pulled away. There was a tear in her eye.

Sam looked concerned. "What is it?"

Maggie shook her head, forced herself to smile and wiped the tear away. "Just me being silly. Just thinking about how lucky I am to have found you. Now - you go on and get to work before they call the police on you."

Sam laughed, kissed her and then headed towards his car. Maggie watched and waved as they disappeared down the street. She wondered how many more times she would be able to do that.

She locked the door and headed up to her bedroom. She took a long hot shower hoping that would make her feel better. Was she coming down with something? Was that even possible?

She put on her jeans and a pull over, grabbed her purse and headed downstairs and into the kitchen. She stopped and looked around. It really did look like her grandmother's kitchen. In fact, almost identical. She smiled. She then opened one of the kitchen drawers and took out a knife. It was the largest one she could fit into her purse.

She picked up the car keys and headed out.

Before she knew it, she was already at the diner. She was surprised because it felt as though she had just left the house. Obviously her mind had been somewhere else.

She parked the car and went into the restaurant. She waved hello to Robin who motioned to the booth in the back. Soon she and Patty were eating their lunch.

"Okay - so what's up? I've known you long enough to know when something's up." asked Patty as she took a sip of her soda.

"I'm going to need your help."

Patty studied her for a moment. "This is going to be one of those things I'm not supposed to tell Sam about, isn't it?"

Maggie smiled and nodded.

Patty let out an exaggerated sigh. "Okay I'm ready. Shoot."

"I need you to sit with me, in your car. There's someone I need to talk to, but I need to catch them at home, so we may have to wait in your car for a while until they show up."

A few seconds passed.

"You know that sounds weird, right? Why not just call — Oh, right, I forgot. No questions. Okey dokey. And you're not cheating on Sam?"

"Oh God no. I swear. I'd never do anything like that."

"Well then, let's go sit in my car!"

Patty flagged Robin to bring the bill.

"I have to say one thing though...," said Patty as she took another sip of her soda, "... being your friend is a very strange experience."

Maggie smiled. She was about to do something that terrified her. She wondered how her friend would feel about her then.

They left the diner and got into Patty's car. She started it and then looked at Maggie.

"Just drive in that direction until we get about four doors away from the hardware store. Please."

Patty nodded and then pulled out. Maggie just stared at the window.

"What?" asked Maggie as she turned to look at her friend.

Patty looked surprised and shook her head. "I didn't say anything."

"Oh. I could have sworn you said something." Maggie brushed it off. She just wished she felt better. With what she was about to do, she needed to be able to think clearly.

"Alright, there's a parking spot there." said Maggie as she pointed to an empty parking spot about half a block away from the hardware store and a bit less than that to the door that led to the apartment above.

"Now what?" asked Patty as she turned off the car.

"Now, we wait."

Patty shrugged and tilted her seat back. "Well I'm going to close my eyes for a bit. You let me know if anything happens."

"I will." mumbled Maggie as she scanned the street. She didn't know his schedule. Didn't know if he'd be leaving his apartment or going to it. She would wait and if she didn't see him, she would go through that door and wait for him by his apartment door. She assumed the door outside was a community entrance, so she should be able to get in. She felt better now that she had a plan - sort of. She opened her purse and looked at the knife. Her stomach was doing flips. She had to do this. She had to protect these people she loved.

They sat there for what felt like hours, but Maggie knew it couldn't have been that long. She hoped he would show up soon because she was feeling worse by the minute.

Just as she was about to tell Patty that she was going to wait inside the building, she saw him. She held her breath. He was walking towards them. He was holding a bag in his hand. He was bigger than she had imagined. She prayed her little trick would work when she needed it to, because if it didn't, she'd never be able to fend him off. She watched as he walked past the hardware store and then to the door that led to the apartments. He looked around for a second and then opened the door and walked inside.

Maggie could barely catch her breath. She shook Patty awake. Patty looked at her.

"I'm going into that door. I need to talk to someone. If I'm not back in about 20 minutes - call Sam."

She was out of the car before Patty could say anything. Her heart was pounding. She ran up to the door and reached for the doorknob. She saw her hand almost touch it. And then ...

Patty sat in her car for a moment, adjusting her seat. She looked at herself in the rear view mirror and fixed her lipstick. Putting the mirror back in place, she started her car and pulled out into traffic. She wondered if she'd ever be able to sell that house she just listed.

In another part of Rosedale, Wyndham was admiring the sketch he had hung in his living room. It was a beautiful landscape. But something was bothering him. Why did he do so many landscapes when it was portraits he loved so much? He decided to focus more on portraits. That made him smile.

Slowly the darkness began to lift. She heard someone calling her name. What were those other sounds? Voices, a lot of voices. Someone was holding her hand.

She slowly opened her eyes. It was like a fog lifting. Her eyes couldn't focus. She blinked. She felt confused.

Every so slowly people came into focus. They were standing around her. She looked around. Who were these people? And then she saw Vicki. Vicki was smiling.

"So what's everybody doing here?" Maggie said softly. It was hard to talk. Her throat felt raw. "Water."

Someone held a straw to her lips. They were saying things but she couldn't seem to concentrate. She took a small sip. It felt amazing. She started looking around the room - as much as she could. She was still having trouble. There were doctors and nurses, her friend Vicki and some other guy she didn't recognize. He didn't seem to be a doctor but it didn't matter. Gradually it hit her and she realized where she was - and why. She started to cry. David and Laura were gone.

33

A few days later she was released from Piedmont Hospital. They said she was good enough to go home, but she was terrified of what was waiting for her there. The memories. An empty house filled with memories.

The doctors had her begin counseling sessions, which was something she would have to do for a while. She was willing to go through it to make everyone happy but deep down knew it wouldn't do anything. It wouldn't bring them back. It wouldn't take away the pain. At the end of the day, she would still be alone with an unbearable feeling of emptiness.

They wheeled her out to Vicki's car. Luckily she would be able to stay with Vicki for a while instead of having to be in her own house. She was grateful for that.

The ride to Sandy Springs was quiet. Maggie felt tired and embarrassed by what she had done - or tried to do. She could sense how awkward things were between her and her friend.

"Listen," she started, "I'm sorry for what I did. I know it was stupid and I know it hurt you. That was never my intent. But truthfully, that night ... it was as if it all hit me at once - the shock, the loss, the loneliness. In that moment, I really didn't see any reason to carry on. I just wanted to sleep. Just sleep and never wake up. So, please don't feel like you have to avoid talking to me about anything. Seriously. If you want to yell at me - have at it. Whatever you need to say."

She looked at Vicki. Her blond hair swept back in a ponytail, the lack of makeup - she looked tired. Maggie knew she had done that to her friend. How would she ever forgive herself for what she had put Vicki through.

Vicki looked at her and smiled. "I'm not going to yell at you. I completely understand. What you've been through - I don't know if I could have handled it. I'm certainly not going to judge you. You're my friend and I love you. I just wish I could take away the pain. But since I can't, I want you to know that if you ever need to talk - or you just need to scream - I'm here. I mean that."

Maggie wiped a tear from her eye. "Thank you." she said softly.

"Hey that's what friends are for." replied Vicki "And thank God you gave me Power of Attorney after ... well, I would have been out of my mind not knowing how you were."

Maggie smiled weakly. "If it's okay with you, since I promise never to do this again, I'd like to keep it that way. I don't have anyone else. And I trust you."

Vicki reached over and squeezed Maggie's hand. "We'll be home in a minute."

Maggie cleared her throat. "Would you mind if we did something before we go back to your house?"

Vicki looked at her. She knew what Maggie was saying. She nodded and turned on her turn signal.

Before long, Maggie was standing in the cemetery looking down at two headstones. Vicki had moved off so as to give Maggie the privacy she knew she wanted. Maggie felt numb. She had cried so much. She had been angry, then made deals with God and then tried to kill herself when she couldn't take it any more. But now, as she stood staring at the headstones, she just felt empty. Empty, tired and beaten down. It had never occurred to her that David and Laura might leave her one day. Now as she thought about her future, it just felt bleak and lonely. She took a deep breath and brought her fingers to her lips. She kissed them and touched each head-stone. How she wished things had been different.

Finally she walked towards Vicki. She had done what she needed to do. She no longer had a choice. She had to get her life together. She had to learn to live again.

The two friends walked back to Vicki's car. Driving away, Maggie watched out the passenger window, as the cemetery slowly faded into the distance.

Vicki waited a couple of minutes before speaking. "By the way, do you remember Paul?"

"Who?"

"My friend - Paul Treadway. He was at the hospital with me the day you woke up."

Maggie thought for a moment and shook her head. "I can barely remember anything from that day. I'm sorry."

"Well don't worry about it. But I hope you don't mind ... I invited him over for dinner tomorrow night."

Maggie smiled. "Anything you want to do is fine with me. So is he a friend or a "friend" and why haven't I heard about him before?"

Vicki laughed. "He's a friend who I wouldn't mind having as a "friend", if you get my drift."

Maggie smiled. She was glad to see Vicki laughing. She needed to hear laughter.

Before long they had arrived at Vicki's house - a comfortable three bedroom ranch with an enormous front yard and huge trees. It didn't take long for Maggie to unpack the suitcase Vicki had brought for her. After a relaxing shower she started feeling more like herself again. She dried her hair and put on her t-shirt and borrowed robe. She was looking forward to meeting Paul. She noticed how much Vicki smiled when she talked about him. But tonight, what she was looking forward to the most, was sleeping. She was exhausted.

She walked out to the kitchen where she heard Vicki putting away dishes. She put her arms around her friend and hugged her. "I want to thank you. And to tell you I'm just so sorry I put you through all of this. I don't know what I'd do without a friend like you."

Vicki tried not to cry. But even still, one tear had managed to escape down her cheek. She brushed it away. "You don't have to thank me. Friends are there for each other. And you are more than welcome to stay here with me for as long as you'd like. Truthfully, I'd enjoy the company."

"Thank you." replied Maggie. "And if you don't mind - as much as I would love to stay up, I really am exhausted. You'd think being in a coma, I would have had enough sleep, but I guess not."

Vicki stared at her friend for a minute, a smile on her face. "You go to bed. Get some rest. And sleep in as long as you'd like. I'll see you whenever you get up tomorrow."

With that, the friends said goodnight and Maggie retired to her room. It didn't take long before she fell into a deep, restful asleep.

The next day Maggie was surprised she slept as late as she had. After a relaxing breakfast and conversation with Vicki out on the back porch, before they knew it, most of the day had passed and soon Paul would be over for dinner. Maggie took a shower, put on her makeup and jeans and joined Vicki in the kitchen. Even though Vicki kept insisting Maggie rest, she wanted to help. She needed to do something. She didn't like feeling as though she was a burden. She was just finishing up setting the table when there was a knock at the front door.

"That's Paul. I'll be right back."

Maggie continued setting the table, trying not to think about what she was going to do with her life now that it had changed so completely. She tried to push those thoughts out of her mind. She had time to think about that. Tonight, she was just going to enjoy the evening. The sadness would be waiting for her tomorrow and the day after. She would deal with it then. She heard voices coming from the foyer and then saw Vicki walk into the kitchen with a man following behind her.

She immediately liked him, which was something that took her by surprise. Shaggy brown hair and glasses and a wonderful smile. She couldn't help but smile in return.

"How are you Maggie? You're looking well."

"Thank you. I'm feeling good, really. I'm happy I have the chance to officially meet you. Vicki speaks very highly of you."

"That's always good to know!"

Vicki hit him in the arm with a dishtowel and smiled. "If you could open the wine for us that would be great."

"My pleasure." responded Paul as he made his way to the counter, taking the corkscrew from Vicki.

"So, what is it you do?" asked Maggie.

"I'm a therapist actually."

"Oh, well that's … appropriate."

Paul smiled at her. "Please no. Don't feel awkward. We all go through things. That's certainly not why I'm here. If it would make you feel better, I could tell you I was a construction worker."

Maggie pretended to think it over. "Perfect! Got any funny construction job stories?"

Paul laughed.

Before long, the three were enjoying dinner as if they had all known each other all their lives. The more Maggie got to know Paul, the more she liked him. Conversation and laughter flowed freely. It was the perfect evening. After they finished eating, they retired to the living room where Maggie got comfortable in the over-sized chair, letting Vicki and Paul get cozy on the sofa.

After a while, she noticed Paul was looking at her, but not saying anything. The expression on his face had changed slightly.

"What is it?" she asked him outright.

"I was just thinking. Have you ever been under hypnosis?"

A little taken aback by the question, Maggie laughed. "No. Can't say I ever tried it."

"Well, in my practice, I use hypnosis a lot. It really helps my patients deal with a variety of issues. Not to mention they feel rested and renewed after they come out of a session. I'm thinking maybe it might help you feel better."

Maggie looked at him, not sure what he was asking.

"Why don't you try it Maggie?" asked Vicki. "It can't hurt and who knows, you might feel like a new woman. You've been through a lot. What have you got to lose?"

Maggie considered what they were saying. She was starting to feel a little pressured by them, but Vicki was right, what did she have to lose? She certainly wouldn't mind

feeling better. She felt anything but. "Okay …
what do I do?"

"Lift up the foot rest. I want you to get
comfortable. Completely comfortable. I'm
going to shut off a few of these lights."

Maggie settled into the chair, feeling a
little silly.

"You aren't going to make me cluck like a
chicken or anything, are you?" she asked him,
smiling.

"Not today. I only do that on Wednes-
days." replied Paul.

He pulled a small stool closer to her and
sat down. He looked at her. "Maggie. I need
you to trust me. Can you do that?"

Maggie took a moment to answer. "This
is going to sound strange considering I just
met you, but I do trust you." She took a deep
breath.

"Alright. I'm going to handle this the
way I would a past life regression. I'm going
to ask you to visit places that your conscious
mind can't remember but your subconscious

should. So I'm going to need you to simply go with what I'm saying and not question it. Can you please do that?"

Maggie nodded and glanced over at Vicki for support, who gave her a thumbs up and a reassuring look.

"Alright then. Let's get started. Uncross your arms and legs, close your eyes. With your eyes closed, start by rolling your eyes gently upward. Begin by taking a deep breath in … hold it … and just let it out slowly now… And again … All you hear is my voice, nothing else, just concentrate on my voice."

Maggie did as she was told. As she started taking in the breaths as he was instructing, she was already starting to feel different.

He went on to tell her to relax her muscles starting in her feet and then her legs, her hips, her back … to feel her arms hanging at her sides …

Soon she found herself drifting. It was as though she would hear his voice and then realize she had gone somewhere and needed to come back to hear his voice again. She was floating. His voice was the only thing she was aware of. It was soothing and soft.

He continued. "You're standing in your kitchen. But not the one here in Atlanta, you're in your kitchen in Rosedale. It's white. It reminds you of your grandmother's kitchen doesn't it?"

Slowly Maggie nodded her head. In her mind she was walking around the room, looking out a bay window at a backyard.

"You're putting the kettle on the stove. You feel the handle in your hand as you pick it up. Breathe in ... and out ... Sam walks in. He smiles at you. Do you see him?"

Again Maggie slowly nods her head and there's the slightest smile.

"You're in Rosedale. Jordan walks into the kitchen and gives you a hug."

Maggie smiles and then drifts off once more.

"You have friends ... think of your friends ... all of them. Remember them ... remember the things you talked about with them. Remember their faces ... their voices ... remember everything Maggie. Wyndham. Patty. Remember everyone in Rosedale. It's safe. You're safe. You need to remember. Breathe in ... breathe out ..."

Maggie felt as though she no longer had a body. She had no idea of time. She was adrift. She was in Rosedale. Her friends were there ... all of them. She remembered them ... she remembered their names. She was remembering everything. Again she drifted away and then found herself drifting back to Paul's soothing voice.

"I'm going to count backwards from five. When I get to one, you will open your eyes and feel refreshed. You will remember everything we did here. You will remember everything. Five ... you can feel yourself starting to rise to the surface; Four ... you're starting to feel the chair beneath you and beginning to feel a bit more aware; Three ... you're starting to wake up. You are here in Vicki's living room in Atlanta; Two ... you're almost awake now; One ... open your eyes Maggie.

Maggie's eyes opened. It took her a minute to get her bearings. Slowly she turned her head and looked at Paul. "I didn't kill him. I never had the chance. But I know who he is."

34

A couple of days had passed since her hypnosis session with Paul. She needed time to adjust. She needed time to organize her thoughts. Time to let her mind accept two completely different realities. Suddenly it was as though she was living in two worlds. And, she needed time to deal with the guilt. How to mourn the loss of David and Laura while at the same time mourn the loss of Sam and Jordan. It was all very confusing and was tearing her up emotionally.

On top of that, she had some decisions to make. She needed time to think things through and figure out what she wanted to do - what she needed to do - without anyone influencing her. This had to be her decision alone.

She had told Paul everything she remembered and knew about the killer. She was grateful she remembered the name Wyndham had told her. The question was however, was that his name in this world as well? Paul thought there was a good chance of that, pointing out Maggie's subconscious wanted the family back that she had lost, so taking on Sam's name would have been necessary for her illusion to work. The same wouldn't necessarily be so for Robert Kraus. Maggie agreed, although she resented him referring to her experience as an illusion. Rosedale wasn't an illusion. It was real. So was Sam.

She had just finished making her bed when she heard the doorbell ring. She could hear Paul and Vicki talking in the foyer. She went out to meet them.

"Hi there. How are you holding up?" asked Paul.

She noticed he was carrying a duffle bag. "I'm good thank you. Better every day."

"Maybe we should go sit at the kitchen table." said Vicki. "It might be easier to set up in there."

The three walked into the kitchen. While Paul took out his laptop and a pad of paper, Maggie poured herself a cup of coffee. Her stomach was in knots. Part of her couldn't wait to hear what Paul had to say and the other part of her just wanted to run away.

She took her coffee and sat down opposite Paul and waited. Vicki joined in, looking nervous.

"Well," started Paul as he was typing on his laptop, "you'd be surprised how many Robert Kraus's there are. I narrowed it down based on the general age and the description you gave me. And then I started thinking about those other things you said ... the crowds, the music. Is it possible it was New Orleans?"

Maggie thought for a moment. "I guess so, I don't know."

"Well that's what I thought. So ..."

"Paul?" interrupted Vicki.

"Yeah?"

"As terribly interesting as all of this is ... maybe you could just jump to the end?"

Paul smiled at her. "In that case, drum roll please - is this your guy?"

And with that, Paul turned his laptop around to face Maggie. Her breath caught in her throat. There, on the screen was a photo of Robert Kraus staring back at her. His eyes. Those dead eyes staring through her. Suddenly she felt ill. She ran from the table, into the bathroom down the hall and threw up. Seeing that face again affected her in a way she never expected.

"Are you okay?"

It was Vicki calling to her from the other side of the door.

"Yeah, just give me a second. I'll be right there."

After a few minutes, Maggie, looking a little pale, returned to the kitchen. "I'm sorry."

"Do you want Paul to stop for now?" asked Vicki.

Maggie shook her head. "No. It just took me by surprise that's all."

She sat back down at the table. "So what's his story?"

Paul took a deep breath before starting. "Well definitely not a good guy. This was actually his mug shot. Apparently his side hobby was being a peeping tom. He was charged with loitering and prowling, but I guess the charges were eventually dropped because I couldn't find anything more about that."

"How does a guy go from being a peeping tom to murderer?" asked Maggie, looking a little confused.

"Well, this guy had issues - big issues. The family moved to New Orleans from some small town in North Carolina - that's why you were sensing the music and the crowds. When he was nineteen years old, he killed his mother - with a sledgehammer no less - and then set fire to the house. Luckily his brother who was asleep at the time, managed to get out. The local paper ran the story but it never made national news. Guess it was just another murder in a sea of murders."

"Nice guy." mumbled Vicki.

"Real nice. Apparently later they started taking another look into unsolved murders in the area - primarily in the 9th Ward, thinking maybe this guy was responsible for those too."

"So what happened to him?" asked Maggie

"Well," continued Paul, "the next day, after killing his mother, he comes back to the scene of the crime and is spotted by police. They chase him down, tell him to stop, he refuses, he runs at them with a knife. And of course they shoot. The officers were investigated and they were all cleared."

"So ...?"

Paul looked at Maggie. "He survived. They operated, but he never woke up from his coma. He's still alive. He's in New Orleans."

Maggie thought for a moment. "Nineteen? How is that even possible. He looked like he was in his thirties."

Paul just shrugged.

"Wait a second." said Maggie, still thinking through what she was about to say. "The timing is off. When did all of this happen?"

Paul crossed his arms and looked at Maggie. "Two years ago."

Maggie sat back in her chair. "What? No that doesn't make sense. I was there and THEN the killing started. I can't believe he was in Rosedale, what, two years before me? Unless he was there but didn't do anything until after I showed up ..."

Paul shook his head. "That I can't tell you. Maybe he kept his nose clean for a while

... maybe he was better at hiding his activities and no one noticed till later ... or, I don't know - maybe you just can't judge time in Rosedale like you can here. Remember, it's like a dream. You thought you'd been there for years, when in reality, it couldn't have been more than a couple of weeks. So I can't answer that. But what I can say is - if this is the face you saw - then this is him."

Maggie stared at the computer screen and into the eyes of Robert Kraus. Finally she looked up. "Well then, I guess I have to go."

Paul looked confused. "Go where?"

"To New Orleans. I have to find him and I have to kill him."

"Whoa whoa whoa!" exclaimed Paul. "Let's back up here for a second. Ok? It's one thing to talk about killing him in Rosedale - I mean that's like killing someone in the Land of Oz - but this is the real world! We have real laws, real police and real prisons! Geez Maggie you can't just go around killing people."

Maggie got up from the table and started pacing. "Listen, you may think Rosedale is the Land of Oz, but it's not. It's very real. I was there. And this guy isn't just killing people in some sort of dream world. They are dying right here, in what you call the real world. The only difference is, no one realizes it's him doing it. They're thinking it's heart attacks and strokes. But does that make him any less dangerous? Does that make what he's doing any less real?"

Paul sat at the table thinking about what Maggie had said. He looked at Vicki who was just staring at him and not saying a word. His mind was spinning. "I hate this. I really do hate this."

Vicki took his hand. "I can't believe I'm going to say this, Paul. But you know she's right."

Paul nodded. "Yeah - and that's the part I hate."

Maggie sighed in relief. "We're going to have to figure out where he is right now. He's obviously still alive and still in a coma. Once we find out where he is exactly in New Orleans, I'm going to have to come up with a plan."

35

Within 24 hours, all three were on a flight heading to New Orleans. She wondered what they might face when they got there. It didn't seem right to involve Paul and Vicki. This was her battle and she felt it should be hers alone to fight. But, there was no talking them out of helping her - although she made it clear that only she would be the one responsible for his death.

If they could find him.

An hour and a half later they were landing at Louis Armstrong New Orleans International Airport. They only brought carry on luggage, so it made the whole process easier and quicker. She rented a car from the airport kiosk and before long, they had checked into their hotel and were on their way to grab a quick bite to eat.

It was already dark outside as they walked down the street heading towards the restaurant. Maggie was taken aback by the sounds and smells of the city. They reminded her of what she had experienced when she was connected to Robert. This was definitely the place. She could feel it. She could feel him. It made her skin crawl to think he had walked these streets. That this is where he had killed his mother and possibly countless others.

She heard music playing somewhere in the distance as they entered a quaint restaurant on one of the side streets, called Belleville's. The food took their minds off of what they were there to do - but only temporarily. After their dinner of shrimp étouffé, they sat silently at the table, sipping coffee. They hadn't uttered a word for some time. Each of them lost in their own thoughts.

It was Paul who broke the silence. "I know where he is."

Maggie looked surprised. "Why didn't you say something earlier? I've been panicking wondering how we were going to figure that out."

Paul sighed. "I guess ... I guess I just wanted to think about it before we stepped off the cliff. But the more I thought about what you said, I realized we have no other choice. This is the right thing to do."

"So where is he?" asked Vicki

"A place called St. Aloysius Nursing Home. It's a long-term care facility in the 9th Ward. That's where they sent him after they took him out of East Hospital."

"So now we just have to go there, figure out what room he's in and ..." Maggie was at a loss as to what came next. "Has anyone thought about how exactly I'm going to do this? I know it's a little late in the game to ask that question..." She lowered her voice. "Do I unplug something or ... what?"

Paul raised his hand. "I may have some answers for you."

"We're all ears." responded Vicki, leaning closer to him.

"First of all, we don't have to figure out what room he's in. I already know what room he's in."

"How?" asked Maggie

Paul shrugged. "We're assuming this is a lot more complicated than it really is. I called them before we left Atlanta. It's like any hospital. You ask what room a patient is in and they tell you. He's in Room 210. It's not a private room, but it's a nursing home. I'm going to go out on a limb and say we probably won't have to worry about whoever else is sharing the room with him."

"So how do I do it?"

"Well that I'm going to have to get back to you on." He looked at his watch. "In fact," continued Paul as he started to get up, "I've got to run an errand. I want the two of you to take a cab back to the hotel. No walking. I'll meet you back there in a few."

"Where are you going?" asked Vicki, looking concerned.

Paul shook his head. "You don't need to know. It's fine. Nothing to worry about. See you in a few." They watched as he walked away from the table and out the front door.

It was an hour later, as they were pacing around Maggie's hotel room when they finally heard a knock at the door. She hurried over to it, looked through the peep hole and opened the door to Paul. Vicki let out an audible sigh of relief.

"So where did you go?" she asked. It was then she noticed the brown paper bag that he was pulling out from inside his jacket.

"What's in the bag?" asked Maggie.

Paul reached into the bag and produced a small vial. He held it up between his two fingers so the women could see it.

"Potassium Chloride."

"Where did you get that?"

He smiled at Maggie. "It doesn't matter."

Maggie stared at him. "So what does it do?"

"This is one of the drugs they use in prisons when they carry out a death sentence. This, injected into a vein, will produce death in under two minutes. It stops the heart. And unless they look for Potassium Chloride, which I strongly doubt they will, they'll just assume he had a heart attack."

Maggie slowly exhaled. "I'm going to need a syringe and ..."

Before she could continue, Paul dumped the rest of the contents of the bag onto the bed. Three syringes and a rubber tourniquet. "Just like when they take blood. Tie the rubber band around his arm, inject the needle into a vein and that's it - of course pushing in, not ... out."

"Three syringes?" inquired Maggie.

Paul shrugged. "They were having a sale - you just need one."

Maggie picked up the vial. "Is this going to be enough?"

"Enough for him and then some."

Maggie barely slept that night. The combination of anticipation and dread made it virtually impossible. She wondered if Paul and Vicki were feeling the same. She only hoped she wasn't too late.

She replayed what she would have to do over and over in her mind. She prayed they would be successful. She also prayed for forgiveness.

Morning couldn't come soon enough. At the first sign of daylight, Maggie was up and showering. She wanted to get it over with. She wanted to go home. She was putting the vial of Potassium Chloride securely into her purse when she heard a knock at her door.

It was Paul and Vicki.

"Okay. I'm ready. How did you guys sleep?"

"What sleep?" asked Vicki. "I couldn't sleep a wink."

"Yeah well neither did I."

She looked at Paul. "So what's the plan?"

He sat on the edge of the bed and looked at them. "Well first, let's have some breakfast and a lot of coffee so that we're awake. There's a restaurant here at the hotel. Then, well I guess we go pay a visit to the nursing home. Get this over with."

The three of them walked out of the room to head to the restaurant. They didn't speak. Maggie looked into her purse as they rode the elevator down. One vial, all three syringes, just in case, and the rubber tourniquet. She was going to do it. She was ready.

After breakfast which consisted of a lot of coffee, they headed down to the parking garage to the car Maggie had rented. They got in with Vicki taking the back seat. Maggie started the car and put her hands on the wheel. That's when she noticed her hands were shaking slightly. She leaned forward and rested her forehead on the steering wheel. She needed to calm herself down.

Paul reached over and took her hand in his. "You're doing the right thing. You're going to save a lot of lives. It'll be fine."

Maggie was grateful for the words of encouragement. "How are we going to get in?"

Paul smiled. "I'm pretty sure we're going to be able to just walk right in. This place isn't security central. It's not one of the high end facilities. Just have a little faith. It'll be alright."

Maggie smiled gratefully and started the car. They headed out of the parking garage and onto the street. They were on their way to Bienville Street which was located within the 9th Ward.

"I was just thinking," began Maggie, "if he dies here, on this side..."

Paul cut in. He knew what she was wondering. "If he dies on this side, no one in Rosedale will remember there had ever been a serial killer at all. Nothing."

"But what about the people he killed?"

Paul sighed. "Not positive of course, but my guess is they would have to forget those people ever existed. The Wizard's curtain remember? It all has to go away in order to make sense."

Maggie thought about what Paul was saying. It was all so strange.

"So what's the plan?" asked Vicki as she propped herself up between the two front seats.

Paul looked at her and smiled. "Well the plan is - you are staying in the car."

"What? No way. We're in this together."

Paul shook his head. "I need you to stay in the car. That way, you can pull up and get Maggie and me the second we step out of the building. Besides, I don't want us to go in there as a group. Too much chance of drawing attention. You wait in the car, ready to pick us up at the door. Maggie and I will go in, get up to Room 210. I'll wait at the door making sure no one is coming and Maggie ...

you'll do your thing. As soon as you inject the potassium, remove the tourniquet, put it in your purse, along with the empty vial and the syringe. Oh, that reminds me..."

Paul reached into the inside pocket of his jacket and handed Maggie a plastic tube with a lid.

"What's that?"

"You can put the syringe in this when you're done. Obviously don't want to take any chances of you getting poked."

Maggie nodded.

"Just be calm and take your time. It's going to be just fine. I'll have plenty of warning if someone is coming. People only make mistakes when they rush. So take your time and be methodical."

"Got it."

She pointed in front of them.

"And I think that's where we're going."

They looked in the direction she was pointing and saw an old red brick building. As they got closer, they saw the sign - St. Aloysius Nursing Home. It looked to be maybe three stories high with a sweeping circular driveway in the front. Parking it seemed, was in the back. Luckily with Vicki staying in the car, she could wait in the street with a clear view of the glass front doors and be in position to pick them up as soon as they walked outside.

As they got closer, it became clear the building wasn't in the best of condition. The grass had yellowed in patches and other areas were overrun with weeds.

Maggie stopped the car on the road in front of the Home, making sure she had a clear view of the entrance. She and Paul got out while Vicki moved up to the driver's seat.

"Good luck." said Vicki quietly as Paul and Maggie headed towards the building.

Maggie's stomach was twisted in knots. She had to keep herself calm otherwise she knew she'd draw attention to the two of them. Paul must have sensed her stress level because he took her hand and made a couple really bad jokes to help put her at ease.

They walked into the building. The antiseptic smell was the first thing Maggie noticed. The lighting was harsh and the chairs in the waiting area looked as though they had come from the local Salvation Army. In front of them was the reception desk and to the right of that, were three elevators. There seemed to be only one person working at reception. She was a young girl perhaps in her 20s. She didn't notice them come in because she was staring down at her phone smiling. Maggie's first instinct was to go up to her, but Paul gently took her arm and guided her to the elevators. He pressed the button and in no time, the elevator door opened. They got on, pressed the button for the second floor. The second the door shut, Maggie let out a sigh of relief. She looked at Paul. He nodded and smiled.

They felt the elevator slow and finally come to a stop. The door opened. The sign on the wall in front of them gave the room numbers with arrows pointing in both directions. Room 210 was to the right.

Without saying a word, they continued walking towards the room as though they knew exactly where they were going. As though they'd done it a million times before. Other than the girl at the front desk, they hadn't seen any other staff. Maggie prepared herself to see a nurse in Robert's room.

They read room numbers as they walked by until they saw the one they were looking for. Room 210. They walked in. There was no nurse in sight. Maggie was grateful.

There were two patients in Room 210. Maggie looked at the first one to her right. He didn't look familiar at all. He was an elderly man who was fast asleep with his mouth agape.

She looked at the second bed - the one closer to the window. The dark hair, the protruding forehead. It was him. It was Robert Kraus. She couldn't stop staring. It was as though the world around her had ceased to exist. It was the same man, but different. He was a shadow of the person she had seen in Rosedale. Being in the coma had caused his body to become weak and misshapen. His hands were twisted and tucked up close to his face. But it was still him. There was no denying it.

A tube was in his nose that Maggie guessed was a feeding tube and a heart monitor was beeping next to him. She was concerned about that, but knew it would take time for someone to get to his room and by then, she and Paul would be gone.

She nodded at Paul. He took his place by the door while Maggie reached into her purse. She took out the rubber tourniquet and tied it tight on his arm. She then took out a syringe and filled it with the liquid from the vial. She grabbed his arm and looked for a vein. After what felt like forever, she finally saw it. She was ready. She looked at him once more and bent over him so that her mouth was close to his ear.

"Remember me? This is for Mary Haskins, Father McNeal, Alice Topper and anyone else you hurt, you sick son-of-a-bitch."

And with that, she stuck the needle directly into his vein and pushed the liquid into his blood stream. It didn't take long. As soon as the syringe was empty, she put it into the plastic container Paul had given her, then put it, the empty vial, and the tourniquet into her purse and closed the zipper. She turned and left the room in a hurried yet controlled walk. Paul followed suit. Suddenly, behind them, they heard the alarm sound on the heart monitor. In that moment, Maggie knew for sure she had done it. She had killed him. They didn't say a word to each other nor did they slow their walk. Instead of taking the elevator, Paul took her arm and guided her to the stairwell. Down one flight of stairs, past the girl at the reception desk - who was still staring down at her phone - and then out the front doors. Vicki was waiting for them. The second they got in, Vicki pulled out and they were on their way back to the hotel.

It was done. Robert Kraus was dead.

No one said a word during the drive back to the hotel. Each was dealing with what had just happened in their own way and needed to find a personal way to comes to terms with it. They had taken a life. Even though doing so had saved innocent lives, they had done the unimaginable. Still, they were relieved it was over and relieved he would no longer be able to hurt anyone else.

36

"So let me get this straight," grinned Maggie as she took a sip of her drink, "you're a hypnotist, therapist and psychic medium?"

Paul laughed while Vicki giggled next to him. They were sitting in the hotel lounge, finally shaking off the tension that had built up during the day.

Paul nodded, finished off his drink and motioned to the waitress to bring another. "Yup, that's right. And I do windows too."

"And he's very nice." added Vicki.

Paul smiled at her. "I was waiting for you to say incredibly handsome or sexy, but very nice will work too."

"So where did the two of you meet?" asked Maggie.

Paul and Vicki looked at each other, decided who was going to answer that question. Finally Vicki responded. "On a dating website!"

"No!" laughed Maggie

"Yes! And it was 'like' at first sight." laughed Vicki while Paul pretended to be hurt.

The waitress came back to the table with Paul's drink. She looked at Vicki and Maggie, but they waved her off. The laughter subsided.

"So what made you try to reach me while I was in the coma?"

The smile left Paul's face as he looked at Maggie. "Well, when Vicki told me her best friend was in a coma and not waking up ... that's when I told her about the abilities I have. It's not really something you want to lead with when you first meet someone.

But, I'd been curious about comas for some time - doing research, reading as much as I could. And then about a year ago, a friend of my sister's was in a coma following a car accident. That's when I first tried to reach out to someone like that. It wasn't as good of a connection with her as it was with you, I think probably the fact that you're gifted helped, but that was the first time I got a glimpse of another world. The other side, as you like to call it.

So, anyway, I told Vicki I'd be willing to try to connect with you and see if I couldn't help in some way."

There was silence at the table for a while until Maggie looked up.

"Well I want to thank you. Both of you. For reaching out to me and for all your support since then."

"So what's the plan moving forward?" asked Paul as he took another sip of his drink.

Maggie shrugged. "Live. I guess. Just keep putting one foot in front of the other until I remember how to walk. It's so strange. I miss David and Laura so much. But I have to tell myself they're gone and there's nothing I can do about it. And at the same time, I also miss Sam and Jordan. But at least I know that with Robert Kraus gone, they're as safe as I can make them. And - there's some sort of comfort knowing they don't remember me, you know? I wouldn't want them to miss me. I just hope I got to Robert Kraus in time."

Maggie finished off her drink and looked at Vicki and Paul. "I'm thinking another of these would be a seriously good idea."

Paul smiled and flagged down the waitress once more.

"There is something that's been bothering me, though." said Maggie as she nervously played with the small napkin under her glass.

"What's that?" asked Paul

Maggie took a deep breath before starting to speak. "Well, once Robert died here, on this side, he would have just vanished from Rosedale. Right?"

Paul nodded, unsure of where this was going.

"And of course," continued Maggie, "that would mean no one in Rosedale would remember there had ever been a Robert to begin with and they would also completely forget his victims - like they never existed either. It would be as though the entire event never happened."

"That's right."

"Well then, isn't it likely, there have been others in Rosedale, like Robert? And in all those other places you said are like Rosedale? There's no way he was the only dangerous person to ever be in a coma. This has happened before, Paul. But as soon as the killer either wakes up or dies -"

"Everyone forgets..." said Paul slowly.

Maggie nodded. "Nothing ever happens in Rosedale. Everybody said that. Everybody believed that. But what if a lot happened in Rosedale - it's just that nobody remembers?"

Vicki moved closer to the table. "We learn from our experiences. If no one remembers anyone ever being killed ..."

"They wouldn't realize they needed to protect themselves." whispered Paul.

Maggie looked at her friends. "How many people of died because of their medical conditions ... and how many have died because they were actually murdered on the other side?"

And that's where the three of them sat for another two hours. Quietly sipping their drinks ... lost in their own thoughts.

The television was on in the hotel room the next morning while Maggie was packing her bag, getting ready to head to the airport. She became aware that one of the news anchors was reading the story that Robert Kraus, the man who killed his mother and attempted to kill his brother had passed away from a heart attack at a local long-term care facility. A quick flash of his photo and that was that. Maggie smiled.

A short time later she was with Paul and Vicki in the rental car, heading back to the airport. They had seen the same news broadcast. After navigating the traffic around the airport, the rental car was returned and soon they were standing in the terminal checking to see if their flight was on time.

"I'm looking forward to getting home." sighed Vicki. "Not that I don't like New Orleans. But it would be nice to come back under better circumstances. And eat beignets!"

Paul laughed at her and put his arm around her. "I'll make it up to you. We might as well make our way over to the gate."

They started walking in that direction, but noticed Maggie wasn't following.

"Maggie?" questioned Vicki.

Maggie hesitated for a moment and then smiled. "I have something I need to do first.

I'm fine. Really. You go on and I'll be back in Atlanta in a day or two. I promise."

"What?" asked Vicki, looking concerned.

Maggie just shook her head. "I don't want to get into it. I just need to take care of something and then I'll be back in Atlanta. I promise."

Vicki looked at her friend and then hugged her. She pulled back after a minute and looked Maggie in the eye. "Call me the second you get back. I'll be waiting for you."

Maggie nodded. "I promise."

Slowly Vicki turned and joined Paul. Maggie watched as they made their way through the terminal and then out of sight. She looked up at the flight information display. She still had another hour before she could board her flight to Chicago.

She walked around the terminal, going into the small shops that offered magazines, books and candies. Finally it was time. She felt a strange mixture of excitement and dread

- but that wouldn't stop her. Three hours later she was hailing a cab at the airport in Chicago.

"Northwestern Memorial on Huron Street please." she told the driver as she settled back in her seat.

"The hospital?"

"Yes."

He flipped on his meter, quickly checked his side mirror for oncoming traffic and then aggressively pulled out into the lane. Maggie silently stared out the window, not really seeing anything at all. Not really thinking anything at all.

He drove into the heart of Chicago, cutting through traffic as only a seasoned cab driver could do. About 20 minutes after they left the airport, he pulled over and announced they had reached their destination. She sighed. Was she doing the right thing? She handed the driver his fare along with a tip and got out of the cab, pulling her carry-on bag behind her. She looked around. The hospital was enormous and imposing, made up of what looked like, four different buildings. He was here. Somewhere. Sam was here.

She started walking until she found herself standing at the front doors. She paused. She was about to go in, but instead, decided she needed to go for a walk first. Fresh air might help her feel calmer. Besides, she needed to think.

As she walked she looked around at the wide sidewalks, busy streets and perfectly groomed trees that were framed by tiny decorative wrought iron fences. She saw a patch of green up ahead. It looked like a park, perhaps. She walked towards it.

A bus went roaring past. Yellow cabs darted in and out of traffic. Maybe she could sit at the park, or whatever it was, for a while. As she walked she thought about Sam walking these very streets. This was his city. This was where he lived. She was seeing the things he saw.

She thought back to the last time she saw him at home in Rosedale, when she held onto him at the door.   The connection had been strong and immediate.   She saw everything.   She didn't want to let go.   She learned things about him his own subconscious wouldn't share with him.   The scar on his elbow was as a result of a fall from his bicycle when he was nine.   That made her smile. He was real. In that instant, she knew everything about him, including where he lived on the other side.

As she walked, she fought back the tears. She should feel happy.   She was finally going to see Sam. But was she? She got to the patch of green and saw benches lining the sidewalk. She sat down and stared at the hospital in front of her.

Which window was his?   What was she going to see when she walked into his room? She remembered Robert Kraus and what being in a coma had done to him.   He was a shadow of the man she had seen in Rosedale. What would Sam look like? She remembered what he looked like in Rosedale. Strong, muscular, beautiful.   And his eyes.   She remembered his beautiful, blue eyes. What was she about to see here, on this side?

She sat there on the bench, trying to sort out all of the thoughts she was having. They were just spinning in her head. Slowly a tear filled her eye and spilled out onto her cheek.

She looked up at the hospital. Who was she kidding? The man in this hospital wasn't her Sam. This man belonged to someone else. Her Sam lived in Rosedale ... in a cute, little, yellow house with purple flowers out front. She didn't know this man ... not really ... and he didn't know her.

She wiped the tears from her eyes, straightened herself, walked over to the edge of the sidewalk and flagged down a cab. She needed to get to the airport. She needed to go home.

37

She had the music playing as she was getting ready. Light jazz filled the house. That always made her feel good. She closed the clasp on her necklace. She stood back and looked at her reflection in the large mirror. She hadn't worn that dress in forever. Maybe not since she went out to dinner with David to celebrate their wedding anniversary. It was David's favorite dress on her. He always liked red.

She sat on the edge of the bed and looked around the room. Had it really been that long? The room still looked the same. The house still looked the same. She had spent the past year working so hard decorating other people's homes, maybe she should have done something different with her own. Maybe it was time she did that. Maybe she was finally ready to do that.

She had managed to pick up the pieces of her life. One foot in front of the other and she did, in fact, remember how to walk again. But even still, she couldn't shake the sadness. She pretended a lot. She forced herself to smile when in public. She realized as long as she smiled, people wouldn't look any deeper. A smile and a joke and everyone thought all was fine. End of story. She didn't want anyone worrying about her. It wouldn't change anything anyway. Vicki had been wanting her to start dating again. So far she had managed to come up with an endless list of excuses not to do so. But maybe she needed to jump back in the dating pool. Why was she so hesitant? In some strange way, dating again felt like admitting defeat - like she was accepting the loss of David and Laura ... of Sam and Jordan. And those were things she would never just accept.

She shook her head when she thought about the saying 'what doesn't kill you makes you stronger'. She hated that saying. It was stupid. She had thought about it and decided they needed to change it to 'what doesn't kill you leaves you with bruises'. That's how she felt, still after all this time. Bruised.

She was meeting Paul and Vicki at a new Italian restaurant that had opened in Buckhead. It had gotten wonderful reviews. She had the feeling Vicki was itching to tell her something. She smiled to herself. She had a good idea what that 'something' might be. Vicki and Paul had been together almost non-stop for the entire year. They made a great couple. They seemed to make each other happy ... and that's all that mattered. Life was fleeting. Plot twists happened without warning. Being with someone who made you happy, even if it was just for a day, made it all worthwhile.

She shut off the music, turned on a few well placed lights and headed out to her car. She was looking forward to spending the evening with her friends. She actually hadn't seen much of Vicki recently so this would be a good time to catch up.

She backed out of her driveway and started heading towards the restaurant. It was already dark outside. She liked driving at night. She could imagine she was anywhere.

By the time she got to her destination she was surprised to see how busy they were. Obviously the great reviews meant a huge uptick in business. The valet parking was backed up but luckily she saw an open parking spot across from the restaurant on the street. It was perfect. She didn't have the patience to wait in line.

She parked her car, checked her side mirror for traffic before opening her door. There was a slight breeze and the night air felt refreshing. She was looking forward to the evening. She was actually feeling a little excited.

She crossed the street and walked up to the entrance. Not seeing Vicki or Paul she walked inside and checked in. She was immediately taken back to a table where they were waiting for her.

They stood as soon as they saw her walking their way.

"Oh my God you look wonderful!" gushed Vicki as she hugged her friend. "I've missed you so much!"

"I've missed you too." smiled Maggie, feeling flattered by the warm welcome. She turned to Paul. He was standing there grinning at her.

"Well I'm hugging you too." he said as he wrapped his arms around her. "It's been a long time. You do look great."

"Thank you!"

They settled into their seats. Maggie looked around.

"Have you been here before?" asked Paul

Maggie shook her head. "First time. I can't believe how busy they are!"

"I know. It was a miracle we got a reservation." said Vicki.

A waiter came by the table asking for their drink orders. That handled, he presented each with a menu, gave a slight bow and hurried off.

"So what have you been up to?" inquired Paul as he turned the pages of the menu.

Maggie shrugged. "Actually ... well let me show you."

She took her cell phone out of her purse and pulled up some photos. She held the phone so that Paul and Vicki could see the images.

"Just finished decorating this house and now they want me to do their offices and their corporate apartment. So business is going very well."

Vicki examined the photos.

"Wow that's gorgeous."

Maggie nodded, smiling. "It's amazing what you can do with a budget of 'money is no object'. That carpet alone is worth almost as much as my house!"

Paul let out a low whistle. He looked at Vicki. Vicki cleared her throat.

"Well, Paul and I have something that we'd like to tell you."

Maggie couldn't help but smile. She knew what was coming but there was no way she was going to take the moment away from them. She put her phone down on the table and folded her hands on her lap. She looked at Vicki. "Yes? I'm all ears."

Paul took Vicki's hand in his. Vicki took a deep breath and then held her left hand out for Maggie to see. Maggie looked down and saw an absolutely beautiful engagement ring on Vicki's hand. They both looked so happy Maggie couldn't help but be excited for them.

"Oh my God that is beautiful! Congratulations to both of you! I can't think of two people more perfect for each other."

Vicki beamed. "Thank you. And then there's the second part."

Maggie looked confused. "The second part?"

Vicki glanced at Paul and then back to Maggie. "I'd like you to be my Maid of Honor... If you'd consider that."

Maggie couldn't help but grin. She couldn't have been happier for them. It was the first time she felt joy in a very long time. "I would be honored. Really. So when's the date?"

Just then the waiter returned with the drinks.

"Are you ready to order?"

Vicki and Maggie both looked at Paul.

"If you could give us a few minutes please?" responded Paul

Again the waiter gave a slight bow and vanished into the crowd.

"May 18th. We figure that still gives us time to get things ready. Truthfully though I wish it was tomorrow."

This time it was Maggie who got up and hugged both of them. It was going to be a wonderful evening.

Dinner was delicious. The reviews didn't do the restaurant justice at all. They talked and laughed the entire evening. By the time they finished their dessert, they were stuffed.

"Well we definitely have to do this again." said Paul as he retrieved his credit card from the folder and put it in his wallet.

Maggie sighed. "Well I have to tell you, I had an absolutely wonderful evening. And again I'm so happy for you guys."

They got up from the table and slowly started to walk to the door.

"What color were you thinking for the wedding? And how many people are in the wedding party?"

"I'm thinking sort of a champagne color, but I don't know. Maybe you and I could do some shopping and see what's out there. Maybe if I actually see some dresses I'll be able to decide on a color."

"That sounds like fun." smiled Maggie.

Paul opened the door so that they could step outside. People were still lining up to go into the restaurant.

"Good heavens this placed is crazy!" exclaimed Maggie as they managed to weave through the crowd.

"There's only two bridesmaids and you. I didn't want to go overboard." said Vicki, answering Maggie's earlier question. "Where are you parked?"

Maggie motioned to her car across the street. "Over there. I didn't feel like getting in the middle of this."

"Well dear friend," said Vicki as she hugged Maggie again. "You drive safe and I'll give you a call tomorrow and maybe we can plan a day to go shopping."

Maggie smiled and nodded. "Sounds perfect." She looked at Paul and then hugged him good-bye. "I'm so happy for you. You'd better take good care of her. I'll be keeping my eyes on you." she said, laughing.

Paul smiled too and kissed her on the cheek.

She turned, looked for cars and then started to walk across the street. She opened her purse to retrieve her keys. She was digging around in her purse and almost at her car when she realized she had left her cell phone on the table. She was irritated with herself. Why was she always forgetting things? Still checking in her purse, feeling annoyed and a little panicky about leaving her phone behind, she immediately turned and started to hurry back to the restaurant. And that's when it happened. Suddenly a bright light appeared out of nowhere and washed over her, followed by an instant of excruciating pain and then a scream. At least, she thought it was a scream. And then there was nothing.

Vicki and Paul looked on in horror as the ambulance pulled away with Maggie in the back. Vicki had wanted to get into the ambulance with her, but they wouldn't allow it. She and Paul needed to finish telling the police officer what they had witnessed before they could leave for the hospital. The driver of the car was also there being interviewed by police. He looked distraught. Everyone looked distraught. Vicki couldn't stop crying.

After what felt like an eternity, Paul and Vicki were finally able to get in their car and drive to the hospital. Vicki still had power of attorney so at least they had no problem getting information from the medical staff.

They sat in the waiting room for hours. Vicki resting her head on Paul's shoulder silently crying while Paul simply stared off in the distance, trying his best to comfort her.

Finally a doctor walked into the waiting room. He was a man in his 60s, balding and looking exhausted. He scanned the room until he saw Paul and Vicki and then started walking towards them. Paul nudged Vicki and the two of them stood up, waiting to hear what the doctor was going to say.

"I'm Dr. Spence." he said as he looked directly at Vicki. "I understand you have Power of Attorney?"

"Yes." answered Vicki, holding on to Paul for support.

Dr. Spence looked at the two of them. His face softened.

"Let's sit down over here so we can talk." He motioned to a table that was in the corner of the waiting area. They sat. Paul and Vicki waited for him to speak.

"Your friend, Maggie, suffered catastrophic injuries when the car hit her. We operated and for all purposes, we were successful."

"Oh thank God." uttered Vicki under her breath.

Dr. Spence looked at her and shook his head. "No. There are spinal injuries and she's on a ventilator. Currently she's in a coma. I am really sorry to have to tell you this, but she's not going to wake up. Not with the extent of her brain injury.   She can't breathe without life support. I'm so sorry."

Vicki looked at Paul.   Tears filled her eyes. Paul looked devastated.

Dr. Spence gave them a moment before continuing. "I need your permission to shut off life support. It's the only humane thing to do. She's not going to get better. She's not going to wake up. This is no life for her."

Vicki straightened.   The tears had stopped flowing. Her mind was racing. Slowly she turned her head and looked at Paul. Together they had the same thought.   Vicki smiled at him. He smiled back. She looked back at the doctor and through her tears, she answered his question. "No. You do not have my permission. Don't unplug anything. Do everything in your power to keep her breathing. Everything."

*   *   *

She found herself standing there, staring out a bay window, out onto a backyard. Slowly she turned, trying to understand what she was seeing. A white kitchen. It looked like her grandmother's kitchen. She started to cry. They were tears of happiness. She touched the countertop, the cabinet doors. Her hand slid across the sink. She started to giggle. Was this really happening? Her heart felt as though it was going to burst through her chest.

She ran into the living room and up to the painting that hung over the bombay chest. She looked in the bottom right hand corner. She grinned. It was signed by Wyndham Hart. Yes, it actually was signed by Wyndham Hart. She ran up the stairs and flung open a bedroom door. The room looked like teenage girl's room complete with posters and perfume bottles. Maggie could barely control her excitement. She turned and ran into the master bedroom and into the bathroom. She saw a bottle of cologne - men's cologne. She knew what it was called. She had seen it before.

That's when she heard it. The sound of the front door opening.

"We're home!"

She thought she was going to scream. It was Jordan. She ran out of the master bedroom and as soon as she turned the corner, she looked down and saw Jordan walking into the kitchen. And then, at the doorway stood Sam - smiling up at her. Sam with those blue eyes of his. She couldn't help but cry as she ran down the stairs and threw herself into his arms.

He started laughing. "What are you doing?"

She pulled away and looked at him, unable to stop smiling, unable to stop touching his face, unable to stop laughing. It was contagious. Soon they were both laughing.

"I'm just so happy to see you. So happy to see both of you. It's been a really, really long day."

Suddenly a thought crossed her mind. There was just one more thing to check on. "Hey I was thinking - would it be okay with you if we had a barbecue or something? Invite some friends? Maybe Wyndham ... maybe Patty?"

She waited for his response. She felt a little tense.

But he looked at her and she saw the joy in his eyes. "If you want to invite Wyndham and Patty for a barbecue that would be just fine with me."

Again she threw herself in his arms and hugged him. She pulled back and looked into his wonderful blue eyes. He was perfect. Absolutely perfect. He stroked her hair and kissed her.

"So Mrs. Cooper. What happened today?"

Maggie smiled and shook her head. She was over the moon.

"Nothing, Sheriff Cooper. You know nothing ever happens in Rosedale."

www.ingramcontent.com/pod-product-compliance
Lightning Source LLC
Chambersburg PA
CBHW020821030726
47496CB00001B/28